1

Argent Myst: Avowed

Written By: L.R. Sherwood

ARGENT MYST

AVOWED

L.R. SHERWOOD

Argent Myst: Avowed

Written By: L.R. Sherwood

Prologue:

Salem, Massachusetts May 1693

Juliette entered the town just before midnight expecting the streets to be deserted, the villagers secure in their homes, safely tucked away from the perils of the dark night. Instead, she came upon the streets teaming with people all anxiously waiting outside the prison. Something had taken place while she had been out in the forest with her wolf; perhaps another witch had been discovered.

She hugged the rocky church wall and peered into the small, crowded village square. The people of the township, illuminated by an eerie glow of burning torches and darkened by plumes of acrid smoke, gathered closely together, some murmuring quietly to one another, others completely silent as a weighted fear settled on the hamlet.

Unable to see over the heads of the crowd, she quickly surveyed her surroundings to locate a better place to keep hidden from the mortals and view the trial.

She wondered where Marek could be. He must be a great distance away, otherwise, she would be able to sense his location. He would be disappointed at missing the trial; it was, after all, the reason they had come to Salem.

They were attempting to locate a coven of witches but so far, the alleged witches in this town were nothing more than unfortunate victims, accused by a group of troublesome young girls. There had been no deaths during their short time in the village and for that, Juliette was thankful. She hated to see anyone get hurt and Marek had

10

given strict instructions that they were not to interfere in any way. They must only observe so as not to reveal their true nature to the mortals.

Scaling the rough and rocky wall of the building next to her, Juliette reached the thatched roof and froze, every nerve in her body was flooded with an icy dread as she felt his anxiety and heard his voice echoing through her mind. He was calling for her, searching for her... she crawled to the edge of the roof on her stomach, unobserved and a fierce growl escaped from between her bared teeth.

The double doors to the jailhouse had been thrust open and from them emerged Marek, held between two Salem officials and being dragged towards the town square where a tall wooden pole had been driven into the earth. Another prisoner, a young woman, was pulled from the shadows of the jailhouse and pushed to her knees not far from where Marek was being taken. Juliette did not recognize her and barely spared her a glance as she tried to make sense of what was happening before her.

The crowd surged forward as the prisoners were being brought out, focusing their fear, their hatred, and their guilt onto one lost soul, one man, and one immortal... her beloved Marek.

He was barely conscious; his head hung limply between his shoulders, his feet dragging in the dirt behind him as he struggled to clear his head of the dark cloud pulling him under. Juliette felt the rage tear through her as she noticed how badly he had been beaten. Blood caked in his hair, his face was stained with bruises that had not yet healed, and one of his arms was bent at an unnatural angle.

How had he come to be there? How had she not heard his mental voice until now? How was it possible that

11

these mere humans had managed to capture and abuse him? Why had he not vanished into vapor long before they were able to make a spectacle of him in front of the entire village? So many questions running through her mind simultaneously, but all thoughts were lost the moment his head lifted, and his gaze locked on her position.

He felt Juliette's presence and his eyes met hers through the pungent smoke and flickering shadows that danced from the torches illuminating the arena. Their gazes held, communicating an unspoken fear of the situation they now found themselves in.

"Juliette, stay where you are," he commanded, his mind reaching out to her. His mental voice was weak and weary; it seemed a struggle for him to connect with her. Juliette's heart shattered at that moment, and an enraged sob escaped her lips.

She sprang to her feet, squatting low on the overhang above the crowd, ready at any moment to push aside her qualms of hurting another and vault into the mob to eliminate any who should try to stand in her way.

"No! Juliette, stay where you are. I need you to stay safe...stay alive! Promise me Juliette!" Marek's mind screamed for her to understand; anguish reflected in the depth of his eyes.

"Disperse Marek, please! Let us leave this place!"

Marek shook his head in response to the outraged plea only he could hear.

"I cannot. They have cast something on me; I cannot break free. I do not know why this is happening or by whom, but it is too late for me and too dangerous for you. If they find you too, they will kill you."

"I cannot watch you burn, Marek. I cannot allow them to hurt you... fight with me; there is still a chance."

12

Tears filled his eyes as he begged her to heed his command.

"I have already lost this battle... I need you to stay out of sight until dawn is almost upon you. They will dispose of my remains in a shallow grave near Gallows Hill or in the rocky crevice at its base. You will need to resurrect my remains. It is the only way Juliette, you know this."

The fury and agony she felt only increased at the knowledge that Marek was right. If they fought and lost, that would be the end of them both.

Tears openly streamed down her face. Silently, she agreed. "I will not fail you, my love. We will be together again... I promise you that."

He nodded his understanding as the minister approached him with a burning staff and set the straw at his feet aflame. The flames engulfed her beloved Marek within seconds.

The pain Juliette saw in his eyes, his tortured screams, and the probing thoughts he desperately sent to her mind reverberated through her entire being. He fought to push the pain away, to rise above the agony that consumed his body and heart, to focus on his power, trying to command his tortured body to burst into vapor and leave the flames; but something was crippling his abilities.

Through her tears Juliette noticed, as his back arched against the burning pyre, that there was a talisman hanging from a chain around his neck. Golden stones engraved with runes shimmered wickedly in the firelight.

Almost as if another power had taken hold of the fire, it erupted towards the black, starless sky, soaring to great heights; black smoke billowed, obscuring the gruesome fate of the condemned. A blood-curdling shriek

13

filled Juliette's ears as the fire's flames thrashed violently,
tearing the life from her beloved.

The bond of their blood had linked them together
and his pain became her pain. It was not until the flames
had died down that Juliette realized the tortured cries that
she heard were her own, and the blaze that had engulfed
Marek had seared her flesh as well.

As she lay there on the roof, consumed with agony
and rage, Juliette could not bear to look towards Marek's
body. She could feel the empty space that his essence had
once filled. No longer did she feel the warm pulse of his
presence or sense his unyielding devotion for her. The loss
was crippling.

A flash of lightning tore across the sky, and
darkened clouds moved in swiftly. Juliette's wrath brought
with it an unyielding storm that doused the town and
Marek's remains in pelting rain and hail.

Thunder rolled across the sky as the town's people
scrambled for the safety of their homes. Terrified of the
squall that had appeared out of nowhere, they fled from the
storm that raged around them. Through her grief, Juliette
felt a slight thrum of power and heard the softly spoken
familiar words of a binding spell floating in the thick
oppressive heat of the night. She rolled to her stomach,
ignoring the crisp burnt skin that tore as she dragged her
body to the edge of the roof to see down into the nearly
vacant courtyard.

Only the Salem officials remained in the square.
Fear lit in their eyes as they listened to the soft chanting of
the young witch at their feet. One man kept a firm grasp on
her shoulder, holding her down to continue kneeling in the
dirt next to the burning pyre.

14

Juliette's eyes flared with the knowledge of what had kept Marek from dissolving and escaping the horrors of this night.

The town of Salem, known for its swift persecution of anyone accused of using witchcraft, had used what they feared most to capture, abuse, and destroy her beloved.

It was at that moment that she vowed to take vengeance on the ones responsible for the horror unleashed this night. The seething rage she felt at that moment was so immense it would carry her through the centuries, spurring her on to seek justice, to find retribution and to reclaim the life that had been stolen from her.

Chancellor, Oregon Present Day

Traveling the winding roads through the mountains of Oregon, on the outskirts of the small town of Chancellor, Juliette reflected again on the reason she'd come to be here. For centuries, she had been tracking the bastard who had stolen Marek's remains, but she was always one-step behind.

She had been traveling the world, hunting in the most unimaginable places... searching in cemeteries, tombs, and other crumbling burial grounds, stalking him like prey. Yet still, he eluded her.

Contrary to myths, there was not a sensible vampire on earth who would choose to live among the rot and decay of the dead. Why he chose to hide in these places, Juliette could not understand.

Walking the earth alone with no end in sight was at times unbearable. Choosing to live in the presence of death would be a constant reminder that everlasting peace would never be within your grasp. That was enough to make anyone go mad, but Juliette knew first-hand that this particular monster had been insane long before he had found immortality.

Now, with the strength of his vampire powers fueling his madness, he had become a terrifying sociopath. He fed from the pain of others and would stop at nothing to wreak agony wherever he went.

She had traced this vampire to Chancellor following the trail of ravaged bodies he had left scattered in his wake. It was not enough for him to simply feed from the humans' blood, but from their fear and suffering as well.

16

Juliette did not know how he had found his immortality. She often wondered if he had somehow discovered how to resurrect Marek's flesh and steal his life's blood to become the fiercely powerful vampire that he was today.

Whatever way he had been turned, she took comfort in knowing that his strength did not surpass her own, as she was older than he was by at least a decade.

She also carried within her abilities that had been handed down to her by a long line of witches. However, even with all her gifts, she still had not been able to destroy him or even get close to him. He had the uncanny ability to escape her grasp whenever she was near. It seemed as if he were toying with her, leading her on a maddening game of cat and mouse, only pausing long enough for her to catch up and then disappear again.

However, this time was different. Juliette could feel a change coming. Something hovered on the edge of her sight, something pivotal. Whatever it was, she would use it, she silently vowed, to end it… to end him.

She had arranged for a residence in the Chancellor area to call home. A sanctuary, to regroup while she developed a course of action, and gathered the power and tools that she would need to complete this final battle. She had purchased a small chalet about five miles from the outskirts of town.

The cabin was perfectly secluded. She would be sheltered from the prying eyes of meddlesome neighbors. It was the ideal place to set in motion her plans for retrieving Marek's imprisoned body and put an end to the monster that had destroyed her life.

As she turned off the highway onto the gravel road that would take her to her new home, a faint whine from

17

the back seat drew her attention. Juliette turned her head slightly to glance at the large white wolf taking up much of the back seat in her sport utility vehicle. Tenderly patting the wolf's great head, Juliette murmured reassurance to her companion.

"Calm, Ambrosia. We will be there soon, and then you can hunt for us."

Ambrosia had been orphaned during Juliette's first hunting trip as a newly turned vampire. She had worried herself sick that she would not be able to hunt, that she would not have the strength to feed from or take the life of a living creature. Being an empath carried a great burden for a vampire. She suffered the pain and fear that her victims experienced, making it nearly impossible for her to ever harm another living creature.

Nevertheless, if she wanted to live eternally at Marek's side, she had needed to learn to block that part of her power; it was the only way. Her first and last hunting trip had ended in disaster with Marek having to kill the large she-wolf Juliette had tracked before it mauled her.

She had meant only to take enough blood that the animal would recover, but the wolf had been fiercely protecting something and fought back with a vengeance. Granted, Juliette would have healed within just a few hours, but Marek could not stand by and watch her be hurt.

She had been frightened and ashamed after that, and Marek knew that they must find another way for her to feed.

Until that point, he had always shared his own blood with her, but that had begun to take a toll on him. As her powers continued to increase, she needed to feed more often, and it had become impossible for him to be able to sustain her hunger.

18

The small wolf pup she had found, after unwillingly killing its mother, had caused Juliette to feel even greater remorse, and it only increased her reluctance to kill another living creature. However, to Marek, finding the pup had seemed like a godsend.

They took in the small beast, solving the problem of it being orphaned and created a new donor for Juliette. The animal was trained and transformed to quench her thirst as well as to be her companion and protector.

It had never been done before, but Marek had seen the remarkable abilities of vampire blood. He had hoped that, in time, the wolf would become an extraordinary creature.

As the pup grew Juliette had formed an unforeseen bond with the animal, and they had become inseparable. The animal had been fed a natural diet of raw meat as well as vampire blood daily as it matured and had become accustomed to the powers it would possess once the transformation was completed.

By then the pup had grown to an immense size weighing well over two-hundred pounds and had been completely transformed into a vampire wolf.

Ambrosia, as Juliette had named her, had been the perfect solution for her donor. She hunted throughout the night for wildlife that lived in whatever region they visited, staying clear of humans, and returning to Juliette who would then feed from her host.

The blood from the wolf's hunting trips, combined with the mystic properties of the animal's vampire blood, gave Juliette the strength she needed and left Ambrosia completely unharmed.

Ambrosia settled her enormous head on her large paws as the SUV rambled on down the dark tree-lined road.

Cloaked in darkness, she could still make out the giant cedar trees and lush green ferns that grew rampant blocking the view of the cliffs that lay just beyond the property. Juliette had driven three-quarters of a mile when the cabin came into view.

It was a spacious log cabin that had been built on a raised platform, with stairs leading to the wrap-around porch. The front door was inlaid with a beautiful cut glass window; it glimmered like ice crystals in the small amount of moonlight that had managed to weave its way through the treetops. There was also a second story with a balcony that stretched along the back of the house facing the cliffs.

Juliette parked in the gravel drive and stepped out of the vehicle. As she pulled open the back door of the truck, allowing Ambrosia to leap lightly to the ground, she could smell the salt blowing in from the sea and hear the waves pounding the beach below. After pulling her bags from the rear of the vehicle, she proceeded up the few stairs that led to the porch. She paused briefly and bent towards Ambrosia, "Go love. Go and hunt. Dawn is near and we need to feed." The wolf trotted silently into the trees and disappeared beneath a veil of shadows and fog while Juliette continued up the stairs and unlocked the front door.

Just as she had requested, the house had already been furnished with her belongings which had been delivered weeks before her arrival. She had given strict instructions for every window to be entirely concealed behind the heavy draperies she had provided.

As she entered the house, she was pleased to see that her demands had been carried out.

Juliette glanced at the large opulent fireplace, empty aside from the cold logs stacked in the center. As she set her bags in the foyer and strolled into the room, Juliette gracefully gestured towards the barren hearth and smiled slightly as a warm and inviting fire quickly erupted within.

She looked over the interior of the cabin recognizing items that she had collected over the centuries.

The living room, off to the left of the front entry, contained a newly acquired wrap-around sectional upholstered in ivory suede. The coffee table was an antique chest, adorned with carvings of entwined roses, polished, and gleaming in the dim firelight that now penetrated the interior of the cabin.

Bundles of elegant red roses, tied together with a black silk ribbon, were centered in the middle of the chest. Another one of her frequent requirements fulfilled. Juliette loved the fragrance and the semblance of the red roses. It reminded her of the life she now lived... beautiful and delicate, but with an aura of mystery, danger, and loneliness.

The fireplace that contained her fire was positioned across from the sofa between the kitchen and the living room. It was set inside a grey brick hearth with a white marble mantle. The mantle was bare aside from an ancient amethyst crystal urn, bejeweled with polished stones.

The stairs that led to the second story were located to the right of the front door. Both the floors and stairs were constructed of dark polished wood. Juliette enjoyed the echo of her boots on the floor as she moved from room to room inspecting the décor.

The kitchen was rather elegant with its stainless-steel appliances and marble countertops. The dining room contained her massive, ancient, solid wood table with matching benches. She had spent many nights at this table, stirring and concocting potions, and spells, practicing her craft.

Caressing the polished wood as she circled around the table, Juliette turned towards the stairs, curious to see what charming secrets the second floor held. At the top of the staircase the floor opened to a large landing that overlooked the front entryway; the glow from the fireplace cast ghostly shadows upon the walls.

Opening the door to her right, Juliette entered what was to be her bedroom.

The floors were covered in thick, luxurious, Persian rugs. The entire west wall consisted of two large picture windows with opaque scarlet and plum silk draperies hanging on a twisted black iron curtain rod. A pair of French doors let out onto the terrace between the large windows, these were also carefully concealed behind silk. Opposite the French doors was her king size bed, sheathed in the same fabric as the windows.

Smoothing her hand along the cool silk that clung to the bed, she turned towards the wall that stood between the bedroom and bathroom.

From below, the fireplace continued up through the floor where another crackling blaze warmed Juliette. It was centered in the wall separating the two rooms. Juliette bent down peering through the flames dancing in the fireplace, she could see through to the tiled floor and claw-foot bathtub.

Strolling into the bathroom through the door on the right, she was delighted to see an open shower set in the corner carved out of the same white marble as the fireplace. Everything in the bathroom matched the rest of the house, right down to the crystal urns on the vanity filled with roses.

After her stroll through the house, Juliette stepped out onto the terrace and walked to the railing to face the ocean.

The cliffs that led down to the sand and surf below were approximately one-hundred yards away. A narrow pathway led from the backdoor in the kitchen through the trees and foliage to a lookout point. From there a rickety wooden staircase led to the black sand beach she knew stretched a mile in each direction. The shoreline gently curved outward to create an inlet.

Juliette's vampire enhanced vision made it easy to see through the curtain of shadows that hung from the trees. She could see the ferns gently swaying in the cool night air. She could hear the foam fizzing from the surf crashing against the seashore below, and she could smell danger in the tranquil Oregon night.

She knew it would not be long before she finally caught up with her rival. It wouldn't be long before she faced the possibility of death. Would she find Marek alive, suffering within the confines of his petrified body? Or would he be dead?

After all these years she did not know which circumstances she preferred to find. She had been mourning his loss for centuries, and she needed closure. One way or the other she needed to carry out the vengeance she knew that foul creature deserved.

She could feel his presence near here, somewhere to the north of the town. This was the closest she had ever come. To be able to sense his black heart was both encouraging and terrifying.

She could feel his impatience with her pursuit of him and knew that he would soon face her to end this little game. She wondered about this change, worried that he had finally stopped running because he had something terrifying planned for her. Whatever his reasons were, she would face him here… in this small peaceful fishing village.

That was the only reason she had brought along her belongings and set up residence here in Chancellor.

There was something stirring in the quiet night. A foreboding feeling settled around her. Like the calm before the storm, she knew the serenity of the moonlit beach would soon be disrupted. The silver light falling from the sky, painting the forest in muted tones of emerald and onyx, would erupt in fearsome crimson blood. The fear, floating in from the sea, was dense and carried with it a great burden that weighed heavily upon her shoulders.

She prayed for the strength and courage she would need to at last put an end to this ancient struggle and at finally find the peace that she so desperately craved.

The last patron had finally stumbled out into the crisp September night. The bar stools had been stacked and the last shot glass dried and placed on the gleaming tower of jiggers.

Evan Gallient the bartender and owner of The Waterfront Pub, was counting out the cash register. He was weary from another long Saturday night filled with breaking up brawls, pouring booze, and avoiding Tori's inexhaustible advances.

The voluptuous and very flirtatious Tori Sumner was one of The Waterfront's employees, and Evan was forever asking himself why he had ever hired her. She was an exceptional waitress and very popular with the male patrons, but her constant flirting and not so subtle sexual innuendos were beginning to wear on his patience.

His little sister April, and partner behind the bar, was probably the only reason Tori still had a job at the pub. She was constantly reminding him that good help in this town was hard to find.

Unfortunately, she was right, but if he had to be grabbed or groped one more time... he didn't think he'd be able to stop himself from tossing her out on her pretty little ass.

"Hey Evan, you want some help stocking the bar tonight?" Evan looked up from counting, irritated that he was now going to have to start over.

Tori was leaning across the bar, her full breasts pressed firmly to the counter giving him a very generous view down her low-cut t-shirt.

"No thanks Tori, I think I'll close up here and just come in early tomorrow." He grabbed the drawer, deciding to count it in the office where he would be left alone; he turned and left the common room.

"Go ahead and go on home Tori. I'll finish wiping down the bar tops for you while Evan closes." Sensing Evan's annoyance with Tori, April completed her list of beers that needed to be restocked and came out from behind the bar.

"I can help Evan restock for tomorrow too, so no need for you to hang around." Tori, glaring at April, snatched her coat and purse from under the counter.

"Fine… I'll just go say goodbye then." April stepped in front of her before she could head towards the office.

"Trust me, the last thing you want to do is keep pushing your luck with Evan. Try to remember, he is your boss and call it a night."

Tori opened her mouth to respond but seeing the protective anger glittering in April's green eyes thought better of it. Turning on her heels, she walked out of the bar letting the door slam closed behind her.

After April had finished cleaning up the front and locking the doors, she headed to the back dreading the mood Evan would be in after Tori's behavior. She pushed through the swinging kitchen doors and was surprised to hear laughter coming from the office.

"Come on man, why don't you just give her what she wants? She's only been throwing herself at you for the last seven months. Live a little. You've been alone way too long!" April heard Trevor's drunken remark. Not impressed, she stomped into the office,

26

"Trevor Helms quit giving Evan advice that could land his ass in the clinic! Who knows where that girl has been? Or perhaps you have more insight into her extracurricular activities…we all know you're a lot less picky than you should be about who shares your bed!"

Evan and Trevor both turned toward the door where April stood with her hands braced on her hips, tapping her foot in annoyance.

"Don't worry beautiful, I only have eyes for you." Trevor reached out, grabbed her around the waist, and pulled her onto his lap.

"Don't you ever give up? I told you, you're not even my type." April wriggled away from him and walked across the small office to stand next to Evan.

Sadly, that was a lie, and it was getting harder to avoid her feelings. But April reminded herself that she wanted more than just a one-night stand… much, much more.

Evan was the only one who knew of her secret infatuation with Trevor. It had started as a schoolgirl crush when she was twelve and started looking at Evan's best friend in a completely different light. Evan did his best to shield his little sister from Trevor's womanizing ways, but April was neither stupid nor blind. All he could do was remind Trevor to back off when it came to his little sister.

"Hey friend, watch it! You know better than anyone that you've got to get through me first when it comes to my baby sister." Evan commented as he threw the baseball that he'd been toying with up to April, who immediately caught it and tossed it back.

Trevor knew that April was off limits, and although they didn't think he was aware of her feelings, he had known for some time. He cared for her very much. But the

27

fact was, April was Evan's sister, and he wasn't about to cross that line.

Unfortunately, he was also finding it harder and harder to avoid his growing feelings for April.

So instead, he played the part of the womanizing rake, hoping to discourage any deeper feelings that would leave them all angry and hurt in the end. They were his family, and he wasn't about to do anything to ruin that.

"Are you two done playing around so we can get out of here? I'm starving, and I want breakfast!" Trevor stood and, stealing the baseball from Evan's unsuspecting fingers, began to toss it up in the air as he exited the office. April watched him go and turned to her brother,

"Better finish up in here before he loses your lucky ball. Shall we call it a night and stock tomorrow before we open?"

"Yeah, sounds good to me. Sunday's usually start slow anyway." Evan leaned down and closed the safe door.

"Go on ahead I'll be done in a minute." April grabbed her coat off the hook on the back of the office door and hurried out after Trevor.

As Evan stepped out into the frosty night air and turned to lock up the front door behind him, he could hear Trevor and April laughing a couple of doors down from the Pub. They were tossing his lucky ball back and forth, which made Evan more than a little uneasy given Trevor's lack of sobriety.

"Hey, guys… do you mind? It took me three seasons to catch a home run, and you're going to lose it in the drink." Evan caught up to them and attempted to collect his prized possession.

"What's the matter buddy? You don't think I'd lose it do y-ah shit!" Just as Trevor went to toss the ball to Evan, Tori stepped out of the shadows and knocked the ball out of his hand. It hit the ground and rolled into the bay.

"Oh! Sorry boys. I didn't mean to ruin your little game." Evan turned from where his ball had plunked into the water, obvious displeasure written all over his handsome face. Tori, with her lips turned down in a sultry pout, came up to put her arms around him.

"Mm… you're so warm. I've been standing out here forever. My car won't start. You wouldn't mind giving me a ride home would you Evan?" Trevor was leaning far over the pier when he heard Tori's plea for help.

"Sorry bro, I think your ball is gone. But uh, maybe she could make it up to you." With a wink and a mischievous grin Trevor threw his arm around April's shoulders and leaning heavily on her, staggered to the parking lot around the back of the buildings.

It took every ounce of patience Evan had not to shove Tori into the same water his ball now resided in.

"I'll look at your car first. Maybe you just need a jump." Tori wiggled closer as he tried to set her apart from him.

29

"A jump huh… I never thought you'd ask." The smell of liquor on Tori's breath explained why she had the nerve to behave so brazenly. Evan wondered if he was the one funding her nightly drinking binge while she was "working" and his tolerance finally broke.

"Come on Tori. I am your boss, nothing more. Now can we please just go and see what the problem is with your car so I can get out of here? I'm tired and I want to go home… alone. Got it?" Tori's eyes narrowed.

"What the hell is the matter with you Evan Gallient? Most guys would jump at the chance to take me home. What makes you so fucking special, huh? You think you're too good for me?"

Tori turned and stalked back to her car. Without another glance back at him, she climbed into her beat up Honda and pealed out of the parking lot.

"Well, so much for her car not working." April commented dryly as they watched Tori speed away.

"Sorry about your ball Evan. I know how much it meant to you."

"Yeah well… shit happens. Let's just get out of here and go get something to eat before Trevor passes out. I'm driving."

***

Later, after Evan had dropped Trevor and April off at their homes, he headed back to the pub to restock the liquor for the following night. April had asked him to wait until the next morning, but he was suddenly anxious. The thought of going home alone to the house his parents had once lived in wouldn't help his anxiety level. So, he would go back to work and keep his mind busy until he was so exhausted there would be no avoiding sleep. He hoped to get the restocking and kitchen prep done tonight so he could focus on getting the food and beverage inventory submitted for that week's delivery.

He had just parked his truck and was climbing out when he noticed the fog hanging low over the pier. This time of year, it was expected to see fog rolling in off the water. He didn't think anything of it as he began the short walk up from the parking lot. He stopped where his baseball had rolled into the bay.

Disappointment and remorse at the loss almost overwhelmed him, reminding him all too well of another loss that still pained his heart.

His dad had loved the game, and it didn't matter who was playing. If there was a baseball game on, his dad had it blaring on every T.V. in the pub, and occasionally, they even took the time to all drive into the city and go to a game as a family.

It was on just such a trip that he had caught his lucky home run ball. He could still hear the excited crowd cheering for him, taste the salty peanuts on his lips, and feel his dad patting him on the back.

"Good catch kid." Evan looked up at his dad with delight,

"Here pops, you take it. You've always wanted to catch one." His dad looked down at him, pride shining in his green eyes.

"No son. It's your lucky ball, you keep it." It was one of the many memories that Evan had of his parents, one that he cherished deeply.

Only a few years later, his parents had been killed at sea when their thirty-foot catamaran capsized in a freak storm, drowning them both. Their bodies had never been recovered.

Evan was still crippled by the loss of his parents. It didn't seem possible that they had been gone almost three years now. Most days he was lost, floundering, trudging through the tasks of living day to day. He ran the pub with an absent mind. He had stopped doing all the things that he used to enjoy. He had lost track of how many fishing trips with Trevor he had turned down until Trevor had finally stopped asking.

April had asked him to get help, but how could he explain his feelings to a total stranger when he couldn't quite get a grasp on them himself. He was sad, lonely, but most of all scared... scared that anything or anyone he should ever care about would be taken from him just as his parents had been.

Their family dynamic had been destroyed. The only thing that kept him going now was knowing that he had to be there for April.

Evan somberly looked down to where the ball had fallen into the cold dark depths,

"Here you go dad... you finally got your fly ball. Take care of it for me."

The night was eerily still and Evan, suddenly sensing someone behind him, turned and looked up.

The fog he had noticed before now surrounded him in a thick grey curtain. Caught in the midst of the eerie silver cloud appeared to be the silhouette of a young woman. He leaned forward trying to get a better look at her without getting too close. He still wasn't sure what he was seeing.

The mist was churning and glimmering, making her appear ghostly as she stepped closer to him and out of the luminous fog.

Evan was drawn to her and slowly stepped closer, seemingly having no will of his own. He stopped and reached out his hand.

The faint scent of fresh cut wood drifted around him as his dark angel descended from the clouds.

Her eyes were the strangest color, radiant blue topaz with a hint of grey, giving them a silvery glow. Her high cheekbones and finely arched brows gave her a very regal appearance, complimented by full seductive lips that were just begging to be kissed. An untamed mane of exceedingly long mahogany tresses framed the perfection of her elegant features, making her by far the most exquisite creature he had ever seen.

They stood there, eyes locked, caught in the seduction of a raw attraction that seemed to pulsate with a life of its own; the musical chorus of the rise and fall of the ocean lapping against the pier lulling them into a trance.

Evan nearly jumped out of his skin when he heard a deafening crash coming from the back of the pub.

Sorry that the spell had been broken and annoyed at the interruption, he twisted around to see what had caused the loud clatter. Seeing nothing that would warrant his

33

immediate attention, Evan turned back to face the girl, hoping that the noise hadn't scared her too badly.

She was gone. Nothing remained of her but the soft haze that had drifted about her wraithlike form and the lingering aroma of the sweet-smelling forest.

Evan glanced around the empty docks. With the fog now lifting, disappointment washed over him. Who was she, and what had she been doing out here at this time of night? His undeniable urge to touch her had him puzzled and the fact that he didn't even know her, or anything about her, mattered little to him.

Another resounding crash came from the back of the buildings disrupting Evan's train of thought.

Pushing the strange encounter to the back of his mind, Evan turned and sprinted around the side of the buildings to the alley between the Waterfront Pub and the bait shop. There he found a homeless man knelt over the spilled garbage cans looking for scraps of food.

Evan took a deep breath and tried to get his heartbeat to regain its normal pace.

"Charlie, what are you doing old man? Trying to give me a heart attack?" Charlie climbed wearily to his feet.

"Sorry 'bout all the noise Evan, I was just looking for something to eat. Hey, what are you doing here this late anyhow? Young man like you ought to be in bed next to some sweet young thing."

Evan laughed and walked over to put his arm around the withered frame of the old man.

"Afraid not gramps. You know me, business before pleasure. Come on inside. I'll make you something to eat."

34

Evan looked around when they reached the front door, but the girl had not returned. Evan vowed to find out who his beautiful visitor had been, determined that she was more than just a figment of his imagination.

Turning his mind back to the present, he turned the key in the lock of the pub's front door and stepped aside to allow Charlie to go in before him and get out of the cold.

Evan failed to notice the shadowy figure watching them as they entered the pub, and he closed the door behind them.

Charlie was exhausted. Having his stomach full, and his body warmed from the bottle of whiskey he and Evan had shared, made the pain in his bones and the crisp night air a bit more bearable.

Charlie thought back on all the kindness those kids had shown him and smiled.

If it weren't for Evan, April, and Trevor, he probably wouldn't have survived this long. He never let on to the youngsters just how bad it was out here. He had made his bed, and it was time for him to lie in it.

Evan had asked him years before how he came to be homeless.

"I made some very bad decisions lad. I got greedy, and I trusted the wrong people. Listen to old Charlie when I tell you that the only people a man can trust are his family. Hold on dearly to the ones you love, and don't ever let go. If I had followed that very same advice and listened to my Millicent, bless her soul, I might still have a roof over my head and a wife by my side."

That was all anyone needed to know about the life poor Charlie had left behind. God willing the one he now lived would be over soon.

Evan had offered several times for him to come home with him and stay on until he could get back on his feet and had been disappointed by the refusal of his offer each time. But Charlie knew his time was coming quickly, and he didn't want anyone having to clean up the mess he had made of his life.

He could feel the tightening in his chest, he could hear the rattling with every breath he took. He took notice

36

of the weakening in his body and was having a difficult time just getting out of his crude bed every morning.

He wasn't sure how much longer he was going to have to wait but when the time came, he would be ready... ready to leave this world and be reunited with his darling Millie.

"Not much longer Millie, old Charlie will pass through those pearly gates soon enough sweetheart."

Charlie stopped murmuring to himself when he reached the top of the berm. He was relieved to see the old, abandoned lighthouse come into view.

The distance between the dock and the black sand beach was getting harder and harder to cross. Nevertheless, he now called this place home.

The lighthouse tower wasn't very tall, but the bluff that the tower sat on raised the lighthouse well above sea level. It was constructed of wood and had at one time been whitewashed but now it was as old and neglected as its inhabitant. Its paint was chipping, graffiti was painted on the outer walls, and the door hung at an awkward angle having dislodged from its hinge many years ago.

Pushing the door open and stepping in, Charlie sensed something in the atmosphere. Danger reverberated through the interior of the lighthouse causing the hair on his neck to prickle. The cloying metallic odor of blood seemed to pollute the air.

Looking around the door once inside, he could see the staircase that led up to the arc lamp.

Underneath the staircase was the pile of broken-down cardboard boxes and newspapers that served as his bedding. Charlie squinted in the dim light but was unable to see if there was anyone else there.

37

At the sound of the door slamming behind him, the old man turned with a shock and stared at the intruder. He couldn't make out any features. The figure standing before him was nothing but a shadow, a very large and ominous shadow.

Charlie tried to take a step backwards when, in the flash of an eye, the shadow had become as solid as steel. It snatched him up by the throat and held him in the air, his feet dangling pathetically kicking and twisting trying desperately to find solid ground.

Instantly Charlie was paralyzed with fear. His attacker lifted him effortlessly. He tossed him across the room as though he were nothing more than a rag doll.

Trying to regain his senses before the next attack, the old man clung to the wall trying to pull himself up and get to the stairs.

Not stopping to see if the creature was behind him, Charlie began to claw his way up the stairs, desperation making his movements clumsy and weak.

Before he could make it to the landing, he was forced down from behind and crushed beneath a great weight.

He could feel his bones shattering and his lungs collapsing. Incapacitated by the pain, he lay there limp and unmoving as a velvety whisper filled his ears and his mind, washing away the prayers he had been mentally reciting.

"You were anxious to die old man… why now does your heartbeat wildly with fear?" Charlie was yanked up from behind and once again slammed down, pinned to the stairs, this time nose to nose with his assailant.

He was almost unconscious from the pain, yet something held him from going over the threshold and sinking into the darkness that he wished would overtake him. He could now see something of the creature's face. Glowing eyes bore into his and the moonlight glinted off fangs that seemed to grow longer with every word that was spoken.

"Not the way you wanted it to end. It's too late for regret Charlie. Even now I can smell the blood filling your lungs." Charlie tried to speak, instead, he began to cough and choke, blood filling his mouth.

"You want to know what I am." Charlie stared in bewilderment trying frantically to breathe.

"No old man, I can't hear your thoughts. But I've heard that pitiful question countless times over the centuries." Charlie closed his eyes to the terror that now gripped him, desperately praying that it would be over soon. The creature laughed, a cruel and frightening sound.

"It's not hard to guess how desperately you crave death to release you from this pathetic existence... however, I am disinclined to let you join the afterlife... just yet."

The shadow hissed as it leaned back so that Charlie could look fully into the face of his killer. Its teeth bared, it pitched forward, piercing daggers into the flesh above his jugular. He could feel the blood being pulled from his body; the pool in his lungs receded. He took a deep breath then and was struggling to jerk away, when he heard the voice in his mind as darkness began to close in. "You want to know what I am? I am your one-way ticket to immortality!"

***

Juliette gracefully dropped onto the upper deck of her cabin. The images from her encounter on the dock replayed in her mind as she distractedly tried to concentrate on the layout of the town.

Chancellor was the perfect location to end this war. It was small and spread out. The isolation of this place would make it easier to defeat this creature, hopefully without much interference from the humans.

Juliette looked down at the baseball now cupped in her hand. Why had she taken it? What was it about the dark-haired man at the pier that lured her in? Was it his striking green eyes or perhaps the grief that seemed to emerge from behind them? His entire being radiated loneliness and defeat, but he carried within him a great deal of strength.

Generally, Juliette limited her contact with the mortals for the simple reason that she had come to despise them. Mortals had been the ones who had helped begin this war. They were pawns, easily manipulated, and trapped into serving that monster. Juliette was not about to let her life, or her quest be derailed or sabotaged by anyone, least of all a human.

Yet for some unknown reason, she found that she could not escape his image. She was intrigued by his clashing emotions. He was filled with despair, yet it was overpowered by the sheer amount of strength that blazed within him.

It reminded her so much of how she had felt every day for the greater part of her immortal life; yet she buried the pain and forged on knowing she had a duty to fulfill.

40

His aura burned bright, searing her with its glowing essence... but why? What made him so different from the millions of other mortals she had encountered throughout the centuries?

She toyed with the ball, being careful not to smash it like a marshmallow as she rolled it between her palms and gazed out towards the sea. The sun would be rising soon, and she needed to go inside before the sun's rays could cause her skin to burn. But where was Ambrosia?

No sooner had the thought crossed her mind than Juliette saw Ambrosia glide from the forest in her mist form, a dazzling luminescent cloud. Keeping her wolf shape, the great white creature was suddenly weightless as she soared up from the ground and cleared the wooden railing that Juliette now leaned against. Ambrosia landed on the balcony, her mist form becoming solid as she quietly trotted to Juliette's side.

"Good girl, just in time. I can feel the sun, it's rising quickly. Come, let us go inside. I am famished."

As Juliette opened the door and allowed Ambrosia to enter the house, she caught a glimpse of someone walking through the trees. Closing the door behind her she took a step towards the railing and leaned forward, trying to peer through the undergrowth.

It was him. She could smell his skin, hear his heartbeat, and feel his aura. What was his name? What brought him here? Why was he plaguing her?

She hated the fact that she was so curious about him. Was it curiosity? It most closely resembled desire.

Juliette gasped and took an involuntary step away from the railing, the intensity of that emotion now causing her to fear him. It had been centuries since that emotion had made its presence known within her. Desire was a sign

41

of weakness and a sign that Marek was fading from her heart. There was no room in her life for this stranger or the odd yearning she had for him.

Suddenly she felt a searing heat on her face, she looked up towards the treetops and saw that the sun was beginning to rise above the horizon.

Anger and fear surged through her; without a moment's hesitation Juliette dropped the baseball that she had been holding as her body evaporated into vapor and plunged through the wall and into the dark sanctuary of her bedroom, away from the sun and away from the man who now plagued her thoughts.

***

Evan still wasn't tired. After Charlie had left, he finished stocking the bar and locked up to go home.

However, once he pulled into the drive, he didn't want to go in. This evening's events had brought back some very painful memories, and the last thing he wanted to do was enter the home his parents had left to him. It only helped to remind him how empty the house and his heart remained.

He climbed out of the truck and turned towards the woods. Hoping a walk would help him clear his head, he started to hike in the direction of the cliffs that overlooked the beach.

Evan liked living in the middle of nowhere. The nearest property was nearly a mile south of his cabin.

If he remembered correctly, the last time he had hiked past the other cabin it had been vacant. He wondered if the property had been purchased yet. Curiosity getting the better of him, Evan turned south and began the long trek through the forest.

As he hiked through the dense vegetation, Evan couldn't keep his thoughts from returning to the young woman he had encountered on the pier.

He'd seen his fair share of bizarre weather anomalies here in Chancellor, but never a cloud of churning argent mist that smelled of smoked maple wood and timber after a summer storm drifting around a gorgeous woman.

Shaking his head and softly chuckling to himself, Evan tried to steer his mind to a more logical explanation of what he had seen. It was just your normal, average, run-

43

of-the mill fog bank, rolling in from the chilly damp spray of the pacific coast.

But the girl, he didn't know what to think about her. She'd been hovering at the edge of his thoughts all night long. Even Charlie had noticed his preoccupation this evening.

Evan slowed his steps realizing that he was coming upon the neighboring cabin, and that there was someone standing on the terrace. The sun was just beginning to rise over the trees, leaving him still encased in the twilight shadows of the great cedars.

As he stepped into the clearing surrounding the cabin, he looked up to offer a greeting to his new neighbor.

It was at that moment that the sunlight penetrated through the treetops, illuminating the balcony above him… now empty except for what appeared to be falling remnants of glistening diamonds drifting slowly towards the deck and the haunting scent of sweet cut maple.

Evan stood there, rooted to the ground, his heartbeat hammering in his ears as his mind tried to make sense of what he was seeing. His eyes were locked on the balcony above him when he caught sight of something rolling towards the wooden edge of the deck. It fell to the ground with a thump and rolled across the damp earth to come to a stop against his scarred work boots.

Evan was suddenly faint, his skin becoming clammy and his hand shaking as he leaned down and picked up his lucky ball, the ball that by all rights should now be at the bottom of the Cerulean Bay.

April awoke to the sound of someone banging on her front door. Trying to ignore the incessant pounding, she pulled a pillow over her head and snuggled deeper into the down feather mattress.

"April, wake up and answer the door." Evan's voice billowed through her small one-bedroom condominium. April peaked out from under her pillow. Surprisingly, for Oregon, the sun was not held at bay by cloud cover and was just beginning to peek through the slats of her vertical blinds, to cast piercing shafts of light across her room. She glanced at the nearby clock, 6:23 a.m. damn, what the hell was he doing here at this hour?

Tossing aside the covers, April climbed out of bed and stomped off to let him in. Evan had just raised his fist to beat against the door when it was flung open to reveal his very disheveled and irritable little sister.

"I hope to hell you have a very good reason for waking me up Evan. Do you have any idea what time it is?" April stopped her tirade as she noticed the strained expression on Evan's pale face.

"Evan, what's wrong? What's happened?" He looked like he hadn't even been to bed yet. He still wore the same faded blue jeans and his worn Waterfront Pub t-shirt from the night before. His face was shadowed with the growth of a new beard, and his bloodshot eyes were glassy from lack of sleep.

He slowly raised his arm and opened his hand to reveal the baseball that Tori had knocked into the water the night before.

"Where did you find it?"

45

"You wouldn't believe me if I told you. I need some coffee. Mind If I come in?" April stepped back from the entrance, unable to take her eyes off the ball he held out to her. She motioned for Evan to enter the condo.

"You look like you need a lot more than just a cup of coffee. What did you do last night?" She didn't wait for a response as she turned and padded barefoot into the small and cozy kitchenette. Evan closed the front door and dragged his heavy frame to the sofa in the living room. Sinking into the buttery suede, he lay back and draped the arm holding the ball over his eyes.

"I think I'm losing my mind." April began a pot of coffee and turned to look at him from the kitchen entrance. She hadn't seen Evan this ragged since the day he had told her of their parent's accident. Lifting two cups from the cabinet, she continued her silent scrutiny as she waited for him to elaborate.

Suddenly he sat up, rubbing his eyes with his knuckles, he began to relay all the strange events that had occurred the past evening. By the time he was finished with his story, the percolator was winding down and April was pouring them both a cup of the strong brew. After handing Evan his coffee, she took a seat on the matching ottoman opposite him.

"How on Earth did your ball end up on your neighbor's patio after we all saw it roll into the bay?" Evan raked his fingers through his hair in frustration.

"I have no idea. The only thing I know for sure is that everything that happened last night, and this morning has to do with that girl." Evan paused and took a long drink of his coffee,

"I spoke to Mr. Jennings, the landlord of the cabin next door to mom and dad's place, and it's been sold to

46

some foreign woman, Juliette Bellerose. He said she offered to pay him a lot of money in addition to the purchase price if he would see to the delivery of her belongings and unpack them for her."

Evan rolled the ball between his palms as he continued.

"He said she had some real strange requests before she moved in. Apparently, she's a very eccentric and private person."

"So, suddenly, this woman that lives next door to you is the cause of all the fog here in town, and she stole your ball? None of this makes any sense." The sarcasm in April's voice softened a bit when she saw the hurt expression on Evan's face. "I mean fog in Chancellor is really nothing to freak out about, but your ball, that's kind of weird."

"April, you and I grew up here. I have worked on those fishing boats since I was big enough to board a troller. I know fog. I've worked in fog all my life. This was like nothing I have ever seen before. If you had been there, you would know what I was talking about."

Evan stood and walked to the window overlooking Cerulean Bay. The fishing boats had long since departed their moorings, and gulls were sweeping down to salvage what bits and pieces they could find on the docks. From April's apartment, he could see the pier, the docks, even the back entrance to their pub.

April was perplexed. For Evan to go off the deep end and claim that he might have seen something otherworldly was a strange occurrence. Her usually levelheaded big brother was acting odd.

"Okay…describe it to me."

47

Evan turned and looked at her with a haunted glow in his deep green eyes and a tremor in his voice as he spoke.

"This silver cloud, the mist, or fog… if that's what you want to call it, seemed to shift, and dance, almost humming and pulsating with life as it moved around her. Then at the cabin, it seemed to be almost seeping through the walls and into the upper deck. It smelled of soil, wood, and rain. Not overpowering, but very fragrant and subtle, not quite tangible, more like the memory of… ah hell April, listen to me. I know I sound crazy! Believe me, I know! But I saw it, I smelled it. Whatever it was, or whoever she is, she moves fast because one second, I was reaching out to her, drawn to her, and the next she was gone! Just like that, in the blink of an eye, gone!" Evan snapped his fingers.

"I don't know what you want me to do Evan. Do you want me to look into it? Call someone maybe? What? Why are you looking at me like I've suddenly grown another head?" April stood and placed her empty mug on the counter.

"Because that's exactly how people would look at us if we went around talking about this." Evan set his mug next to hers on the countertop and turned towards the door.

"Just do me a favor, be careful, and don't go out alone. Something's not right; I'm not sure what, but I feel it." He turned back to her, one hand on the doorknob and said, "I'm tired, I just want to go home and get some sleep."

She walked to the door to see him out.

"Be careful out there big brother, you're all I have left." With a wink and a smile, Evan leaned in and gave her a quick hug.

48

"Don't worry about me, it's going to take a lot more than some cloud of perfume and a pretty girl to take me down. Get some sleep sis, I'll see you tonight." Evan turned and walked down the steps towards his truck.

As he climbed behind the wheel and began to buckle his seatbelt, he stared out the windshield.

The day was tranquil; there wasn't even a hint of a breeze to rustle the leaves in the cedar trees, almost like the calm before the storm.

Something was going to happen; he could feel it in his bones.

He thought back on April's worried remark as he looked at the ball in his hands; *"You're all I have left"*, and he was suddenly fiercely determined to find out exactly what was going on here in Chancellor, Oregon, and what this Juliette Bellerose had to do with it. He was certain about one thing; he'd be damned if he were going to let anything else in this godforsaken world tear what was left of his family apart.

***

The storm had finally settled into a light drizzle. Nothing but the sound of raindrops falling to the damp earth, and her lone wolf howling in the distance penetrated the quiet, balmy night. One would have never believed that this now peaceful township had only moments ago been teeming with a fiercely terrified mob, hell-bent on retribution and fueled by fear.

Juliette had remained on the roof until the town's minister had led the young witch away and had come back out into the rain to collect the charred remnants of Marek's body. Although they were already drenched from the rain, he poured holy water among the ashes for extra measure. With the help of the local reverend, they gathered the remains from the once smoldering pyre and placed them into a large, ornate silver chest that took both men to carry. After their task had been completed, they headed into the church, locking the door behind them.

Juliette thought it strange that such esteemed gentlemen would lower themselves to taking on the duties of the village undertaker, but none of the events from that night had made any sense. Marek had been burned at the stake without a trial. All previous executions had been by hanging, and one ill-fated man had been crushed to death under the weight of large rocks. A burning execution was no longer permissible, meaning that the people of Salem had broken English law to put an end to Marek's life. But why?

She silently swung down from her post above the entrance to the chapel, and without delay shrank back into the shadows flooding the alleyway. She wanted to inspect

50

the area where he had been burned to see if she could find any clues that would give her the answers she sought. Careful to stay in the shadows, Juliette skirted around the chapel and quickly crossed to the charred ground where her nightmare had begun.

The moment she stepped into the square something within her changed. Her body felt weighted down, her movements less fluid and her senses dimmed. It was excruciating. Swiftly moving back against the church, the smothering sensation immediately vanished. Lifting one arm towards the center of town, she could feel the invisible barrier pressing against her palm. Juliette's eyes shifted uneasily around the perimeter of the town square, looking for anything that would mark the boundaries of the binding spell. It was faint, and to the mortal eye would go unnoticed, but among the pale grains of sand that covered the ground was the telltale ring of salt circling the border of the courtyard.

Juliette stalked around the edge of the barrier; this, along with the talisman that had hung around Marek's neck and the spell that the girl had cast, were the reason for his inability to dissipate.

Fingers of icy dread clawed their way to her heart choking her. This town was dangerous. In it she was vulnerable. Somehow these people had learned what Marek was and had known how to incapacitate him.

She was fully aware that at any moment she, too, could be caught, accused, judged, and sentenced to the same fate that had befallen Marek.

The stench and images of Marek being burned alive would forever be engrained in her mind. If she were to find him and bring about his resurrection as promised, then she

51

was going to have to remain alert and on guard until he was once again by her side.

Looking up at the stars, as the darkness faded and the faint crimson stain of dawn crept across the sky, she knew she wouldn't have long to break into the church and find that silver coffin.

Scanning the stained-glass windows adorning the walls of the building, she realized that the interior of the church had grown considerably darker since the clergymen had gone in.

Wondering what else they had in store that required such secrecy, Juliette swiftly skirted the side of the church and entered through the thick cellar door that she knew to be hidden behind a thick lupine bush.

The dank walls of the narrow tunnel were illuminated by the glow of a single lantern hanging from the low ceiling. The passageway led to a small antechamber steeped in darkness. It contained a single stone slab stained with a wet sticky substance. The unpleasant odor of dead blood painted a gruesome picture in Juliette's mind as to just what that particular table was used for.

Hearing footsteps on the floorboards above, she let her gaze follow the sound to a small alcove just behind the slab. Peering closer, Juliette noticed a ladder carved into the walls of stone that led up to a trap door. Marek was beyond that door; she could smell his ashes.

As she reached for the first wrung of the ladder, anger and fear penetrated the damp wooden flooring above her alerting Juliette to the quarrel-taking place above ground.

Closing her eyes and using all her vampire senses, Juliette strained to absorb every aspect of the conversation, making the conclusion that there were at least four hearts beating in the room... two of them being the men who had carried Marek's remains into the church as they were slightly accelerated from the exertion of carrying the chest.

The voice of the third man she recognized as belonging to the judge who presided over the witch trials taking place here in Salem; his heart thumped weakly. She recognized the sound of a diseased heart. The fourth person she did not recognize as being anyone she had encountered in this town. His voice held a much higher degree of authority over the other three, and his heartbeat was strong and forceful.

"I offered each of you great sums of money to capture Marek Colville, execute him and deliver his remains to me. Seeing that it was I who had to lure him out of hiding, I do believe I am being more than generous in not reducing the amount of gold you will each be receiving. And yet here you stand before me, demanding more?" This coming from the voice she did not know however, Juliette realized, his voice sounded familiar. How did she recognize it, and why couldn't she place it? Her already turbulent thoughts were cast into further confusion.

Who was this person? Moreover, why had he hired these men to harm Marek? And why was the sound of his voice tugging at the outer rim of her memory? This plan had obviously been quite elaborate and had been in motion for some time now. How had Marek fallen prey to these men?

How had they drawn him out into the open? Juliette wanted the answers to these questions however, the sun would be rising soon, and she needed to get her hands on Marek's silver tomb.

Juliette knew what she must to do. Together with the strength of her great wolf, she would kill every one of them. However, moments before she could signal Ambrosia with her mind, thrust up through the floor, and drain every one of these devious men, their dispute took a chilling turn.

"We have all put our positions at great risk to do your bidding, executing an untried man by way of burning, and the witch you say he traveled with did not reveal herself as you had predicted. If she truly exists, she will surely come for us now! How are we to protect ourselves? We deserve an explanation...I demand it!" The Judge took the lead in the conversation, as the clergymen shrank away from the heated voices.

"My reasons are none of your concern. You will all be more than fairly compensated for your efforts. As for the witch, she will follow whoever holds the coffin. Once you hand over the remains, I will be on my way, and you will no longer be at risk."

Before the judge could offer another retort, Juliette heard the familiar sound of a pistol being cocked followed by a gasp and the retreating footsteps of all three Salem officials.

His tone lowered a degree; boredom and disdain dripping from his words.

"My timing is imperative. I must leave as the sun is rising, and I do not have the time to stand here and listen to your self-righteous atonements. Give me the chest, or I will leave your broken and bloodied bodies strewn across the floor of God's house."

Hearing that the sun would soon confine Juliette to the cellar sent her into a panic. How was she going to save Marek and make it out of here without being disintegrated

54

by the sun's rays? The answer was painfully clear. She was going to have to let this fiend take Marek's ashes. This man knew of her and her powers; she would need to rest, she would need to feed, and she would need to prepare before she could take on his abductor. This fight would have to wait; Juliette just hoped she would not be too late.

The decision made, Juliette dissolved into a cloud of vapor and plummeted through the floor, commanding Ambrosia to do the same, finding solace in the deep dark shelter of the earth.

The town was silent when the sun rose above the horizon as an unknown carriage rolled through the deserted streets. The only defining characteristic of the vehicle was the magnificent crest that adorned the side, and the luxurious velvet draperies that hid the occupant and his treasured coffer from the scorching rays of the morning sunlight.

***

Awakening from a deep slumber and her overwhelming recollection, Juliette realized that the sun had set, and Ambrosia had already left for her evening hunt. The haunting memory followed her out onto the balcony, and it took her a few minutes to slow the pace of her rapidly beating heart.

The soft, fresh breeze caressed her cheek and tousled her long, auburn hair. She could still remember the unrest she had felt that night as she settled into the damp soil beneath the church. That had been the first time she had had to slumber below ground to hide from the blistering light of day, but not the last.

Trying to push away the nightmare of that day, Juliette turned and entered the cabin and crossed to her bathroom. She started the shower and let her silk ivory nightgown slip to the floor.

Stepping into the cascade of heated water, Juliette took pleasure in the soothing warmth as it poured down the soft curves of her slender frame. The steam, rising from the fine spray that rained down over her body, carried with it the sweet perfume of fresh cut maple wood as she bathed her silken skin and long thick hair. Reluctant to step from the warmth of the shower, Juliette turned the water off and reached for the heavy, plush towel hanging from the back of the bathroom door.

She dried and dressed quickly, donning a faded pair of blue jeans, a plum satin camisole, chocolate suede calf high boots, and a matching suede, cropped, fitted jacket. She pulled her hair back into a low ponytail and, sweeping her bangs to the side, she secured them with a wide plum-beaded headband. Adding eyeliner, mascara, and glossy lip balm to blend in more with the mortals, Juliette was ready to explore her new hometown and possibly pick up some leads on the whereabouts of the fiend she had come here to destroy.

The drive into town didn't take very long, she headed back towards the wharf she had visited the previous night hoping that what nightlife this small town did have to offer would aid her in the investigation.

Parking her gleaming black SUV behind an old beat-up pickup truck, Juliette took a quick survey of the lot. There were a few young couples milling around in between parked cars and a handful of older men dressed in heavy cotton parka's, worn jeans, and rubber knee boots, smoking cigars, and pipes in the dim glow of the electric lanterns hanging from light poles.

Juliette climbed out of her SUV and walked towards the Waterfront Pub's entrance. She ignored the admiring and curious glances cast her way as she entered the tavern. She located a small bar-top table near the rear of the pub and took a seat.

She opened all her senses, testing the emotions emanating from the patrons and taking in every conversation that was being had. She listened for any clues that might lead her to the town's newest inhabitants.

From the direction of the bar, she felt his aura and tried desperately to ignore him but was failing miserably.

Evan had just finished pouring a beer and was collecting the money due when he spotted her entering the pub.

As she walked past him and sat towards the back of the room, her intoxicating perfume, once again, overwhelmed him. His head was spinning from the memory of last night. He turned to look at her and tried

57

with all his might not to stare. His memory had not done her justice, she was exquisite!

It was then that he realized she was meeting his gaze. An almost wistful look softened her gorgeous features. Abruptly the longing expression was gone, replaced with one of carefully guarded secrets and distrust.

Clearing his throat, Evan approached her, set down a red cocktail napkin on the table in front of her, and leaned forward bracing his palms on the polished wood.

"Can I get you something to drink?" Trying to appear unmoved by their intimate scrutiny of one another, Evan presented her with his ever-popular boyish grin.

Juliette had wanted to get a better look at the man she had seen yesterday, but she hadn't expected to feel the unsettling heat of arousal unfurl deep in her belly.

Her breath caught in her throat and her cheeks flushed. Juliette looked up to meet his green eyes. They were the color of the deep Pacific Ocean that stretched out beyond the pier. His hair looked as though it hadn't been cut in a while with unruly waves as dark as the midnight sky. He was tall and well-built with strong broad shoulders, a powerful sculptured chest that tapered down to a taught abdomen, slim hips and muscular thighs that were encased in tight denim. He wore a faded red t-shirt that had a lighthouse logo and the name of the bar printed on it. His strong forearm was inches away from her, and she could smell the clean fragrance of soap, and warm masculine flesh.

Juliette tried to glance away, but her eyes seemed riveted to his.

"Do you happen to have any hot coffee?"

"Sure." He turned breaking the connection and quickly returned to the bar. Taking an Irish coffee mug down from the shelves behind the bar, he poured the coffee from the carafe and came back to place it on the napkin in front of her.

"You're not from around here." It was a statement meant to inquire as to where she had come from and why. Juliette knew what he wanted and didn't want to play along.

"No, I'm not." Evan raised a curious brow in her direction, understanding that she didn't want to elaborate and extended one hand towards her.

"I'm Evan Gallient, owner and operator of The Waterfront Pub." Juliette paused, placing her hands on either side of the hot glass to warm her cool touch before meeting his grasp.

"Juliette Bellerose."

"Nice to meet you." Evan's words were soft, as his feverish skin embraced her cooler flesh.

Soft waves of velvet heat radiated up her arm and wrapped coils of warmth around her cold heart. She could not let go, yet she knew she desperately needed to. These feelings were wrong; he should not be affecting her like this.

Before she could withdraw her arm, a blond waitress dropped her tray on the worn bar with a loud clatter demanding Evan's attention. Evan reluctantly dropped her hand and turned away. With a disapproving glare at the young woman, he began to help her get her drink order.

Juliette was grateful for the disruption. It gave her a moment to compose herself and try to overcome the sensations that Evan was causing to churn within her. She could not take any chances. It was best that she just get the

59

information she needed and not ever return to his establishment.

Juliette sighed as she turned away from the bar. She'd begun to survey the common room when she noticed the same blond waitress glaring at her while Evan poured the beer she needed to fill her order. Juliette met her gaze, unwavering and unfazed by the animosity surging in her direction.

The girl exuded raw sexuality and was absolutely seething with jealous rage directed at the intimate moment she had interrupted.

Her pretty pixie-like features did little to detract from her overexposed breasts and painted on blue jeans. She had taken her Waterfront Pub t-shirt and remade it into a skintight, navel-bearing monstrosity that left little to the imagination.

It was a wonder they allowed her to work looking like that, yet Juliette could see from the lustful glances of the men in the room that her attire was a hit with the male patrons.

A deep voice next to her ear startled her.

"Don't worry about Tori, she's harmless." Juliette kept her eyes on the girl he called Tori until she turned to collect her tray from the bar as Evan hurried over to help a customer in need of a refill. She turned to look at the man who had somehow snuck up behind her.

She had been so caught up in the sensations that Evan had brought to life in her that she had let her guard down, something she would be careful to never let happen again.

"I'm Trevor Helms, a frequent visitor of the Waterfront and Evan's best friend."

His golden blond curls hung over his wide brown eyes, giving him a playful quality; he seemed harmless enough.

"Juliette Bellerose. I think I've made an enemy of the girl."

Evan noticed the conversation taking place and tried to maneuver himself into eavesdropping distance.

"Wouldn't doubt it," Trevor was saying.

"Couldn't be helped, I'm sure. Gorgeous women tend to make her a bit edgy." He leaned forward and whispered in her ear, "I'm pretty sure she views you as competition." Juliette appreciated his honesty, fortunately, the girl had no reason to fear her as competition. Juliette had absolutely no intention of courting whatever feelings Evan stirred within her. She had another agenda, and it was time she got on with it.

She turned her face back towards the waitress as she strutted from table to table checking on her customers and leaned in closer to Trevor.

"Lucky for her I am not here to compete." She turned and looked him in the eye, keeping her voice low and her stare intent on his friendly brown eyes. "I'm here to find someone, maybe you can help." Evan stepped up to her table and put a fresh beer in front of Trevor.

"Looking for someone, well that shouldn't be too hard, this is a very small town. What's the name?" Swiveling on her stool, Juliette turned to include him in the conversation.

"Devlon Coleville, he has probably only been here for a short time. Do you know anyone by that name?" Trevor stared at his beer, a frown creasing his forehead as he tried to recall anyone by that name.

Evan answered first, "No, I don't know anyone by that name, and anyone new in Chancellor would probably have already been by the pub since this is one of the few restaurants in town." His words only confirmed what Juliette had already assumed.

Devlon was still in hiding. He had not shown his face yet in this small town, but it would only be a matter of time before the disappearances and attacks started.

Evan grasped for anything to keep her talking, but he didn't want to pry and be nosy.

"How long are you planning on being here in Chancellor, Juliette?" His question seemed to snap her out of a deep thought, but the guarded look returned to her unique silver eyes.

"As long as it takes." Her short cryptic answer slightly annoyed him. He could feel the wall she was attempting to keep around herself. She seemed to want to keep him at a distance when all he wanted to do was to wrap her in his arms and be as close to her as possible.

What was it about her that had him wanting her so badly? They had just met. He wasn't even sure if what he had seen in the mist the other night had really been her; maybe it was his imagination playing tricks on him. But how could he explain his imagination conjuring an image of a girl he hadn't yet laid eyes on?

She detected his annoyance and was glad for it. The last thing she needed was this human lusting over her, making it harder for her to ignore him. She refused to admit to herself that she was as equally drawn to him. Their sadness and fortitude giving them equal ground. She did not feel superior to him as she usually did with humans. He was dangerous. She needed to keep her distance from him.

62

They hadn't realized that they had been staring intently at each other until Trevor cleared his throat to break the tension that had been building.

"So, I'm going to go see if anyone is up for a game of eight ball and leave you two alone to finish…" pausing as he searched for the right words, then giving up, Trevor just mumbled, "okay, bye." and headed towards the billiards table.

Warmth flooded Juliette's cheeks, mild embarrassment washing over her. Evan noticed her blush and smiled inwardly, pleased that he had gotten under her skin as well.

She wanted to deny what was happening between them. Well, he wasn't going to give in that easily. He was beginning to reach across the space between them to take hold of her hand, desperate to touch her again, to make a physical connection with her that wouldn't be so easily dismissed, when April came barreling through the kitchen doors.

Juliette noticed the slim girl with long curly blue-black hair and striking green eyes as she flew at Evan, near hysteria. It occurred to her that this girl carried the same features and coloring as Evan. Yet her small, heart-shaped face was pale, and there were tears rolling down her cheeks. Trevor, hearing the commotion near the pool table, dropped his cue stick abruptly and hurried over to the crying young woman.

"April, what's wrong? What happened?" Evan seemed to momentarily forget about Juliette. He pushed away from where she sat and joined April and Trevor at the end of the bar. April was hiccupping and trying to control the tears so that she could speak. With an air of authority, Evan pushed his sister onto a nearby barstool.

"What's going on April? Why are you crying?"
Evan's voice was composed as he handed her a bottle of
water to help calm her hiccups. After April had taken a
few sips, she was calm enough to explain the reason behind
her distress.

"Something horrible has happened to Charlie, Evan.
The sheriff found the inside of the old lighthouse covered
in blood... Charlie's blood!" A stunned expression
crossed his face as Evan slowly leaned against the counter
and looked down at his black work boots.

"I was just with him last night. I asked him to come
back to the house to give him a warm place to sleep; he
refused as usual. If only he hadn't been so damn stubborn.
What do they think happened?" Trevor, now sitting with
his arm around April, looked up at Evan.

"Who the hell would hurt Charlie? He was a
harmless old man." April, sniffling leaned into Trevor's
embrace.

"The sheriff said that they've never seen anything
like it. They are sending out a search party to locate his
body. Oh god Evan, they said body, they don't think they
will find him alive!" That revelation brought on a new
onslaught of tears.

Trevor pulled her against him and let her bury her
face in his chest as he stroked her hair trying to comfort the
distraught girl.

Juliette, who had been listening to the whole
conversation, slid off her barstool and placed a couple of
bills on the table next to her full coffee cup, then she
silently slipped out into the night. She had her first lead.
Now all she had to do was find the lighthouse.

April, Evan, and Trevor were still talking quietly
when Juliette left the pub. The conversation finally broke,

64

and Evan turned to ensure that Juliette was still there. It was then that he noticed the money, the full cup of coffee, and the empty bar stool where she had been sitting moments ago.

***

Juliette left the pub and stopped by her house to change clothes. After reaching the cabin, Juliette exchanged her boots for a sturdier pair, donned a warm black sweater, and replaced her headband for a small knit cap to keep her hair out of her face.

She stepped out onto her balcony and shivered as the frosty night air washed over her. She probed the forest, silently calling for her wolf and located her position far north of the town.

Ambrosia had already hunted and had been scouting the outskirts of town for traces of their enemy. Apparently, she had come across his path, because the serene Oregon night was suddenly interrupted by her piercing howl as she called for her mistress.

Juliette dispersed immediately and spiraled high up and over the treetops barely feeling the fingers of the pine branches sweeping through her ghostly form. It took her only moments to reach Ambrosia and drop gracefully to the ground.

His scent was as clear as though he had just recently passed by. He was so near it occurred to her that she might turn around and he would appear. Fury erupted within her; a burst of power rippled through her body as she stalked the path he had taken.

She silently ordered Ambrosia to take mist form so that if he were near, he would not see her. She couldn't take the chance of him wanting to take Ambrosia from her too.

She followed his trail through the wild undergrowth ducking under fallen logs that leaned upon stronger

66

redwoods and stepping over a bubbling stream that cut through the Oregon hills.

She had been walking for what seemed like ages as her predator eyes roamed the wilderness, raking through the emerald forest drenched in shade from the waxing moon, until the vegetation gave way to rocky terrain that led to a vast cliff.

The moist spray seemed to soar up from the base of the cliff that overlooked the Pacific Ocean to bathe her skin in its damp embrace. Juliette could hear the surf crashing against the stone wall as the water tried to carve its way through the earth.

His scent was quickly lost in the sharp taste of salt and brine that burst from the crashing waves at the bottom of the cliff.

Juliette backed into the forest, thinking maybe he had turned and followed the edge of the wood, but his trail clearly ended where the forest did. She went back to the cliff face and paced back and forth trying desperately to locate where he had gone, but he had simply disappeared over the edge of the bluff. She had searched the area, retracing her steps into the forest well over a dozen times. Even if he had dissipated, she would still be able to track him, but his path seemed to end at the overhang.

Her hair had escaped from under her cap and was blowing wildly in the turbulent wind. She pulled the cap from her head and clutched it in her fist.

Juliette stood on the rim looking out over the edge of the world and snarled in frustration. She had been so close this time. She could still feel his dark pulse throbbing in her heart. But there was no longer any trace of him. It was as if he had simply disappeared into the sea.

She pushed back at the despair that threatened to overtake her, refusing to give in to that weak emotion.

Her mind raced through every possibility of where he could have gone. Perhaps the lighthouse would hold some clues as to his whereabouts. Her mind made up, she dissipated and let the blustering ocean winds pull her from the cliff to twist through the rising squalls and plummet to the surface of the raging sea.

She followed the swells, bursting through clouds of sea foam, Ambrosia following close behind.

By the time they reached the lighthouse it was nearly two in the morning. She had lost track of time and hadn't realized how long she had been in the forest tracking that monster.

It was probably better this way. Maybe with it being so late she wouldn't have to worry about running into anyone.

Her thoughts turned back to how she had heard about the attack at the lighthouse. She was glad she had made the decision to go by the Waterfront Pub to collect information, yet she was still unable to shake the flood of emotions that settled over her every time she thought of Evan. Hopefully that was the last time, she would have to purposely place herself in his path.

The last thing she needed, this close to what she hoped would be the end of her journey, was to get caught up in a tangle of emotions for a human.

She was here to find Marek, the love of her life… the man she had spent much of her immortal life trying to rescue. Then why the hell was she standing here wondering what it would be like to feel Evan's firm lips covering hers, what it would be like to be caught up in his strong, passionate embrace, with his breath fanning out

68

against her cheek, to feel his muscular arms pulling her against his hard body, absorbing his warmth… Juliette stopped her train of thought before it could take her any further.

Evan was dangerous, not because he could ever hurt her, but because the attraction that burned between them could get them both killed.

She looked out towards the ocean where she could see the outline of the cliffs she had just left, far off in the distance. Turning back towards the shore, she surveyed her surroundings.

The wind coming off the surf carried with it the salty pungent odor of kelp beds and seaweed. She could see the frothy white water churning as the waves pounded the shoreline. The sand sparkled like millions of tiny black diamonds. The old, dilapidated lighthouse rested on its rocky throne, ominously keeping its eye on the sea.

Stepping over the crime tape, Juliette began to walk towards the splintered door. She quickly scanned the first floor and found nothing more than the blood spattering on the walls.

This was different. She had been tracking this creature for decades now; he had only left drained bodies in his path. It was not like him to waste the blood and take the corpse.

He was up to something. Was he trying to send a message, giving her a glimpse of the horror he could unleash on this town? Hadn't he figured out that people didn't matter to her anymore?

There had been a time when she considered herself an advocate for humanity. She had never thought she would have the ability to kill or allow the killing of innocent humans. That had all changed the night he had destroyed her life by taking Marek.

His message did nothing to dissuade her from searching him out and putting an end to his dark existence. She headed up the spiral staircase that led to the arc lamp.

Here she found nothing that would lead her in the right direction. She was just beginning to turn and head back down the stairs when she felt the presence of someone else on the beach.

She paused and concentrated on the throb of a beating heart and the radiance of a force so strong it smoldered, Evan! She knew it was him. She could feel the same blaze that had erupted the first time she had seen him at the dock and again when he had passed by her cabin. Even when he had approached her at the bar, she couldn't get past the searing aura that radiated from him, nor the sadness and grief that poured from his very soul.

Juliette knew she should just follow her instincts and dissolve into vapor... leave him alone, without the slightest clue that she had been there. But for some reason she froze. Her breath caught in her throat as Juliette waited to hear him come into the lighthouse. It wasn't long before she heard the hollow sound of his boots on the decaying wooden floor. Her pulse was pounding in her ears, goose flesh was covering her arms, and again she experienced the flames of arousal leaping to life in the pit of her stomach.

Her hands were clammy and shaking with the anticipation of seeing him again. No longer able to resist the pull of attraction that she knew existed between them, Juliette slowly descended the stairs.

***

The rest of the night had passed uneventfully, and since it was still early in the week, business had been slow. Trevor was able to take April home not long after they got the news of Charlie's disappearance and possible murder.

The closeness between Trevor and April hadn't gone unnoticed. When Trevor had offered to take her home, it seemed almost natural to see the two of them arm in arm, walking out the front door. Evan just hoped they knew what they were doing, and that Trevor didn't give him a reason to break his nose. Evan would hate to lose his best friend just because he couldn't practice some self-control when it came to his little sister.

His thoughts had turned back to poor Charlie when he was driving home, and he decided to take a detour to the old lighthouse. Evan planned to drop by the sheriff's station in the morning to get any news they might have and to offer his assistance in the search party.

He felt responsible for Charlie, he should have insisted on Charlie coming home with him. Maybe then he would still be alive. Evan shook himself. They didn't know that he was dead yet. There had been no body. He needed to stay optimistic until the worst could be confirmed.

He had been driving along a narrow, overgrown road when he caught sight of the faded wooden lighthouse sign in the beam of his headlights.

Getting out of the truck, he grabbed a flashlight from the glove compartment and began to follow a trail that led him through the trees and down to the black sand beach. It wasn't a far walk down to the rock jetty that the lighthouse stood on. And from this distance, he could already see the yellow police tape glowing in the darkness marking it as a crime scene.

Stepping into the lighthouse, the beam of Evan's flashlight illuminated the dusty interior. He noticed the pile of cardboard on the floor beneath the stairs, and grief poured through him. He remembered Charlie coming to the pub and asking for the empty cardboard boxes to sleep on. When Evan offered to get him a mattress or have him come stay with him, Charlie had remained firm in his refusal.

Kneeling next to Charlie's makeshift bed Evan found a piece of driftwood that Charlie had fixed to the wall serving as a shelf. On it was a faded miniature of Millicent, Charlie's deceased wife, a collection of polished seashells that he had found on the beach, and an old rusty crucifix dangling from a tangled string of fishing twine.

Evan gathered the few treasures that Charlie had managed to hold onto all these years and wrapped them in a piece of newspaper he'd found on the floor, placing them in his pocket. If the time came to arrange a memorial or funeral service, he would make sure that they were placed with Charlie for burial.

Suddenly he heard footsteps on the stairs above him. Taking a panicked step towards the door, Evan swung the flashlight up the staircase. Juliette stood poised at the top of the stairs, one hand on the railing, the other hanging loosely at her side. Her head tilted, silently questioning his reason for being there.

She was as beautiful as he remembered… maybe even more so, dressed mysteriously all in black, her hair framing her lovely face and the pale moonlight reflecting off what was left of the arc lamp behind her, giving her that unearthly appearance yet again.

"What are you doing here?" she asked in a soft voice.

"I should be asking you the same question," Evan replied, taking a step towards the stairs, drawn to her like a moth to flame. Juliette continued slowly down the steps until she was face to face with Evan, only inches separating them.

Why did she feel this irresistible urge to wrap her arms around him and lean into his warmth? She must fight it; it was wrong... but some unwavering force seemed to be pushing her, pulling at her in one direction only, towards him.

Evan could see the desire burning in the depths of her exceptional silver eyes. He'd never experienced an attraction like this and never so soon. It seemed animalistic, carnal, and too strong to be ignored. He had only just met her, yet here he was reaching for her, leaning in to taste her soft honeyed lips.

He heard her breath hitch as he placed his hands on her hips, tentatively at first. As he slowly moved his face towards hers, shock reverberated through him as she continued to stand there, waiting for his lips to meet hers.

Their mouths touched, hesitantly at first. Juliette gripped the railing knowing she should pull back and break the kiss, yet she found herself unable to move. Evan suddenly grasped her around the waist and yanked her against him, glorying in the way that their bodies fit together. Juliette finally responded, yielding to him, and wrapping her arms around him, one cool hand combing through his thick hair, holding him closer to her, as the kiss turned urgent.

Then as quickly as it had started, Evans arms were empty. Juliette had torn her lips from his and wrenched back. A primal growl escaped her lips as she shoved him from her and backed up the stairs. She leaned against the rough wooden wall, panting, and trying to catch her breath.

Evan also backed away, running a hand through his hair. He blew out a pent-up breath and looked at her in astonishment.

"Wow! That...was certainly unexpected." Juliette gathered her wits and glanced in his direction as he voiced his thought.

Anger, humiliation, and guilt all took hold of her. Suddenly Juliette was seething with rage at Evan for making her feel things she should not be feeling, at herself for being too weak to fight him off, and at fate for placing them in this position. She had no right to feel passion like this until Marek was found and once again in her arms.

"That was a mistake, it won't happen again!" Juliette finished descending the stairs and went to push past him and out of the lighthouse. Evan gently took her arm and turned her back to face him.

"Wait...what just happened, and why are you so angry?" Juliette looked down at his fingers holding her wrist as a cynical sneer touched her lips. Her gaze traveled up to meet his eyes, fury glinting in their green depths. Something in the way she looked at him chilled Evan to the bone. His confusion was quickly replaced with dread as he instantly released her arm.

Juliette knew she needed to frighten him; it was the only way she could guarantee he would stay away from her. However, she feared Evan was not going to be an easy man to scare. She would need to weaken him, body, and

74

mind if she were going to have any effect on him at all and show him a glimpse of the creature that she was.

Juliette stepped towards him, looking into his eyes. She sent a burst of power towards him, occupying his mind, and twisting his thoughts into obscure darkness.

His eyes glazed over as she breeched his mental barriers and enveloped his thoughts in a nightmare that would surely scare him enough to stay away. She pulled in a dark and dense fog to fill the interior of the lighthouse so that she was only a shadow standing before him.

She leaned in closer to him, her mouth mere inches from the throbbing pulse point below his jaw line.

Tasting the fear that was beginning to take hold, Juliette probed deeper, churning his thoughts, and spinning them into dark and incoherent delusions.

She felt his body shudder and he began to slump to the floor. Bracing him against the wall, she maintained her unrelenting hold on his body. Her mind instructed him to open his eyes as they were trying to flutter closed, she cleared his vision long enough to allow him to see her razor-sharp fangs glinting in the shadows before plunging them into his neck.

As Juliette sank her teeth deep into his skin, the copper-sweet flavor of his blood flooded her mouth and poured through her veins. Her body pulsated with his strength and smoldered from the intensity of their attraction for one another, casting her into a euphoric trance. It had been over a century since she had last fed from anyone other than Ambrosia. The strength, the heat, and the salt of his flesh captured her in a merciless grip, and she had to struggle to stop feeding.

She inhaled deeply, trying to clear her mind of the taste of him on her lips. She retracted her fangs and bit down on her own tongue, letting her blood flow into the wound. The fusion of their blood would allow him to heal quicker and ensure that the blood loss would have minimal damage.

As she began to pull away, she suddenly witnessed the faint stirring of awareness flickering in his mind. She quickly realized that the fog she had placed in his mind was beginning to lift. His intoxicating blood had caused her to momentarily loosen her grip on her powers.

She had accomplished what she had set out to do. He was weak from blood loss and unable to hold himself upright. She placed her hand on the back of his head, once again marveling at the feel of his soft curls against her palm, and leaned forward, pushing him to take a seat on the stairs.

Moving away from him, she stared into his pale face, so stark against the shadows of the lighthouse. She had taken a great deal from him... more than she had meant to, but not enough to hurt him if she stayed away and didn't take any more, he should be fine.

Unfortunately, she couldn't say the same for his state of mind.

She had done everything in her power, short of completely revealing herself to him, to show him that he needed to keep his distance. The memory that he would be left with would show him that danger followed her, and he needed to stay away from her.

Juliette knelt down, knowing that she needed to get out of here before he regained consciousness. She cupped his face and looked longingly at his silent features. She was sad that it had come to this. If only circumstances hadn't been as they were, she would have reveled under his golden touch and vibrant essence.

76

But that was never to be. Marek needed her and she had a promise to uphold. Juliette leaned forward, placed her cheek against his, and whispered a final farewell... "Forgive me. This is what is best for us both."

Juliette turned and flung open the door that led out onto the beach, and just as the cold salty air flooded the interior of the lighthouse Juliette's form faded into the wind. For the second time that night, she let the ocean breeze sweep her out into the darkness, far away from Evan, the tempting heat he invoked within her body, and the forbidden longing that invaded her heart as his blood flooded her veins.

Evan was aware of the throbbing pain in his neck, but he was incapable of remembering why it was there. He rubbed at the area that hurt the worst and felt the tender ache as his fingers met the bruised skin where tiny puncture wounds had been.

He could have sworn that Juliette had been there only moments ago. But now all he could see was the hollow wooden core of the lighthouse, the shadows that drenched the black sand beyond the open doorway, and the glowing burst of sea foam as the waves staggered and fell upon the beach.

It felt like he didn't have a single bone in his body. His movements were slow and deliberate as he tried to climb to his feet. He had to lean heavily on the wall as he crept towards the door. Nausea caused Evan to falter, and as he breathed deeply trying to calm his rolling stomach, the stench of Charlie's blood still painted on the walls was almost his undoing.

The earth beneath his feet seemed to pitch and sway, causing him to stumble. Finally, he reached the entrance of the lighthouse and deeply sucked in the clean salt air to clear his mind, all the while he searched the seashore for tracks that would lead him to Juliette. The only footprints crossing the sand were from where he had entered the lighthouse not even an hour before.

He turned back towards the stairwell, wondering if Juliette had gone back up the stairs. He looked up towards the arc lamp as dizziness washed over him, and he broke out in a cold sweat. What strength he had left quickly failed him as his legs buckled and sent him crashing to the floor.

Moaning in pain and frustration, Evan tried to recall what had happened that had left him feeling so sick and weak. He remembered holding Juliette in his arms. He could still taste her lips on his own, but everything after that became a blur. He lay there on the floor trying to form the broken images in his mind into something tangible. But the more he tried, it seemed the more tangled his thoughts became.

Once more Evan pulled himself into a sitting position and waited for his head to clear. It took him the better part of an hour to leave the shelter of the lighthouse and cross the wet sand. The damp and bitter wind whipped through his t-shirt and jacket, leaving his skin numb and stinging.

By the time he reached the path that led him to his truck, Evan was ready to collapse again. He stumbled and fell heavily against the hood of his truck just as the sky opened and rain pelted the rusted body of the pickup creating a deafening patter.

Evan pulled the door open and used the very last of his strength to hurl his body onto the worn bench seat and close the door behind him. The rhythm of the downpour colliding with the windshield and the fear that something horrible had happened to Juliette haunted Evan as the darkness finally came to claim him.

***

Thunder rolled in the distance, threatening rainfall, as the dark clouds covered the night sky and blocked the rays of the waning moon.

The oppressive humidity of the evening dew and the muted tones of the township settling invaded the solitude that surrounded Juliette in her resting place beneath the church, waking her from her slumber.

She could hear the soothing whispers of children's voices as they recited their bedtime prayers. She could feel the low drumming of the villager's footsteps as they retired to their homes escaping the perils that crept in the night, hidden in the thick shadows cast by the darkening skies.

The dirt and rock that sheathed Juliette quivered with the movements of nocturnal creatures and slithering insects, spreading gooseflesh across her body.

She paused for a moment, concentrating on the interior of the church cellar, making absolutely certain that there wasn't anyone present to witness her assent from the earth below.

The cellar was empty except for the corpse of a young woman resting on the stone slab. Markings from the hangmen's noose scarred the soft ivory skin below her jaw. Her clothes were that of a peasant, not made from the same fine cloth the clergymen were privileged enough to drape themselves in. The soles of her shoes were worn from the long days of farm duties and everyday household tasks.

Juliette stepped up to the table, looking down into the girl's delicate pale features. Pain struck her heart at the realization that this was the young witch from the night before.

It seemed that Marek's death had inspired the town to commit another brutal murder. Regardless of how the girl had aided in his capture, Juliette could not bring herself to feel anger for the part that she had played. She had simply been another pawn in the grand scheme to steal Marek from her.

Instead, Juliette mourned the loss of the girl. Her young life cut short, and for what? They had used her, used her power when it was convenient for them, to line their pockets with silver, and then when she was no longer of any use, a liability as it were, they murdered her. The only genuine witch they had discovered on their quest now lay cold and lifeless in this godforsaken town, a town that needed to be taught a lesson.

This witch-hunt had stirred curiosity within Juliette and Marek. They had been searching for other witches, trying to find the coven that had provided the vampire serum that had started it all. Their quest had led them to Salem.

But upon entering the town, they had discovered that these proceedings had nothing to do with real witchcraft or magic. They were no closer to having any answers about where their kind originated than when they had set sail from Europe.

Juliette's thoughts had carried her back to the reason they had begun this quest in the first place, and now she stood alone in the cellar of a church, with nothing but the remains of a gifted young woman and the noble memories of the man she loved.

The voice she had heard just the night before still tugged at her memory; it had made the village officials quake with fear. Their impudence had only angered him more. Maybe the humans were the key to finding out who

81

this mystery man really was and why he wanted Marek's remains. He clearly wanted her to follow him; that realization alone was vexing. How did he know about them, and what did he want from her?

It was obvious that they had planned this attack with great care and detail. It was also very apparent that whomever she was up against had known Marek enough to draw him out into the open and let him believe he could lower his guard. Keeping those details in mind Juliette knew she should be looking for someone who was close to them or had been at one time.

Juliette looked down at her attire. The dark blouse, black breeches, and knee boots she wore would help her move more stealthily through the town, but she needed to arouse absolute fear in the judge and perhaps even his accomplices if she were going to get anything out of them tonight.

Juliette looked over to the body lying on the altar and looked down into the pale lifeless features.

Although it saddened her that the girl's short life had ended so tragically, it was also somewhat of a relief that she could not be used against Juliette in the same manner she had been used against Marek. The threat against her had dimmed now that there was no longer a living witch in this town to bind her powers. However, her death had not been deserved, and Juliette would not allow it to be in vain.

Taking each cold hand into her own, Juliette leaned forward and inhaled deeply, closing her eyes. She tried to muster the strength she would need to occupy the girl's dead body. It would be difficult since she hadn't had time to meet with Ambrosia in the last twenty-four hours to feed, but she had to try.

The air within the chamber took on a heavy feeling, and time seemed to slow down with every breath she took. The pressure beneath the chapel felt as if the walls were closing in, trying to wring the very life from her own body. Finally, she broke apart, disintegrating into a radiant current of energy that hovered for a moment above the corpse and then struck like a bolt of lightning to invade the skin of the dead and commanding the limbs to move once again.

The soft lashes of the deceased fluttered open revealing milky lifeless eyes. Juliette tried to stand, feeling the rigor mortis slow her movements. She swung her feet to the floor as pain ripped through the body. Bones groaned and muscles screamed as she stood.

She shuffled through the corridor and grasped the wooden latch in the stiff, ashen hand. She needed to be quick about this. The excruciating pain of death was almost more than she could take.

It took her much longer than she had anticipated, creeping along through the shadows so no one else in the town intercepted her gruesome message.

She found the judge's cottage near the courthouse. The only light visible from the exterior of the house was the soft glow from the hearth in one of the rear bedrooms.

Juliette crept closer to the window; the judge slept just beyond the thin pane of glass, completely oblivious to the corpse standing just outside his home.

She continued to the next room and carefully pushed open the windowpane. The rigor was getting much worse and more painful by the second. Juliette knew that the only way she was going to get the information she needed was by using the fear of the undead and witchcraft against the judge.

83

After climbing through the window and into the adjacent bedroom, Juliette walked with difficulty towards the dimly lit room and its slumbering occupant.

Once she stood beside the bed, Juliette looked over the conspirator. He was aging and rather portly, his large abdomen protruded from the folds of his nightgown. His head was turned towards Juliette, his mouth hanging open as phlegm-rattling snores filled the room.

She bent placing her face mere inches from his. The stiff, icy hands of the borrowed body were braced on either side of his pillow. She spoke, drawing her words out in hissing syllables, breathing her dead fetid breath upon his mouth.

"Open your eyes and witness the terror you have brought upon this town."

His eyes flew wide, disbelief and then terror written across his pockmarked face. He slid down beneath the bedspread as though the woolen blankets would protect him from the nightmare he saw standing before him.

Juliette screeched in pain as she climbed onto the bed to straddle the swollen male form that shivered violently at her cold and unrelenting touch. She hissed as she ran the stiff fingers through his thinning gray hair, grasping it by the root, and snapped his head back so that he had no choice but to look into the face of the girl he had ordered to be hung that afternoon.

"Tell me of the conspiracy…tell me of the man who traded money for your soul…TELL ME!" Juliette screamed with all the rage she carried for these men. The judge clutched his heart, fearing that this nightmare would surely cause a heart attack.

"Colville…" he stammered, "His name is Devlon Colville!" Juliette sat back on her heels; the shock of that

84

name reverberated through her entire being almost causing her to lose her grip on the corpse.

"Why did he come here?" His face crumpled, he whimpered,

"He said that he hunted a creature more dangerous than anything we had ever encountered. He... he said the creature was guarded by a powerful witch and that they came to destroy our town for all the witches we had put to death. He said they must be destroyed!" The judge swallowed hard, the fear thick in his throat, sweat beaded on his balding head and tears filled his yellowed eyes.

"Please... I only meant to-" Juliette's impatience with the judge caused her to jerk his head back again. His eyes flew wide in pain at the ruthless grip she had on him.

"Where can I find him?" The magistrate paled, knowing that his lack of knowledge would almost certainly be the death of him. He shook his head, tears rolling down his face as his chin pathetically quivered.

"I...I don't know. He left this morning at dawn. He could be anywhere by now. Please... you must believe me... in truth, I do not know!"

His terror was making his heartbeat rapidly. Juliette could see his pulse leaping wildly. She was not satisfied with his answer, but he knew nothing more that could lead her in the right direction.

"You will end this madness. You will cease to condemn innocent people because you fear what you cannot accept. Not another life will be lost because of your tyrannical reign on this town, or so help me God, you will be cursed to walk this earth in eternal damnation!"

She closed her eyes, resting her chin on her chest, she breathed deeply. Suddenly arching her spine and throwing her head back, Juliette let out an unearthly ear-

85

piercing shriek. As the pressure grew, the walls pulsated with electrical energy, and just the same, as she had entered the body, a crack of thunder, a bolt of lightning, and the corpse fell away from her.

Juliette hovered over the bed, taking in the scene of the judge whimpering like a child, too terrified to move as he lay there, pinned beneath the body of a dead witch.

***

Juliette awoke from yet another memory and experienced the strange tug of remorse.

She had never used her powers to manipulate the dead until that night, and she had never done it again. It was something no one else that she knew of had the power to do.

Losing Marek had turned her into a creature she wasn't at all proud to be. Nevertheless, it had been necessary, she told herself, a necessary and short-lived bout of evil… one that she had promised herself would never happen again. Marek would have never condoned such malicious behavior.

Now here she was, over three centuries later, and again using her powers to put fear into the mortal soul.

What was the matter with her? True, the feelings that were occurring between her and Evan would only cause trouble in her quest to free Marek. But she shouldn't have handled the situation as she had. She had left him out there in the pouring rain, weak and defenseless against any who should come upon him.

She needed to check on him and see that he had survived the night. She had to make certain that the spellbinding sample of blood that she had drained from him had left no lasting effects.

Juliette crawled from her large comfortable bed and began to undress for her shower when she heard someone knocking on her front door.

Grabbing her ivory silk dressing gown off the back of the bathroom door, Juliette gingerly crept onto the landing and peered down into the foyer. Ambrosia stood at

87

the bottom of the stairs, a menacing growl sounding deep in her chest.

A tall figure with a shock of dark hair stood in the yellow glow of the porch light distorted by the crystal windowpane. She knew immediately that it was Evan.

Juliette padded barefoot down the stairs and paused at the threshold to the entry, unsure if she should let him in… yet drawn to him.

The excitement at seeing him again caught her off guard. She tried to tell herself that the unexpected leap her heart made was just due to the relief that he was okay.

"Open the door, Juliette. I know you're home, your car is in the driveway." Evan pounded on the door once more to emphasize his impatience.

Finding no reason to ignore him other than their mutual attraction, Juliette knelt looking Ambrosia in the eye.

"Go love, I will be fine. Go and feed." The large wolf whined in refusal to leave her mistress alone, unsure of the dangers. "I'll call if I need you. Go now." The wolf turned towards the back of the house and dissolved into her vaporous form as she leapt through the far wall. Juliette stood and unbolted the door. She pulled it open and stepped back to allow him entrance to her house.

Evan looked down into Juliette's upturned face. The passion from the night before came flooding back.

He knew that he must look terrible, he hadn't even been home to shower and change clothes.

He had finally regained consciousness as nightfall began to ascend on the trees. The rain had slowed, falling in a light drizzle, creating silver lines running down the windshield as Evan sat in the truck and tried to remember what had happened the night before.

He remembered the fierce passion that had blazed between him and Juliette. He remembered the anger he'd felt afterwards, but most of all he remembered the fear he had undergone just as she disappeared, leaving him alone in the lighthouse.

He had been sick with worry, scared that whatever had attacked him, rendering him so weak and useless, had done something horrible to Juliette. He had driven straight here, ignoring speed limits and stop signs, anxious to learn that she was safe.

Now that he had found Juliette, he couldn't seem to take his eyes off her. He drank in the sight of her, noticing the way her hair fell around her shoulders in wild disarray. She looked like she had just crawled out of bed. He noticed the silky cream-colored robe and the way it clung to her supple form until it fell from her narrow hips in shimmering folds around her tiny bare feet.

Juliette recognized the flare of desire in his piercing green eyes. The sand in his hair, the shadow of a beard that dusted his jaw line, and the rumpled clothing he wore did little to detract from the aura of resilient masculinity that set her blood to boiling.

"Are you going to come in or do you enjoy standing outside in the cold rain?" Juliette asked, tilting her head to one side. Evan noticed for the first time that a slight accent rolled her words, soft and French. He recognized the emphasis on certain syllables spoken, comparable to the accent of French-Canadian tourists that passed through town from time to time, but softer... melodic.

As Evan stepped into the foyer, Juliette closed the door and leaned back, pressing her shoulders against the smooth glass.

Evan turned towards her, and his palms began to tingle in anticipation of caressing her silken flesh, held captive by the heady aroma of the forest that seemed to emanate from every pore on her body.

"It seems that the cold has had less of an effect on me than it obviously has had on you. Or is it *me* that caused this desirable effect?" Evan glanced down at the taut, ample peaks that pressed against the delicate material of her dressing gown.

Juliette understood his meaning and quickly pushed off the door, ending their appraisal of one another as she crossed her arms over her chest.

Evan admired how she tried to hide the way her traitorous body seemed to respond to him and enjoyed the faint flush of color that painted her high cheekbones.

He stepped towards her, and grabbing her by the waist, he pulled her into the circle of his arms.

"What happened to you? I've been worried sick about you ever since I woke up in my truck. I haven't even gone to the sheriff's station yet. I needed to see that you were all right first." Juliette tried to pull away yet found herself entangled in the web of temptation he wove around her whenever he was near.

She looked up into the depths of his eyes, trying to probe his mind, finding only remnants of memories from the night before... bits and pieces of the emotions he had experienced and not the reasons behind them. She hadn't expected that a need to protect her would overcome the fear she had placed in his mind. Her plan could not have gone more awry.

"I'm fine Evan. I can take care of myself. Why were you going to the sheriff?"

He pulled back holding her at arm's length, "I'm going to the sheriff to report that I was attacked last night. That's two attacks in the same place. At least I made it out alive! Poor Charlie… I'm beginning to think that he wasn't as lucky. You never told me why you were out there. You could have been hurt, maybe even killed!"

Juliette finally found the strength to pull away from Evan and walked over to the fireplace. She longed to feel the warmth of flickering flames as she stared silently at the oak logs that lay cold in the hearth. But she dared not light a fire knowing that the ability to ignite a fire with a wave of her hand would surely alarm him. She also feared that the glowing embers would only add to the heated atmosphere and ignite the passionate blaze that was crackling between them.

"I told you, I can take care of myself." She tried to find a plausible excuse for why she had been at the lighthouse, and she decided that staying as close to the truth was probably the best road to travel with Evan. "And I was there to find out what happened to that old man."

"Why? You didn't know him, and you couldn't have done anything. Juliette, something could have happened to you. What were you thinking?" She felt his body close behind her.

The heat that exuded from him bled through her robe to inflame her bare skin.

"I know you're new around here, and this town is probably tiny compared to wherever it is you came from, but you can't just go running out to a crime scene by yourself. It isn't safe. Look what happened to me!" Evan pulled the collar of his shirt down to reveal a purple welt where the puncture wounds had been.

91

Abruptly she turned towards him, her eyes narrowing with resentment and passion at the same time. The sight of the wound she herself had inflicted made her wince. Whatever remorse she felt, was outweighed by the urge to taste his flesh, and engorge herself on his blood once again.

"You should stay away from me. You don't know anything about me, it's not safe... *I'm not safe!*" She tried to brush past him and escape the warmth he seemed to radiate. Evan's arms lashed out to snake around her waist and pull her back against him. His silver wristwatch caught on her arm and tore a gash in the sensitive flesh of her wrist, no more than a scratch, but just enough to draw blood.

Juliette hissed in pain and brought the wound up to inspect it as she tried to struggle out of his grasp.

"Damn it! I'm sorry Juliette... here, let me see it." Evan held her hand lightly in his own. He marveled at the difference in size. She was so tiny, yet so full of strength; her small delicate hand was dwarfed by his own.

Once again, she turned towards him, unable to resist leaning into his warmth. Evan held her wrist up softly and traced his thumb along her arm as he looked over the damage he had done. She closed her eyes and rested her forehead against his shoulder, enjoying the feel of being cared for.

Suddenly the erotic sensation of his lips on her already-healed skin yanked her from her lethargic trance and sent her hurling over the edge of heightened desire.

He kissed her where she had bled and gently lapped at the scarlet smear that stained her petal soft skin. He had meant to only kiss away the pain, as his own mother had done when he was a reckless young boy. Yet for some unknown reason, the moment her blood touched his lips he had the undeniable urge to devour her whole...

Juliette jerked back, cradling her arm to her body, trying desperately to ignore the hammering in her heart and the quickening in her veins.

She was enraged at the emotions he was generating inside of her. Liquid heat shot through her, pooling in places long forgotten in her years of solitude.

She should make him go. He was tempting her, touching that inner part of her heart that she had long ago locked deep within her, and getting far too close.

But her body screamed at the sensations that he was stirring to life. She yearned to feel his powerful body straining against hers in the timeless dance of desire, ached to feel the stroke of passion only he could provide, and the comforting warmth of his tender embrace.

Evan was caught off guard by the strange emotions that seemed to be prevailing over his better judgment. She had told him to stay away, but he just couldn't. He was overwhelmed by the need to feel his body pressed against hers.

She reached for him and grasped his shirt in agony, torn between passion and duty.

Her lips were only inches away from his, their breaths mingling, their hearts pounding in unison.

His gaze dropped to her mouth as her tiny pink tongue slipped out to caress her lower lip. His hands skimmed down the length of her back, reveling in the sleek curves of her delicate body.

Juliette let loose of the grip she had on his shirt. Once again, she was overcome with the desire raging within her. She slid her hands up, caressing his muscular

93

chest, his powerful shoulders, and slipped her hands around his neck, plunging her fingers through the raven dark curls.

Their lips met in a hungry clash of desire and insatiable hunger. Juliette could taste her own blood on his lips and the pleasure of it almost brought her to her knees.

She tugged at his hair; he pulled at her hips. The desperation in their movements relayed the need to merge their bodies into one.

Juliette felt the couch at the back of her knees. She pulled Evan down, enjoying the feel of his weight pressing her into the plush cushions.

His lips left hers to taste the soft skin behind her ear and trailed down her exquisite neck, past her collarbone, pausing briefly at the pulse point where her heart was beating furiously, and then further down to kiss the hollow between her breasts.

She threw back her head, arching her body to expose her warmed flesh to his ravenous kisses.

Juliette raked her nails down his back, and grabbing the hem of his shirt, began to pull it up and off. He took her cue and once his shirt was gone, began to undo the knot in the belt of her robe. Once undone, Evan pulled back to push aside the silky fabric and feast his eyes on the sculptured wonder that was her body.

She arched again, reaching for him, calling out to him, desperate to feel him skin to skin. The scorching heat of his chiseled body against her much cooler flesh, and touching her so intimately, was almost too much for Evan to bear.

The proof of his arousal painfully strained against his jeans, pressing against Juliette in the most sensitive of places. She gasped at the electric current that tore through her body.

The shock of him touching her *there* and the knowledge of where this was leading brought Juliette plummeting back down to earth. This was wrong... *he* was the wrong man. How could she have let things get this out of hand? She needed to stop it now!

Evan immediately felt the change in her. The body that was once searing liquid beneath his had turned instantly into cool steel. Her palms came up to press against his chest, and with considerable force, sent Evan crashing to the floor.

Juliette quickly sat up, pulling the folds of her robe closed around her body.

How could she have done this to Marek? She was wracked with guilt and humiliation, and at the same time, in awe of the feelings that Evan had brought to life within her.

Not even had she experienced such free abandon with Marek, the love of her life. Why then did she feel this strange all-consuming need for Evan, a man she didn't even know?

Only one thing was certain, Juliette was going to have to get Evan out of here and out of her life. If only she knew how.

"I can't do this. You need to go Evan. Please." He looked up at her from where he sat on the floor. She looked tiny and vulnerable curled into the cushions of the couch. She seemed afraid to touch him, afraid he would touch her.

Her brilliant silver eyes were huge in her small pale face and glistened with tears that threatened to fall at any moment. Evan ran a hand through his rumpled hair, sighing in bewilderment, unsure of how to proceed without upsetting her further.

"I'm sorry Juliette. That was… are you okay?" Evan pushed himself up off the floor and stood, pulling his t-shirt on in the same fluid movement.

"I'm fine! I can-"

"Yeah, I know, you can take care of yourself. Damn it Juliette, you don't look fine, and it won't matter how many times you tell me that. I am not going to let you push me away. If I hurt you, tell me." He sighed in frustration. Anger was making him raise his voice, something he seldom did. Evan made a conscious effort to calm his temper.

"I don't know what it is about you, but I feel this mind-blowing connection between us. And I know you do too. I don't want to ignore it, couldn't even if I tried. But if I hurt you, in any way…I'm sorry."

Juliette sat on the couch staring at Evan, and for the first time in centuries, she didn't know how to respond.

Where were the walls she had so painstakingly built around her heart? Where was the strength she needed to send him away? Where was the burning hatred for *all* humans, the vengeance that had consumed her for all these years, and the rage that had kept her going when all seemed lost?

Where was the image of Marek that she had been carrying in her heart for three centuries?

Juliette was lost.

A single tear escaped, rolling down her cheek, to splash silently on her hands that lay folded in her lap. Evan knelt in front of her and kissed the moisture that clung to her thick lashes.

"I'm going to leave because you asked me to, but I will be back. This isn't finished Juliette. We've only just begun." He kissed her once more, tenderly on the lips, then

96

stood and walked out the front door, closing it quietly behind him.

For hours, Juliette just sat there, staring into space, trying to resurrect the emotions that had gotten her this far in her quest for vengeance.

She tried to conjure up an image of Marek and wondered how she could have let it slip away in the first place.

Juliette knew she needed to avoid Evan at all costs. If she didn't it would only put both of them in grave danger.

She just hoped she could trust herself enough to stay away. All their lives depended on her, even Evan's.

***

Evan entered his parent's empty house and tossed the truck keys down on the counter next to the blinking answering machine... no doubt full of worried and frantic messages from both April and Trevor.

Weary from the flood of emotions that he had experienced since closing the bar the night before, Evan dropped his tired body into the worn brown recliner that his father had always dozed in.

His head was pounding, and his loins still burned from unquenched desire.

He had meant to go to the sheriff as soon as he had checked on Juliette, but after their stimulating encounter, he just didn't have the energy to sit under the florescent lights and be grilled by the incompetent group of men that passed as Chancellor's law enforcement.

He would go in the morning he promised himself. Right now, all he wanted to do was take a hot shower and lay down in his lonely bed... if he even made it that far.

The images of Juliette, naked and melting in his arms, kept churning through his mind. The sound of her gasping his name in ecstasy, and the feel of her nails raking down his back, followed him into his dreams as he drifted off to sleep.

They were in her living room, a fire blazing in the hearth behind them, as he took her in his arms and purged their bodies of all barriers.

Her skin gleamed in the firelight, like porcelain; her hair hung over her bare shoulders, a silken mantle that

98

shadowed the most sensitive parts of her glorious body, teasing and taunting him. He quivered in anticipation, longing to feel every part of her.

He lowered his lips to hers, tasting the sweet nectar within. She sighed as he traced his tongue down the velvety column of her neck, coming to that place where her pulse leapt with rapture.

She clung to him, and gripping his hair in her hands, Juliette murmured, encouraging him; he heard the words whispered in his mind. Unsure of what she wanted, he began to pull back, looking into the silvery depths of her eyes, and heard her voice in his mind,

"Drink," she said. One word, one syllable, was all the direction he needed. Somewhere from deep within him, Evan knew what it was she was asking of him. Again, she arched her slender neck to expose the delicate cream of her skin. It was then that he saw the puncture marks in her neck, already red and bleeding.

How had that happened he wondered? Then he knew. His teeth had grown as sharp as daggers, primal urges tore through him as he took her in his arms and drank.

The shrill ringing of the telephone jarred Evan awake. The dream had left him feeling disturbed and disoriented, as the ringing persisted.

Where was that damned phone? Evan cursed as he dragged his heavy frame out of the recliner and searched for the culprit that had slammed him back into reality.

He found the handset beneath a pile of unread newspapers that cluttered the dining room table, just as the answering machine was picking up. He could hear April's voice full of worry coming loud across the little machine.

"Evan, goddamn it, where the hell are you? I swear to God if you don't answer this phone right now-"

"Hey, I'm okay, calm down." Evan walked down the hall towards the bathroom as he held the phone to his ear. He reached into the shower and turned the faucet on as he listened with half an ear to April's ranting.

He understood why she was angry. He should have called her sooner, but his cell phone battery had died sometime the night before, and he had passed out as soon as he reached the house. He hadn't even called to let her know that he wasn't coming in to work tonight.

It wasn't like him to ignore his responsibilities; he hadn't been feeling quite like himself since the attack.

After a brief explanation, and numerous apologies, Evan was finally able to get April calmed down and off the phone.

Not wanting to worry or upset her any more than he had to, Evan had lied and said that he had been in bed all day with the flu. Guilt tugged at his heart for lying to April, but how could he explain something he himself really didn't quite understand?

After he had stripped out of his clothes, Evan stepped into the shower enjoying the hot spray on his tired body.

As he lathered his sore muscles with the fragrant bar of soap, his fingers encountered the swollen wound on his neck.

Caught in the midst of a flash back, Evan's dream came rushing back, causing him to lose balance.

His heart beating rapidly and his breath coming in short gasps, Evan clung to the shower walls for support.

He was shaken to the core having been shown through his dream what had happened to him in the lighthouse. But in the dream, he had bitten Juliette. That didn't make any sense, but then again, none of this made any sense.

Because who in their right mind would think they had been attacked by a vampire?

***

April hung up the phone and turned towards Trevor, a worried expression marring her pretty face. The bar hadn't been very busy tonight, and with the help of Trevor and Tori, everything had gone smoothly.

"He said that he's been sick all day and in bed. Why is he lying to me?" She sat in the office and stared blankly at the computer screen. She had driven out to the cabin after she had been unable to get him on his cell that morning. He hadn't been there, and she knew he wasn't telling her the truth.

Trevor, who had been leaning against the desk, squatted down in front of April and took both her small hands in his. Holding them encouragingly, he began to run the pads of his thumbs along her knuckles.

"Maybe he *was* in bed all day, he just didn't specify whose bed he was in." Trevor's attempt at humor brought a slight curve to April's lips.

"Very funny, you know he hasn't been involved with anyone since before mom and dad passed. I don't know why he wouldn't tell me what's wrong. He has never hidden anything from me before, and he's never missed a shift without calling me and letting me know. Something isn't right Trevor." The thought that Evan was hiding something from her had April's stomach in knots. They had always been so close, and she didn't understand why he sounded so distant on the phone.

"Do you want me to go over there and check on him? Would that make you feel better?"

"I'd feel better going over myself, but he sounded so wiped out. He said he was just going to go to bed. I don't want to bother him."

Trevor stood and came around the back of April's chair and began to gently massage the tense muscles in her neck. He hated seeing her worry like this. He knew Evan well and he had to agree; it wasn't like him to neglect his responsibilities to April or the pub, but he couldn't tell her that.

"Maybe tomorrow when he's feeling better, he'll come clean. Until then, let's just close and get out of here." April had been quietly enjoying the massage and was too tired to argue. She tilted her head back to rest against Trevor's stomach and looked up at him.

"Thanks for sticking around to help, you didn't have to do that. I know you must be tired, and you must have to be out on the docks early tomorrow." She was always amazed at how Trevor could spend all night here at the pub and then wake up and be out on his fishing boat at first light.

He called his job a labor of love. He said there was nothing more liberating then heading out to sea just as the sun was beginning to rise over the horizon, with nothing before him but the wide-open water, the songs of the gulls that followed him out to sea, and the fresh gentle wind bringing in the promise of a good day's catch.

"You know me, never could ignore a damsel in distress-"

"Well, if that's the case, then you wouldn't mind taking a look at my car, would you? It's not starting." Tori stood in the doorway of the office dangling her keys from the tip of her finger and looking over the cozy scene with keen interest.

103

Trevor turned towards the unwelcome interruption, and the urge to wipe the annoying smirk from Tori's face was almost overwhelming.

"Are we supposed to fall for that again? Evan's not even here for you to throw yourself at, and you're still pulling this crap. Sorry Tori, it didn't work on Evan, and it's not going to work on me." Trevor pulled April's chair around to face him and extended his hand to help her from her seat.

"You ready to go?"

"Yeah, let me just close up in here, and I'll meet you at the door."

April began to shut down the computer as Trevor pushed Tori out the door and into the common room.

"Looks like you two are getting awfully close. How does Evan feel about you shacking up with his little sister?" Trevor stopped and tried to keep a grip on his temper. It had been a long night for all of them, and the last thing he and April needed was for Tori to stick her nose in where it didn't belong and cause trouble.

"What happens between April and me is none of your damn business. And as for Evan's feelings on the situation… well that's also none of your damn business." Trevor opened the front door of the pub and led Tori out into the night.

"Go home Tori." Closing the door in her face, he turned and headed back towards the office just as April turned off the lights in the pub.

The lamps in the glass racks hanging above the bar cast a romantic glow, sending spears of light glinting off the crystal glassware. April came sweeping through the swinging doors that led to the kitchen and stopped short when she saw Trevor standing there alone in the dark.

104

"Oh, sorry I turned out all the lights! I thought you had gone outside with Tori."

"I escorted her snooping ass out and had the pleasure of closing the door in her face. I swear she gets nosier and more annoying by the day." April set her purse on the bar as she shrugged into her jacket.

"You and Evan let her get to you too easily. Just do what I do... ignore her."

"It's easier said than done." Trevor held the front door open for April as she fumbled with her keys.

He had spent all night behind the bar with April, their movements in tune, as they poured drafts and built cocktails, but he wasn't ready to say goodnight just yet.

"Are you hungry? We could go back to my place for one of my world-famous smoked salmon omelets?"

After bolting the lock on the heavy wooden door of the Waterfront Pub, April turned to look up into Trevor's handsome face.

His deep even tan, the natural golden highlights in his hair, and his boyish dimples almost melted her heart every time she looked at him. How was she going to keep her distance from him when he was so devastatingly gorgeous?

She had been sensing something profound growing between them, but she was still unsure about how to proceed. For as long as she could remember, Trevor had always gone through women as if they were something to be easily discarded once he had tired of them. He wasn't purposely mean about it. It was just the way he lived his life, playful, living in the moment, no ties, or bonds holding him down. He even ran his business with the same reckless abandon.

She and Evan were the closest thing he had to a real family. April was scared that all he would want from her was just a fleeting romance, something that would leave her alone and desperately heart broken in the end... not to mention it would ultimately destroy the friendship between him and Evan if things went badly.

They began the short walk around the back of the pub to their parked cars.

"Sounds like heaven, but it's getting late. I should go home so I can get up early and go check on Evan." She longed to take him up on his invitation, but she was afraid. Trevor casually shrugged off her refusal, ignoring the disappointment that tugged at his heart.

"Okay, maybe some other time then." Draping one arm around her shoulders, almost in a brotherly hug, he led her to her car. April wished her stomach would quit doing that strange flip-flop whenever he touched her.

"Be careful going home." He leaned down and lightly kissed her on the forehead, as he playfully tugged on her ponytail.

She climbed into her car as he sauntered over to his jeep, he turned towards her one last time as she started the engine and drove away. Trevor watched until the red lights faded around the corner as she headed into town.

He sighed to himself. It was getting to be unbearable, being around her, and not being able to hold her and kiss her. He was aware that Evan must suspect something by now. The mild flirtations and long lingering looks that they had been sharing more frequently these last few weeks couldn't have gone unnoticed. Evan knew them both too well to have not caught on.

Trevor decided that he needed to talk to Evan and get his thoughts on the whole situation before he could do anything about his feelings for April. But it would have to wait until tomorrow.

He dug his keys out of his pocket and turned to unlock his jeep when he noticed that Tori's car was still parked under the lamppost near the alley. She was nowhere in sight. Assuming she had found someone else to con into a "ride" home, Trevor climbed into his jeep, pulled out of the parking lot, and drove home.

***

Somewhere in the darkness, a faint whimpering broke the silence. A hand clutched Tori's throat in a vise-like grip, holding her off the ground. She was pinned against the side of the building, her feet dangling. Light glinted off dagger like fangs, and glowing pupils shot out of the shadows like some predatory creature frozen in the headlamps of an oncoming car.

Tori's windpipe was being crushed, she couldn't call out to April and Trevor even though they had been only a few yards away.

She shivered, her body as cold as ice, the fear sinking into her bones.

"I've been watching you, and I can see that the pain in you is great. Do you have any real friends, any family, anyone in this world to mourn you?" The voice came out of the darkness. Terror and lust wove in and out of her thoughts, spinning her mind into confusion. Tears filled her eyes confirming that she was indeed alone in this world.

"Do you want it to end? I can help you... take away the suffering. Is that what you want?" Tori's thoughts were muddled. The fear that had turned her body to ice was melting away, desire taking over. A welcoming heat consumed her, curling upwards like wafting smoke, spreading through her bones until the pain had receded completely.

"You hide behind scorn and seduction... but I can see past that. I see your desire for a man who does not want you. Do you hold resentment for those who look at you as nothing but a common whore? I can change all that

Tori. I can give you the power to take from those that cause you the most pain." The grip that had only moments ago seemed like a tight band squeezing the life from her, suddenly turned sensual, caressing the sensitive skin along the column of her neck, and evoking a dark desire that reverberated through her body.

A lust she had never felt before made her blood boil, her loins throb. Tori's body ached with need; a need she didn't understand.

The moon finally surfaced from behind a cloud illuminating Tori's captor. The silvery light shown upon a straight and narrow nose, high cheekbones, an arrogant chin accented by a slight cleft and framed by midnight black hair that floated around his broad shoulders. Thin lips sneered back at her, and eyes as black as the night penetrated deep into her skull.

"Either way you die tonight. It's your choice on whether you are to be reborn." The spell he had spun around her would not loosen its hold on her mind. Her body cried out for release; a strange thirst overtaking her.

"Yes," she whispered, giving in to the euphoric trance. Without even the slightest hesitation he swept her to the ground, cradling her limp body in his dark embrace and savagely impaling her with his vampire fangs, turning all that had been human into his child of darkness, a slave to the lust for blood, revenge, and all that was evil.

***

Evan awoke late the next morning, his body feeling weighted down as he walked into the kitchen to begin brewing his morning cup of coffee. Wondering if there had been any interesting leads in Charlie's case, Evan went out onto the front porch to collect his newspaper. As soon as he stepped outside the house, he was nearly blinded by the bright colors of the wooded area outside his door.

No sunlight filtered through the treetops, but the forest was awash with vivid greens and reds. The purple plants that bloomed this time of year in his mother's flowerpots seemed to glow periwinkle against the vibrant vegetation.

Staggering backwards, Evan sheltered his eyes from the piercing bursts of color. He had never seen the forest look like this. He felt like he had been drinking quite heavily the night before, when in truth he hadn't had a drop of liquor. He must be coming down with something, he thought to himself, as he stooped down to pick up his paper. Spending the night in damp clothes in his old pickup had probably done him in.

He started to head back into the house, taking note that the clouds above were dark and thunder rumbled through the trees. Large drops of rain began to fall as he entered the cabin and closed the door behind him.

He returned to the kitchen and poured a steaming cup of strong coffee. He began to settle into his worn recliner to read his paper just as there was an abrupt knock on the front door.

110

Swearing aloud for spilling some of the hot liquid on his t-shirt, Evan stood just as April strolled into the living room.

"Hey big brother, how are you feeling this morning?" April looked fresh in a pastel pink sweater, white jeans, and soft leather boots with matching belt and jacket. Her hair was pulled back in a French braid, and a few curling wisps that had managed to escape being tied back, hung loose, surrounding her freckled face. She shook the rain from her jacket and laid it over a nearby barstool.

"I wasn't sure you would even be awake yet... thought I'd come and make you breakfast. I used my key; hope you don't mind." Evan had walked over to the counter to set his coffee down and dab at the dark stain on his shirt.

"That's fine. I'm feeling better, just out of sorts a bit. I think I have a cold. What's for breakfast?" April walked over to the fridge and leaned on the door as she stared at its contents.

"When was the last time you went shopping?" His refrigerator contained a gallon of milk that was way past its expiration date, cola, juice, an old pizza box with the remnants of a dried-up pepperoni pizza, a bottle of ketchup, and a Styrofoam container of leftover food from the bar.

"Well, I don't think we're going to be able to make anything from your sour milk and crusty pizza. Want to just head into town and stop off at the diner?" She asked as she poured herself a cup of coffee.

Evan sipped from his mug as he contemplated his list of things he needed to accomplish before heading into work later that day, all of which required him to be in town anyhow. Breakfast sounded like a good idea.

111

"Yeah, sure. I have some things I need to do in town this morning anyway. Let me just change my shirt and we can get out of here." April took her cup and sat at the dining room table, glancing at the pile of newspapers that had accumulated there. This morning's paper was right on top; April leaned forward and briefly scanned the front page.

The cover story captured her attention right off. The title stated, *"Murder in Chancellor"*. April's quick intake of breath alerted Evan that something was wrong the moment he re-entered the kitchen.

"What's wrong?" She snatched the paper up off the table and thrust it towards Evan.

"Read this! Charlie wasn't the only one attacked!" Before Evan could take the paper from his sister, she yanked it back and began to read aloud.

"The remains of an unknown hiker were discovered near Emerald Lake just northeast of Chancellor, Oregon. The recent discovery of the body has local law enforcement scouring the nearby forest and beaches for clues that could lead to the identity of the killer. So far, nothing has turned up. This is only the second in what sheriff officials fear may be a string of random murders along the northern coast of Oregon. The first victim, identified as local transient Charlie Combs, has yet to be found. The details of the attacks, as well as the identity of the hiker, have not yet been released. Although speculations have been made that the cause of death of the hiker was severe loss of blood and trauma to the neck and throat, Don Wellington, the town medical examiner and mortician, has not commented on these reports, and therefore, these theories remain unsubstantiated."

112

April stopped reading and peered at Evan over the top of the paper. His face had turned ashen, and he looked like he might be sick.

"Evan! Are you all right?" April dropped the paper back on the table and led Evan into the living room to sit down. He was shaking and April was afraid he was going to lose consciousness.

Evan felt his sanity beginning to slip. He remembered his dream from the night before, and he could still feel the throb in his neck every time he turned his head, yet his brain kept telling him that it was impossible. There is no such thing as vampires. The stories of them were legendary, but also fiction, created to scare and entertain. Vampires are not real, he told himself.

Then why did his gut twist with fear whenever he remembered the ache of having his own blood drained from his body, to feel the weakening in his limbs, and the pain in his chest as his heart worked to pump the blood that was no longer there.

Evan tried to focus on that memory, tried to recall who it was that had stolen his blood, but the image was still blurred. It remained at the very edges of his memory, taunting, and teasing him, refusing to reveal the face of his attacker.

He shook his head trying to clear the fog and leaned forward bracing his head in his hands. He tried to remain calm. The urge to let panic consume him was almost overwhelming.

"Evan, you look like you're going to be sick. Do you want me to take you to the doctor?" April was worried about her brother. He was usually the resilient one in the family; she couldn't remember the last time he had been sick. A green pallor had turned his once olive complexion pale and waxlike.

The thought of going to a doctor and having his head checked almost made Evan laugh at the absurdity of the situation. How would he explain to a physician that a vampire had bitten him, and that the very same vampire was most likely also responsible for the disappearance of Charlie and the murder of the hiker? He would almost definitely be committed.

The only way to prove he wasn't losing his mind was to get the details behind Charlie's disappearance. Only then would he be able to comprehend what had happened to him.

"No doctor is going to be able to help me. I need to find out what happened to Charlie. I need to know exactly how the hiker died." Having a plan made it a little more bearable to deal with the realization that a creature that couldn't possibly exist was killing people here in Chancellor, and that Evan had somehow escaped with his life when the only other two people that had encountered it hadn't been as lucky.

He needed answers, and something told Evan that he needed to get them before the sun set. He didn't know much about vampires, but he did know they only came out at night, and he needed to make damn sure that he and April were inside well before then.

The trip to the morgue and to the sheriff's office had proven useless. The medical examiner and officer on the case had relayed the same information that the paper had disclosed.

April had remained by Evan's side all day, a worried expression creasing her brow. Evan had barely picked at his breakfast, claiming that his stomach was still upset from his illness the previous day.

But throughout the day, she could tell that there was more to it. There were dark shadows under his eyes, and his skin had taken on a chalky appearance. He also seemed to be bothered a great deal by bright light, squinting whenever they were indoors, and rarely removing his sunglasses even though the sky outside was overcast.

She had called Trevor before they left the diner to make sure he would be able to help her out at the pub just in case Evan couldn't make it through his shift. He promised he would meet them there as soon as he finished with today's fishing charters.

April was both relieved and eager at the thought of bumping elbows with Trevor again all night behind the bar. The last couple of days they had been spending a lot of time together, yet she never tired of seeing him.

She wondered if she should broach the subject with Evan, let him know that her feelings for his best friend were getting stronger and harder to avoid... but thought better of it. With everything going on here in town, her own feelings seemed miniscule in comparison. This was not the right time, her worry for her brother taking priority.

115

April glanced at Evan out of the corner of her eye as she drove through the woods back towards Evan's house.

Evan noticed his sister's silent scrutiny of him and peeked through his lashes just in time to catch her jerking her eyes back to the road.

He knew she was worried about him, but he had already relayed his fears to her, and he didn't want to say anything about his attack or the fact that he thought it might be vampires behind it all. The thought still sounded insane even to him. Until he could find some hard evidence, it was just better to keep his thoughts and a few other things to himself.

■■■

***

Juliette returned to the inn to pack up her and Marek's belongings. They always traveled light so it didn't take long to pack the few bags they had brought with them to Salem. She then arranged for them to be shipped to Boston where she would collect them later. She quickly sold the horses, deciding to travel on foot; it would be quicker and make it easier to track Devlon.

Ambrosia joined her on the road, leaving the small town of Salem behind. Juliette paused briefly and glanced back at the town, trying to push down the grief that threatened to overtake her at any moment.

They had come here together, full of curiosity and eager for a new adventure and finally some answers about their kind. Now she was leaving alone, the future uncertain.

She clung to the fury that gripped her when she thought about the man that had betrayed them, knowing that she would need to cling to it to survive this and to cope with the pain until Marek was returned to her. As she fled the town, where her love had been taken from her, one name escaped her lips in a terrifying snarl, Devlon!

Devlon Colville was Marek's cousin, taken in by Marek's parents after his own had been killed in a tragic carriage accident. He had been orphaned just as he was reaching manhood. Too young to be on his own, yet old enough to believe he was a grown man. As children, Devlon and Marek had been the best of friends. But when his parents had died, he had changed.

Juliette later believed that it was because he had to live under the constant reminder that Marek was the heir to

117

the Colville estate. Her beloved Marek Etienne Colville III was the only direct heir to his father's vast fortune and to the title of Duke of Brouillard.

Being Marek's cousin, with no title of his own, had always been difficult for Devlon, but now it was unavoidable... mentioned in every conversation, declared in every introduction and Devlon resented it more than anything.

His bitterness had grown over the years. He had, on more than one occasion, attempted to cause strife in the family.

Juliette now knew that was the only reason he had been so accommodating when Marek and Juliette had fallen in love.

Their romance had caused quite a scandal. If Marek were to decide to give up his birthright for her, then that left Devlon in line for the title and estate. At the time she had been so desperate to escape the clutches of her parents and be with the man that she loved, she didn't care what motivated Devlon to help them be together. She'd never taken pause or stopped to think of the consequences, should Devlon not get what he considered was their debt to him for his assistance in their blossoming romance.

Theirs had been a passionate affair, fueled by forbidden rendezvous, stolen moments, and secret letters passed between Devlon himself to a well-paid servant in the Bellerose household.

Marek's father had plans for him, one that would grant him a very large dowry and a daughter from an equally impressive family. Neither of which Juliette had. Although her father was a count, he did not have the fortune or the diplomatic ties that made Marek's intended such a lucrative match.

118

She was also seen as an odd girl, skittish and uncomfortable in the public arena. Her empath abilities crushed down on her in crowded rooms, the emotions of so many being more then she could endure.

His betrothal had not yet been announced, and Marek had no knowledge of it the night his heart had been claimed by Juliette.

It happened one evening during a spring ball, the first of the season. Juliette was not excited in the least to meet the scores of suitors that were eagerly looking for a bride. Her mother had primed her for this night, ingrained in her the importance of finding a husband with money and title.

It was her duty, and her father had made it very clear that the only good that could come of a daughter was making a beneficial match with someone of great importance.

Juliette wanted nothing to do with it. She pitied the simpering young maids that giggled and blushed their way through the festivities. She prayed she would never feel the urge to lower herself to batting her eyes and smiling coyly through her lashes. She wanted to be left alone with her books and her charts. She longed to travel the world and embark on unbelievable journeys and fantastic adventures and to stay far from the overwhelming excitements that were brought on by society during the season.

A husband would only hold her back, restricting her to mundane afternoon teas, and boring dinner parties. A husband would only shackle her to the marriage bed, making sure that she became swollen with child. It would be her duty to produce an heir and if she failed at that, she

119

would face the same ridicule her mother endured day in and day out for only conceiving one child, and a bookish and odd girl no less.

She suffered the disdain her father had for her mother; it tore at her heart, and she knew she could not live everyday feeling the same resentment from a husband of her own.

No, she wanted nothing to do with marriage and everything that it entailed. And she greatly feared who her father would eventually choose if she didn't make a connection of her own and soon.

It seemed a miracle that within the first few moments of the ball, Marek had come into her life and all her fears, doubts and objections had melted away.

She had just completed a turn around the room, floating along behind her parents and making the appropriate small talk to all the nobles that had gathered for the first soirée of the year.

She only felt the giddiness that all the other girls displayed because of her abilities, she wasn't alive with the anticipation of meeting the man who would make her a bride. Yet she smiled, danced, and acted the way she should when being introduced into society. No one seemed to notice that her smile was a façade, until Marek had bent over her small, gloved hand.

He had been enjoying this night about as much as she had. He hated pretending to be enthralled with every debutant that was pressed upon him for a dance.

If you asked him, these matchmaking rituals were barbaric... to treat your own children as chattel to be paraded around until the perfect blue-blooded bull came around with an offer of marriage, a marriage that would no doubt end in misery. He saw it every night in the gentlemen's club… married men young and old, coming to escape their wives in the arms of well-paid and very willing mistresses.

Not that the ladies were innocent of their own infidelities. The lonely and neglected wives, looking for affection, companionship, and pleasure, had approached him on more than one occasion. Yet he never allowed their seductions to lure him into their sordid affairs.

He was quickly tiring of this charade. He didn't think he could entertain another young woman's ideals of marrying the future Duke of Brouillard. He was weaving his way through the crowd to make his escape when he found her hand being placed in his.

He smothered the groan that almost escaped his lips and attempted to smile and murmur the expected pleasantries for yet another introduction. He almost dismissed her as any other eager young debutant, until he looked down and met her smoldering silvery gaze, not shining with the enthusiasm he had witnessed repeatedly tonight, but glinting with something else, could it be resentment?

Everything around them seemed to disappear, plunging them into silence. The only sound to be heard was the quickening of their hearts and the soft breath escaping her lips. The candlelight flickered all around them causing the room to shimmer.

"I am delighted to meet you," he finally managed to declare. His low voice caused strange sensations to course through her body. The heat from his hand seemed to sear her skin through her elegant glove, and she couldn't tear herself away from him even though polite society dictated that they were bordering on improper behavior.

121

"The pleasure is mine." Her voice rang like bells to his ears as her perfect petal-like mouth formed the suitable response. Suddenly he was aware of eyes upon them and someone nearby clearing their throat. He bowed as was proper and reluctantly let go of her hand.

She was puzzled, he had turned to her with obvious boredom, yet as soon as his fathomless blue eyes met hers, they widened in surprise, his pupils dilated, and her wits left her. Every bit of the training and preparation her mother had taught her had vanished. The emotions from of the other people in the room immediately reduced to a dull murmur, this man gave her the ability to block the constant flow of feelings that normally never ceased, leaving her alone with only his own intense reaction to her.

She had expected another self-involved and arrogant peacock, but instead she had been brought face-to-face with the most dashing man she had ever laid eyes on. His mannerisms screamed propriety, royalty, and wealth. But his eyes and his aura gave away his secret; he was as bored as she was, and he detested these formal mating rituals as much as she did. He had been doing an outstanding job of hiding it, until he met her.

She knew a kinship with him that she had never known before. They shared the same desire to escape this place and escape their duties to their families. She was drawn to him, much the way the moon is drawn to the earth, the way a compass is pulled to its magnetic pole by an invisible force too strong to be ignored.

But it was time to move on to the next prospect, and her mother had woven her arm around her waist and was tugging her away from him.

Juliette looked longingly behind her as he disappeared behind the throng of bodies, the roar of

122

emotions flooding back upon her as the distance between them grew. His jaw clenched with displeasure and a possessive gleam turning his blue eyes a menacing steely grey. He was not happy that she was being placed in the arms of another man to participate in a waltz.

She was his, and no other man should have the audacity to touch her, to smile down into her upturned face and breathe in her intoxicating aroma. He stalked the outer rim of the dancing couples, never taking his eyes from her slender form as she was passed from one partner to the next. Her spine remained rigid, her lips smiled, yet her eyes flashed with annoyance and at times panic as the men made every attempt to draw her into conversation.

She caught glimpses of him over her partner's shoulders, and it took everything she had, not to leave the dance floor and rush to his side... for she knew already, without a shadow of doubt, that was where she belonged.

Devlon had taken notice of the exchange between his cousin and the enchanting Ms. Bellerose. He also knew of his uncle's intentions to betroth him to another. This may be the opportunity he needed, to cause the upheaval he knew would be the only way he could gain the title and fortune that he deserved.

"She is not like the others, is she cousin?" Marek turned to see Devlon's gaze following Juliette on the dance floor and knew at once, of whom he spoke.

"No, she isn't. Do you know of her, of her family?" Devlon laughed and lifted his champagne to his lips, taking a slow sip before turning and answering Marek's questions.

"She is beautiful, well-spoken and the daughter of a wealthy count. I have just been introduced myself this evening. Unfortunately, I do not have more information. I

123

do, however, know that your father has made other arrangements for you… one that would supersede any offer her father, the Count Montagne De Glace, could propose I'm afraid."

Marek froze, how was it that his cousin was privy to such information, and he had no knowledge of it? His gaze frantically scanned the crowd searching for her when, out of the corner of his eye he saw Juliette being forcefully led away from the dance floor by the Viscount Arnaud who had clearly had too much to drink and not nearly enough brains to know when he was making a grave mistake.

"We will have to see about that." Marek all but growled to his cousin as he pushed his way through the surprised couples swirling around the dance floor. One brief meeting with her and he knew that he could not live without her in his life.

Arnaud was a heavyset older man who was well known for his mistreatment of the whores that were often in his company and was notorious for raising his hand to any woman who should dare to defy him. Somehow, this drunken rat had been given the opportunity to pull her from the room.

Marek was livid. Where were her parents? Marek followed the path he had seen them take to the rear balcony. The curtains were billowing in through the French doors due to the warm spring breeze, and he could hear the discomfort in her request to rejoin the other guests before he had set foot outside.

"Come my dear, it is such a beautiful night, although it pales in comparison to your beauty. Come now, let me show you the stars and whisper in your ear of the life we will have now that I have struck a bargain with your father for your hand."

124

Marek paused slightly at this announcement. So that was the reason her parents had allowed this encounter to go on unchaperoned. Juliette seemed as caught off guard by this new development as he was.

"My hand? You cannot be... I am sure you are mistaken. If you don't mind, I would like the opportunity to address this with my father." She turned to walk away and was snatched at once by the arm and jerked around to face the now red-faced Viscount.

"You dare question my authority and turn your back on me? This is not the way I had hoped to begin our betrothal, but you leave me no choice. I can see that you are strong-willed, I can change that. You need to be broken, and I will have the rest of our lives to bed you and bend you to my will. Your father and I have already made the agreement. You are mine now." He slammed his lips to hers, forcing her mouth open to shove his tongue down her throat. Juliette bit down as hard as she could, drawing blood, the Viscount yelped in pain and shoved her to the polished balcony floor.

The taste of him on her lips and the repulsive images that his emotional state conjured in her mind made her violently ill.

He was already raising his closed fist to beat her when Marek burst onto the terrace, spilling golden light from the open doors, and intercepting the blow that was meant for her.

"You dare to raise your fist to a woman?" Marek's handsome face was darkened with fury as he all but spat the words in Arnaud's face.

"She is of no concern to you young Colville. If you have any sense at all you will go inside and mind your own business."

125

Marek had placed himself between the Viscount and Juliette, standing with his face mere inches from Arnaud's, the fist that had been meant for her still seized in Marek's strong grasp.

"You will never get the chance to make good on those promises; she is not yours and never will be. Leave now and leave with what little self-respect you have and know that, should you ever come near her again, you will pay dearly for that mistake."

Marek released his hold on the Viscount and turned to gather the trembling girl in his arms and lift her from the ground.

Juliette could see that the Viscounts face was beat red with fury, but none of that mattered. Not the bargain that he and her father had made, not the fact that she had almost been pummeled by the man her father had chosen for her to wed, or the fact that she was now being carried into a room full of shocked onlookers.

She was in Marek's arms; he had saved her and was declaring her his by stepping in and interfering in the plans her father had made. Surely, this meant he wanted her, and her father could not object to this match. She would be his.

Ambrosia followed quickly behind her as they flew down the darkened path. Juliette could still remember the tender way he had laid her on the nearest settee, ordering a servant to get her something to drink to calm her. She could recall with great clarity the way he looked her over for injury, acting as if there were no one in the room.

She recalled the way he had stood up to her father, demanding to know what he had been thinking to promise his daughter to such an unworthy lout as Viscount Arnaud.

He had had so much pride and not an ounce of doubt in the face of polite society. He knew that he was doing the right thing by making it known that they would be together. Tears were streaming down her cheeks as this memory spurred on a tide of emotions. She would get him back, she had to; he had saved her and now she would save him in return.

***

Evan had decided to go in to work and was glad he did; Tori never showed and wasn't answering her phone. Trevor and April were a big help, but they kept glancing at him all night, no matter how many times he tried to reassure them that he was feeling better. Their worried expressions were driving him crazy.

The evening seemed to crawl by. Every time the front door opened Evan's heart would leap, hoping that Juliette had come. But she never walked through the door. He was sitting at the bar counting out the drawer while April went to lock up, the last patron had finally wandered out into the night. Trevor was in back loading the last rack of glasses into the dishwasher, and the jukebox was silent.

They worked quickly trying to tie up the loose ends of closing the pub. Trevor went behind the bar, pulled himself a draft from the taps and sat waiting for April and Evan to finish their work.

April went into the billiards room and began to shut off all the lights as Evan took the counted drawer into the office and locked it securely in the safe. He would need to make a deposit tonight. He grabbed his coat and the zippered deposit bag and shut the office lights off.

When he reached the common room, he couldn't help but notice April and Trevor sitting side by side, their heads bent in deep conversation, and Trevor's hand on her lower back. Oblivious to his careful scrutiny, April leaned forward and brushed a strand of hair off Trevor's brow. Evan stood there in shock! Had he been so self-involved that he hadn't noticed this little romance blooming between

128

his little sister and his best friend? How long had this been going on? And why had no one said anything to him?

He took a step back into the kitchen so as not to alert them to his presence in the main room. He didn't know how to react to this, not just yet anyway. He thought it better that he kept it to himself for now, until they were comfortable enough to bring it up themselves.

He cleared his throat and bellowed from the kitchen,

"You guys about finished up in there?" He pushed through the swinging doors and tried not to smile as they quickly scrambled to their feet, putting distance between them. "I'm done in back, now I just need to get this deposit to the bank and get home. I'm beat." April noticed that he wouldn't look her in the eye. She wondered just how much he had seen.

They filed out of the pub into the chilly night. April glanced at Trevor as they walked towards the parking lot and wondered if he'd noticed Evan's odd behavior. They had all driven in their own cars, so there was really no reason for them to linger in the parking lot. April made a quiet escape to her car and said goodnight... her eye's lingering on Trevor for an instant before she climbed in and drove off with Trevor following shortly after.

Evan sat in his ancient truck, hands resting lightly on the steering wheel, and looked around at the vacant lot. He wondered where Juliette was... she had been in his thoughts all night. Placing his head on the wheel, Evan breathed in deep then slowly let out the pent-up breath. He had been feeling very strange ever since the night at the lighthouse.

He couldn't pinpoint what it was; he didn't feel ill. He just felt out of it, and he couldn't focus. He kept losing

129

his train of thought, and he didn't like it. He wondered if the loss of blood had caused any sort of permanent damage.

Evan had heard about vampires, and the mystic powers they were said to possess and what they could do to their victims. He didn't know how one became a vampire, but he was scared to death that whatever had happened to him in the lighthouse had begun to change him.

He needed to know more. The small library in town was probably not the best place to begin his search. He doubted that they carried anything more than town folklore and fishing guides, not to mention that at this hour his choices of where to read up on vampirism was greatly limited. The best place to begin his search would be the internet; it was definitely the most discreet place to find what he needed to know.

Unfortunately, his laptop was in the office inside the pub. Evan climbed back out of the pickup and headed back inside the bar. Once inside Evan noticed Trevor's empty glass still sitting on the counter. He chuckled softly to himself; he must have really startled them. Trevor was usually very good about picking up after himself.

As he rounded the bar to put the glass in the sink, he heard a faint sigh coming from the back of the pub. He glanced up and squinted into the darkness. His eyesight had been extremely sensitive today, but for some strange reason he couldn't seem to see through the thick, inky darkness that filled the interior of the pub. He couldn't penetrate the dimness or see anything in the rear of the bar. Again, he heard a sigh, followed by a soft throaty and sensual voice.

"I was hoping I'd get to have a moment alone with you." Evan's heart leapt. His first thought was of Juliette, but the tone of voice was all wrong. Instead of the

130

whispered bell tones he heard in Juliette's delicate voice, he heard dark and heavy chords, dripping with seduction and was instantly annoyed.

"Tori? How did you get in here? I locked the doors after I left." Tori began to emerge from the shadows. She was stepping very carefully towards him, prowling through the darkness.

"I was hoping you'd be surprised to see me..." A pout marred her once pixie-like features. The hair on Evan's arms prickled. His instincts warned that something was wrong, something was coming from her... something dangerous. He backed up against the counter, and she came around the end of the bar.

She looked like she had not showered in days. Her short blond hair was clumped together with a sticky red substance that looked a lot like blood. There were dirt smudges on her face, and she wore her usual uniform from work, but he knew that she had not been to work in a few days. Her clothes were filthy, torn, and tattered, revealing a brief glimpse of pale skin.

"I was hoping that you had been missing me..." Evan was not certain if he should be concerned at her haggard appearance or alarmed by her strange behavior. He felt as if he were being stalked, as an antelope might feel being hunted by a lioness on the grasslands. Deciding to go with his most basic urge to run, he turned toward Tori fully intending to push past her and leave, yet it seemed that his boots had been rooted to the floorboards.

She advanced slowly. Her eyes seemed different... dark and fathomless, her pupils dilated so much that her eyes were almost completely black when they had at one time been a pale blue. Fear lodged in his throat, making words impossible to utter.

131

Tori snaked her hand up his chest and up around his neck, threading her fingers through his hair, gently at first... then sharp pain shot through him as she dug her fingernails into his scalp and forced his face down towards hers.

"I have been very patient with you Evan." Her breath was icy on his lips as she maintained her unrelenting grip on his head. The curves of her face shaped into a look of wonder, and then quickly turned into a childlike pout as she noticed that his eyes filled with anger and distrust.

Evan, suddenly infuriated, found a strength he didn't know he possessed. Grabbing Tori by the wrists, he shoved her away into the rack of gleaming glassware and moved quickly to put as much distance between them as possible.

The sound of shattering goblets and glasses hitting the floor didn't faze Tori at all. She was around the end of the bar in an instant, too quick for Evan to even see her movements until she was within a few feet from him. She slowed her advancement, pursuing Evan like a hunter stalking its prey yet again.

The hurt and pouting expression had gone, leaving one of determination and annoyance.

Rage overtook him,

"Get out of here Tori! You no longer have a job here. If you don't leave, I'm calling the cops!" To his amazement, Tori began to laugh, a deep sadistic laugh, all the while continuing her slow pursuit of him.

"No offense Evan, but I've received a better offer and the benefits..." Tori ran her tongue along her teeth, "are so much better!" Evan tried estimating the distance to the door as she continued to speak,

"And now that you're not my boss, there is no reason we can't be together. There is nothing standing in our way." Evan didn't stop moving away from her, but he was quickly running out of room, being backed into a corner yet again.

"That wasn't the only reason we're not together. I don't want to be with you. I never have and that isn't going to change now. You need to leave." His words finally made an impact. She stopped moving, her eyes narrowed, a wicked gleam glinting in the dark room. The air became heavy and thick with danger.

"You're making a big mistake Evan!" Her voice was low, nearly a growl.

"My only mistake was putting up with you for as long as I have." The room seemed deafeningly silent. Only the sound of their breath could be heard. Her lips lifted in a snarl baring sharp white fangs; an icy dread consumed Evan as he realized what Tori had become.

"You really shouldn't have said that." She moved so fast Evan didn't have a chance to move.

She sprang from where she had been standing seconds before, launching herself at Evan. He slammed to the floor cracking the back of his skull on the hard wood. Pain spread through him like wildfire as she clawed his shirt with talons that seemed to have grown in seconds.

"You are MINE!" she screeched as she slammed her fangs into his neck, shredding his flesh. The searing pain engulfed him and Evan nearly lost consciousness.

Her hands were everywhere, moving in frenzied movements tearing at his chest arms and shoulders. She pulled back, the frustration clear on her bloodstained face. Again, she sank her fangs into his neck, searching for the vein that would allow his blood to run free.

133

Evan screamed in agony. He was no match for her strength. She finally found the vein that she wanted and after some time she pulled back and continued to straddle his limp form. She mimicked her creator and savagely bit into her own wrist and tried to force her flowing blood into his open mouth.

Evan wrenched his head to the side, avoiding her wrist, trying to fight back with what strength he had left. Through the haze of pain and numbing fog that threatened to take him at any second, he could hear her chanting the same mindless phrase repeatedly.

"You are mine; I will make you mine. You are mine; I will make you mine!"

Without warning, something or someone slammed the front door open, sending moonlight spearing across the floor illuminating the struggle.

Blood seeped into the cracks of the wooden planks. Tori gave up trying to press her wrist to Evan's mouth and let out one last piercing shriek as she flew at the intruder, dissolving into a swirling black cloud before ever reaching the door.

Evan lay there in a pool of his own blood, dazed and in unbearable pain. The attack had stopped, but his head was pounding, and his neck and chest burned and throbbed from the damage her nails and fangs had caused. He tried to turn his head towards the front of the pub to see who had interrupted her.

"Don't move Evan. Let me see how bad it is." He was suddenly lost in luminous silver eyes. Soft auburn tresses seemed to float around him, shutting out the horror, and enveloping him in the sweet scent of smoky wet timber. Her incense immediately calmed his pounding heart.

134

"Juliette... what are you doing here? I told you..." he struggled to speak, "it's not safe for you..." The irony of his statement was not lost on her.

"It seems to me that you are the one not to be left alone." She gently ran her fingers around the wounds trying to gage the seriousness of his injuries.

The claw marks on his chest were deep in the flesh; they would require suturing if she couldn't heal him. The open gash on his neck and the gash on his head were what had her worried most. He was losing a lot of blood and would quickly lose consciousness. She was not sure just how much blood Tori had managed to force on him, if any, but he didn't seem to be healing.

"Do you have a first aid kit here?" Evan tried to answer Juliette's question, but the room was starting to spin; he was nauseous and beginning to welcome the darkness that was quickly surrounding him.

Knowing there wasn't much time, Juliette bit her own wrist and let her blood run free over his wounds.

Hopefully, she could get the wounds to close before he lost any more blood. After allowing enough of her blood to flow into the less life-threatening injuries and seeing them begin to heal, she grabbed a stack of cocktail napkins and held it tight against his throat, but the bleeding wouldn't stop. She tried the same method, but the damage was deep in the tissue; there was only one way to close the wound and save him.

Using her nail, she sliced her already healed wrist, deeper this time to allow more blood to flow before the wound closed. She moved behind Evan and pulled his head into her lap; his eyes were beginning to glaze over, and he would lose consciousness very soon.

135

"Evan, I need you to listen to me. I know you are frightened, but I need you to drink this. It will help you heal." Juliette placed her wrist to his lips; he struggled, his eyes bulging as another wave of terror gripped him. Tori was a vampire; she had just tried to force him to drink her blood. Now Juliette wanted him to do the same. She was a vampire too! Evan attempted to pull away from her, his struggles causing his blood to pump harder, and his neck wound to bleed profusely.

Juliette hated to force him, but it was the only way. She leaned forward, locking her free arm around his neck so that he had no choice but to swallow the blood that was running down her arm. His head began to pound, and his heart thundered in his chest as her blood began to work its way through his system. When he had finally had enough, she pulled back and looked into his frightened eyes.

"I am sorry Evan. This was the only way." His eyes were beginning to flutter closed. The struggle was finally over, his blood loss was finally taking a toll. Within moments, he was blissfully unconscious.

Her blood quickly flooded his veins. The lacerations on his body were already beginning to clot and scab over. She pulled the napkin away from his neck and was relieved to see the gash already starting to heal and bruise.

His breathing was slowing, and she could hear his heartbeat returning to a normal rhythm. He was on the mend, but she needed to get him out of here before that psychotic bitch of a vampire came back.

Tori was newly turned. Juliette could tell that, by the mess she had left of Evan's neck and the fact that she had been human just a few nights before.

136

This was something that Devlon had never done in the past; this was new. Why had he turned her? What did he hope to gain by creating another vampire? One thing was for certain… she was outnumbered now, and this was going to be even harder than she had anticipated.

Juliette silently contemplated the best way to get him out of here. Her truck was just outside the back door; it wouldn't be hard to get him there, but she couldn't leave his bar looking like this. The sheriff was already on high alert because of the other murder that had occurred. If anyone found Evan's pub like this, the investigation would come much too close.

Kneeling next to Evan, Juliette closed her eyes and leaned forward, placing her palms flat against the floor to conjure a spell that would return the bar to its previous condition. The room began to hum, and the wooden planks quivered beneath her hands as she felt the power building within her.

Slowly raising her arms, she pulled a gleaming current of power from the earth and sea below the pub, using the elements to harness her strength, she sent a gentle wave of light careening through the bar. The low vibration that strummed through the building built until she could feel the rumbling deep within her chest. Every corner of the building that was touched by her brilliant pulsating light gleamed anew. When the humming subsided, Juliette opened her eyes to see that the bar looked as if nothing had transpired. The shattered glass that had lain scattered and broken on the floor now gleamed whole in the racks of hanging goblets. Evan's blood that had soaked the floor was nowhere to be seen, any evidence of his attack was gone.

Weakened by the spell, Juliette sat back on her heels and breathed deep trying to clear the dizziness that was brought on by the surge of power she had summoned. She would need to feed, but first she needed to get Evan out of here and back to her cabin where she could keep a close eye on his recovery.

***

Deep in the forest Tori was clawing her way through the shrubbery, tears streaming down her face. Her encounter with Evan hadn't gone anything as she had imagined it would. She had pictured in her mind how pleased he would be to see her alive and well. His face should have lit up at the possibility that they could be together forever.

He should have looked at her in awe of her strength and beauty. Instead, he had gazed at her in horror and disgust, he'd turned her away again. No, not turned her away... he'd shoved, he'd pushed, he had told her to get out, and that he didn't want her now or ever!

The fury and pain that his words had caused her sent her into a frantic rage. She blindly flew through the forest ignorant of the limbs and branches that clawed at her as she ran, until she noticed a light through the trees and caught sight of a campfire on the other side of a creek.

She landed gracefully in the middle of the campsite and took notice of the tackle box and fishing pole resting against one of the giant cedar trees. A small ice chest that smelled of fish rested next to it, and a torn faded tent sat just beyond the firelight.

A middle-aged man had just stood up from the campfire, teapot in hand, and turned at the sound of her sudden entrance into his camp.

"Well now little lady, where did you come from?" The man seemed genuinely kind, and as he took in her tattered appearance, worry crossed his weathered features.

"Has someone hurt you darling? Who were you running from?" Tori's fury would not let her see that this

139

man cared, and had she truly been in danger he would have come to her aid.

Without answering his questions, she charged him and began to pummel his face, shoulders, and torso. Taking her rage to new heights, she savagely beat the man near to death with her new vampire strength.

The pungent odor of fresh spilt blood enraged her already ravenous thirst. She plunged her fangs into his neck, striking his jugular on the first attempt; she drank from his mangled body like a savage beast, only stopping once she was full. His heart faltered and beat one last time.

Tori stood and surveyed the now quiet camp. The only sound was the crackling and popping of the fire and the gurgling creek beyond it. She breathed in the fresh night air as the despair of this night's events began to catch up to her.

What had she become? What had she just done? She had wanted so badly for Evan to see her in a different light, but all he saw was a monster. She walked to the edge of the water and rinsed the blood from her arms and face.

She would change that, she *needed* to make him see that he couldn't live without her. She stood and looked up at the night sky and swore silently to herself that he would be hers. No matter what it took, no matter who got in her way, in the end he would belong to her forever.

***

He was warm, almost too warm. He felt like he was floating, the pain he last remembered was gone and the cold had been replaced by velvety warmth that had spread throughout his entire body.

Evan tried to open his eyes to see where he was, but his mind was refusing to surface. Darkness weighed him down as though he had been sleeping for days.

It took a moment for his vision to clear. He could see that it was very dark in this room, apart from a warm fire in the hearth to his right. He was in a large, very soft bed, and there was a soft silk bedspread pulled up to his bare chest.

His chest!

Evan bolted upright in the bed and looking down, he knew that he would surely be covered in deep lacerations and possibly bandages.

Why didn't it hurt?

He pulled the coverlet down to reveal flawless skin, not a nick a cut or a scrape on him... that was impossible. He remembered very vividly the attack that had almost killed him.

Evan swung his feet over the side of the bed to rest on the cool wooden floor. He was wearing soft black pajama pants that tied at the waist and nothing more.

Where was he?

Who had dressed him, and how had he survived without even a scratch? He tried to stand, and his head began to swim, the room was spinning, and there was someone trying to push him back onto the bed. Evan sat,

141

closed his eyes, and waited for the room to quit moving before opening them again.

Juliette was kneeling before him, her cool hands holding him firmly down, trying to prevent him from standing again.

"You need to lie down and rest. You've been through a lot tonight."

Evan jerked back at her touch, recalling what had happened before he had passed out, but the moment his gaze fell on her delicate features, the fear simply fell away.

He took in her appearance, the terror pushed to the very back of his mind. He was suddenly struck with awe by her seamless beauty. Her hair hung in soft waves to her waist, she was dressed in white satin pants that flowed to the floor with a white satin lace camisole that almost appeared translucent with the glowing firelight behind her. Her delicate white feet were bare, her toes not painted as he would expect, but perfectly manicured and flawless. There wasn't anything he could find fault in.

"You're beautiful."

Juliette smiled slightly and shifted to sit on the bed next to him.

"Thank you."

She looked him over, his midnight black hair falling in wild chaos over his forehead, his strong jawline was shadowed by his beard, and his magnificent flesh, taut over rippled muscle, warm and sculpted, blazed in the light of the nearby fire. His deep green eyes held in fixation as she scrutinized his body.

He had never thought it possible to be caressed by a woman's gaze, but that is exactly what she was doing to him. His skin felt every shift of her eyes, every nerve

142

tingled, and he had never been more aware of anyone... ever.

She ran her fingers through his hair, gently feeling for the bump that remained on the back of his skull. Her fingers were feather light, causing gooseflesh to rise on his arms and chest.

"This will take time to heal. I would suggest taking some time off work to recover."

He was reminded again of the attack.

"What are you?" his question was spoken quietly, but the demand to know the truth carried volumes.

Juliette dropped her hand and stood. She walked to the windows where the silk draperies had been pulled aside to reveal the shadowed forest beyond the balcony. She wasn't sure how much he would remember. Was there any possible way to keep him from knowing the truth? She would need to handle this delicately to gauge just how much he knew.

"What is the last thing that you remember?" Juliette turned to see Evan looking again at his hands, his arms, and his chest which carried no sign that he had been mauled by Tori.

He was struggling to see through the haze of his memory. He thought he could recall very clearly what had happened to him, but there was no proof of it on his body. Had it all been a dream? Had he made the whole thing up in his head? He had been feeling odd lately. Was he losing his mind to the point of hallucinating? Evan met her unwavering gaze, a worried and perplexed expression marring his handsome face.

"I don't really know... I was going back to the pub for... my laptop. I thought I saw...I mean Tori was there but there was something wrong with her..." Evan stopped and placed his face in his hands, "I don't know." Juliette came around the foot of the bed, to sit by his side once again.

She could see the struggle and what it was doing to him. He was starting to piece everything together but was doubting himself. She would need to probe him more to see just how much he could recall; maybe she could persuade him to think that the things he had seen were only nightmares and not real.

"Tell me Evan; tell me what happened." Evan dropped back onto the pillow. The sore spot on the back of his head sent flashes of memories through his mind… Tori attacking him, pushing him to the ground, his skull splitting on the hard wooden floor, her fingers, like talons tearing into his flesh.

As the images came flooding back, he told her everything… of the light glinting off of her fangs, the pain as she plunged them into his neck over and over again, the rivers of blood that flooded the floor, of Tori trying to force her own blood into his mouth. He stopped talking and looked at her, measuring her response to his last statement. He remembered what she had done; she had succeeded in forcing him to drink her blood.

Juliette sat quietly waiting as he bravely remembered the battle he had fought and had been losing until she had come to his aid. He knew of the vampires, knew that they were here in his small quiet fishing community, but just how much did she need to reveal of herself?

One thing was certainly clear, she would need to keep this newly turned vampire away from him… she was going to have to veer away from her original plan to maintain her distance if she were going to keep him safe.

Tori's infatuation with him had grown into a terrifying situation now that she had become a vampire. She would need to make sure he was never alone.

She knew that he was watching her and waiting for her to explain her part in all of this. Like the coward, she never thought herself to be, she attempted to change the subject.

"Do you want me to call your friend or perhaps your sister? I don't think you should be alone right now; you may have a concussion."

"No, I want you to tell me what happened next. I want you to tell me why you made me drink your blood, and I want the truth."

Their eyes met and held, she was so beautiful it was hard for him to be angry with her, but he didn't want to lose that emotion. It was the only thing that would force the truth from her. Evan slowly sat up putting their faces mere inches away from one another. The anger in his eyes slowly turned to a burning desire.

Suddenly it dawned on him, the situation in which he had found himself... alone, barely dressed in Juliette's bedroom with a warm inviting fire. It created a very sensual atmosphere.

He lifted his hand to touch her hair where it cascaded past her shoulder. Her silver eyes shimmered in the flickering light; her lips slightly parted. She wanted to say something but held back. At that moment, he didn't care what she was, he wanted her still.

Evan leaned in and kissed her lightly at first, then placing both hands on either side of her face, pulled her against him. His need to touch her, to feel her, to know that she was real, grew stronger. He deepened the kiss.

Juliette had known this would happen, yet she

145

couldn't pull away, and she couldn't stop it. He had come so close to dying. Her world had already come for him. She needed to protect him, needed to feel him, and know that he was alive and safe. She returned his kiss and gloried in the way his hands cradled her face. She wanted to feel cherished and treasured, and it had been so very long since anyone had touched her like this, either physically or emotionally.

But Marek was there, always in her heart and on her mind. The guilt came flooding back and doused the passion that was quickly consuming her.

She placed her hands on his and gently pulled them away from her face as she ended the kiss. Juliette rested her forehead against his and inhaled his enticing aroma.

"I am sorry Evan; I can't do this." Evan looked down at their intertwined hands and tried to control the emotions that burned within him. He wanted her, wanted her like no other. He'd never experienced a desire this strong for anyone or anything. It was on the verge of being painful to stay away from her. But something was holding her back, and he needed to know what.

"Why Juliette? Tell me why when everything that we are feeling is so powerful? You can't deny that we have something amazing between us. Why fight it? Why throw that away? Tell me, tell me everything."

She would tell him the truth, he deserved that, after all that he had been through. And she would start with her engagement to Marek. He would understand that. He would honor that commitment, and these feelings between them would not matter anymore.

Juliette placed her hand on his chest, feeling his heartbeat strong against her palm. She drew in a deep breath and looked him in the eye, tears glistening on her

146

lashes threatening to fall at any moment.

"I cannot deny it, you're right about the feelings between us. But I am not free to be with you. I have come here searching for my fiancé." Evan pulled back, slowly dropping his hands in his lap and sucked in a deep breath.

"Your fiancé?" Evan exhaled, trying to force those words away. He sat there for a moment, staring into the fire, trying to keep the disappointment out of his voice when he spoke.

"Why didn't you tell me this earlier? Why did you let it get this far? Damn-it Juliette." Evan pulled away and began to get up, his head was pounding, and he couldn't breathe.

The warmth in the room, that had moments ago been charged and intoxicating, now seemed to be suffocating him. He struggled to free himself from the blankets and stand. He needed to get some air; he couldn't take a breath.

Evan burst through the French doors and onto the balcony. The cool night air helped immensely to clear his head as he drew in a lungful. He gripped the railing and let his head fall. He stared at the ground, the muscles in his arms rigid, as he struggled to hold it together.

What was wrong with him? He felt out of control, his emotions were governing his body and every thought.

The wood planks were cold against his bare feet, but he hardly noticed as he tried to piece together the times she had pushed him away...the night at the bar when she had told Trevor that she wasn't competition. He had ignored it, too consumed with his attraction for her. They had already made a connection at that point, or so he had thought.

That night in her living room, she had been crying

and angry, but not at him, at herself. Now that he thought back on it, he could see it so much more clearly, she had been ashamed of herself.

He sensed her presence as she came up next to him on the balcony. She held a shirt in her hands, the same material as the pants that he already wore.

"You should put this on, it's cold out here." He numbly took the shirt and put it on.

"Are these clothes his?" he asked quietly, hating the bitterness he heard in his voice, once again looking out at the still Oregon night.

"Yes, but he won't miss them. He's never worn them, and I don't know that he ever will. They are yours to keep if you like." Juliette's voice was soft, almost a whisper. What did she mean she didn't know if he would ever use them?

Evan finally turned to look at her. She looked so tiny and fragile in the robe that she had put on before coming out onto the deck. He longed to put his arms around her to pull her close and to share his warmth with her.

Juliette turned her back towards him, looking out into the dark forest, her shoulders drooping beneath the weight of what needed to be said. Evan reached for her, turning her to look up into his eyes,

"Is he a vampire too?" Her eyes flew open, the shock of hearing him say it aloud almost caused her knees to buckle. He steadied her, not releasing her until he was sure she would not fall.

"Yes."

Her mind was racing, he knew, he remembered. How was she going to explain everything to him?

"Where is he?" Evan softened his tone, seeing the

defeat clearly in her eyes.

"He was taken by the same man that took your friend Charlie." The blood drained from his face. So that was the reason she had been out at the lighthouse, searching for something that would lead her to her missing fiancé.

"When was he taken? How long has it been?" Juliette looked down at her hands. How much should she say? He knew so much already; would it be wise to keep trying to hide it from him?

This was his home. In her heart, she knew that telling him was the right thing to do. She needed to reveal the entire nightmare of what was happening here in Chancellor and the creature that she was.

"He was taken a long time ago, centuries ago. However, I made a promise to never give up until he was found, one way, or the other. I will not break that promise." Evan didn't know whether to admire her persistence or to pity her desperation in finding her fiancé.

He had begun to assume that Charlie was dead, and he had only been missing for three days.

"Why do you think it's the same person who took Charlie?" Juliette turned and went to sink into one of the chaise lounges that sat in the corner near the door. Evan chose to stay where he was, attempting to keep his distance from her without being offensive.

Juliette took notice of his decision to not follow her and although she was relieved by his choice, it started an ache deep within her chest. This twinge of sadness was something she had only ever experienced when thinking about the loss of Marek.

It shocked her to feel the same depth of unhappiness at the thought of Evan not wanting to be near her. Was it because of her engagement or because he was repulsed that she was a vampire?

Either way it didn't matter, she thought to herself. This was what she had wanted, was it not? This was the way it had to be.

"I need to tell you everything for you to understand Evan, but I fear that you will not be so willing to be my... friend once I am done." The word 'friend' seemed so wrong. It didn't seem powerful enough to describe their relationship, but she knew that it was best to remind him of what they should be, if he chose to remain in her company once he knew everything about her.

"My name is Juliette Bellerose; I was born in Paris, France in 1660. I am 352 years old, and as you've already guessed... I am a vampire. "

Juliette had already confirmed to him what she was, but it still did not prepare him for the shock that coursed through his body at the realization of just how old she really was.

He leaned into the balcony railing, needing support, and ran his hands through his hair while trying to come to grips with everything that he had learned.

He looked her over from head to toe, finally seeing her for what she really was. He recalled the differences in the way that she carried herself. She didn't sway her hips as most women tended to do these days, attempting to entice men to take notice of them. Instead, when she stood, her posture was correct, her spine strait. She moved, gracefully gliding, as she held her head high and kept her back rigid.

She spoke differently than the people today, aside from her slight accent, she didn't use slang, didn't curse and rarely raised her voice. Her mannerisms were those of someone born to wealth and were very refined.

Her face was youthful. The only thing giving away her years of existence was the flicker of secrets and shadows of ghosts from the things she had seen, shimmering in her silvery gaze.

Years of learned patience kept her from pushing him too far until he was ready to learn more. She wondered what he must think of her now. She searched his face for any sign of revulsion and found none. He seemed to take in every detail of her, and at last his green eyes settled on her face and he nodded, giving her the sign to go on.

She told him what life had been like back then, of her yearning for books, knowledge, travel, and excitement… things young women in her day were never able to pursue.

"What was-is your fiancé's name?" He quickly corrected his statement, but he saw the flinch that briefly crossed her features and immediately regretted the slip.

"Marek, his name is Marek Colville." She looked up from her lap and met his eyes. Evan was stunned by the amount of raw emotion he heard radiating from her admission. The tremendous amount of love and pride that shone through her tears was almost staggering.

The way that she said his name was as if she were pledging her undying love and devotion to a god. His heart plummeted. He knew now that no matter what had occurred between them, and no matter how this search for her lost love ended, she would never look at him with that amount of passion or affection.

He couldn't believe how quickly he had fallen for her and was still falling. She was engaged, and a vampire for god's sake. What was wrong with him that he couldn't simply walk away. If he knew what was good for him, he'd leave and forget about ever meeting her. But he knew, without a shadow of a doubt, no matter how much this tore at his heart, that he would do whatever it took to help her find what she was looking for. He would help end her suffering, so that the love and hope she clung to so desperately was not in vain.

Despite the pain that it caused, he encouraged her to tell him more of their life together.

She shared with him the unforgettable moment that she and Marek had met. She shared the fear that she had experienced when Arnaud had raised his hand to her, and the immense sensation of warmth, love and security that had taken its place when Marek had swept her up in his arms and carried her to safety.

"Why didn't you and Marek ever get married?" Juliette sighed, and leaning back on the chaise, she pulled her knees to her chest and wrapped her arms around her legs recoiling from the question. She had asked herself that question many times over the centuries. Before they had turned, their families had been the reason they had never married, but after that, there had always been something more important to see to. Looking back, she could recall all the struggles that they had faced… all the things that needed to be resolved before they could wed, and then… they had run out of time.

She didn't know how to answer that question, so she explained the initial reason for their inability to marry.

"We had been led to believe by his cousin, Devlon, that Marek's father did not approve of our marriage. We discussed running away to be together, but we didn't want to shame our families. So, we decided to stay and face his father. We had hoped that Marek's father would change his mind once he saw how happy we were together, but several attempts on my life caused us to flee Paris."

Evan finally came to sit on the chair opposite her, pulled in by her intriguing history and hanging on every detail of her past.

"We waited for the would-be murderer to be caught, hiding out in the forest, hoping that in time we could return and be married. It wasn't long after our departure that Marek learned that someone was murdering his family. He returned to Paris to try and save them. That was when he learned of Devlon's treachery. He had lied about Marek's father not supporting our marriage to cause us to run away so that he could have his title. When that didn't work, he hired someone to try to kill me. His plan was to place the blame on Marek. But again, his plan failed. That was when he started murdering the Coleville family. He made it look like a plague was the cause of their deaths so that he could inherit the title and the family fortune."

"Is Devlon still alive? Is he behind this?" She nodded in response.

"I have been tracking him ever since the day he took Marek. He has always stayed just out of my reach. It seems that he is slowing his pace, waiting for me to catch up to him."

"His usual approach is to leave bodies scattered, not bothering to hide them, their necks ravaged, and severe blood loss is usually the cause of death with his victims. I am usually too late to find them, all that is left is a drained and decaying corpse." Speaking now as if unable to stop, she relayed the grizzly details of her plight.

"There have been times when he takes someone, and it's very hard if not impossible to find them. No one has ever survived an encounter with him... until now." Juliette paused, wondering if she was being too graphic.

This was the first time she had spoken aloud to someone else about Devlon and Marek in centuries. She supposed that it was something she needed to do, to get it out, hear it out loud and to share the grief that had consumed her for so long.

Tears were openly streaming down her cheeks. It took every ounce of strength for Evan not to gather her close to him and kiss her tears away.

Instead, Evan reached for her and took her small hand in his. He turned it over in his palms and marveled again at the strange sensation of just touching her.

It seemed that every nerve ending was exposed. The feeling of her skin against his seemed to cause vibrations to ripple through to his bones.

It occurred to him that he was more physically aware of everything around him. All his senses were heightened.

He could see the shadows stretching and getting larger as the night grew longer. He could smell the salty sea as it lapped at the beach below the cliffs in the distance, and he could hear the flickering of the flames in the hearth inside.

He dropped her hand and quickly stood to look out into the forest. His head was still pounding, and the strange sensations almost had him reeling.

Juliette noticed him stagger to the railing and quickly went to steady him.

"Evan, what's wrong?" He took a deep breath trying to clear his head and could swear he tasted the flavor of the nearby pine trees, the slight tang of menthol tasted odd on his tongue.

"I don't know, I just feel strange. I guess I am just tired."

154

Thinking that the exhaustion from the evening's events had finally caught up to him, Juliette suggested he lie down.

Evan glanced at the bedroom; the warm fire bathed the walls in dancing shadows. The thought of lying down in the silk draped bed next to Juliette caused a surge of desire that almost brought him to his knees. Evan knew, that with these overwhelming feelings coursing through him, he would not be able to keep from touching her.

Juliette saw the lust leap into his eyes and could taste the raw hunger that emanated from him and quickly suggested another alternative.

"Maybe I should take you home, it's been a long night and the sun will be rising soon." Evan hated to leave her, but he knew he needed to get some distance from her if he was going to be able to get a grip on what was happening to him. He headed towards the French doors and looked down at the clothes that he now wore.

"Do you have my clothes so that I can give these back to you?"

"Keep them, your own clothes were ruined." She wrapped an arm around his waist to help him back into the cabin and placed one hand on his chest. He looked down at her, this angel in white, with her delicate hand still resting on his thundering heart.

He wondered if she could feel it slamming against her palm. Evan pushed down the emotions that tied his stomach in knots and cupped her small hand in his.

"Thank you for saving me. If you hadn't come to the pub tonight, I wouldn't be standing here."

"Please, don't thank me. If I had stopped Devlon ages ago, this never would have happened."

155

He saw the defeat in her eyes and hated being the cause of it. He wanted to protect her, to help end her suffering. She had shared with him everything about herself, something she had clearly never done with anyone before. He owed her his life, and he felt the strength of this new bond with her.

Evan still had the ache and the urge to hold her, but he resisted, knowing that just being near her would need to be enough. He could see that she needed to reach out and wondered how long she had kept this bottled up inside. When was the last time she had let someone get this close to her?

"I will help you, Juliette. I'm in this with you. Together we will find the people that we have lost. You're not alone anymore." Juliette swallowed the tears threatening to fall again. She nodded unable to speak around the lump in her throat and clasped his hand as they went back into the house to gather his things and take him home.

***

Evan had not gone home right away to rest as he had promised Juliette he would. After she had left him at his pickup in the parking lot shortly before dawn, he had headed back into the pub to check out the scene of the attack.

It had taken him quite a bit of effort to convince her that he was fine and didn't need her to follow him back to his place. Had it not been for the imminent sunrise, he doubted he would have won that battle.

He was still very sore, and the odd sensations he had been feeling all night were still there.

He rubbed the now healed skin below his jaw as he entered the pub.

The clouds were thick today, and it would be a while before the sun was high enough for light to stream through the windows enough to illuminate the interior of the bar.

He flicked on lights as he went, searching for any proof that he had been viciously attacked by Tori.

The floors shimmered in the soft glow from the hanging Tiffany lamps, looking more pristine than he could remember them ever being. There weren't any glasses missing from the gleaming racks; there was no evidence of the struggle he remembered.

If he hadn't known any better, he would never have guessed that the bar had been in such disarray just hours before. How had Juliette cleaned up so well?

It occurred to him that he didn't know why she had been there in the first place. Was she fighting the attraction

157

as much as he was, or had she simply been trying to track Devlon?

He recalled the story that she had shared with him about Devlon and Marek Colville. This whole tale seemed to be pulled right out of a historical romance novel or European history book.

Devlon had crossed oceans and centuries to come here and wreak havoc on the small quiet town he had grown up in.

Evan sank down to the floor and, closing his eyes, leaned his head back against the bar. The knot on the back of his skull reminding him that he had one hell of a headache.

His heart sank as he thought about Juliette and Marek. He was torn between wanting her to find him and have the happy ending that she had been fighting for and wanting her for himself. She clearly cared for him, she had saved his life and shared her deepest secrets with him... that had to mean something. She could have left him to die.

She needed help, that much was obvious. She had been at this for a long time, alone, with no one to talk to, and she still hadn't been able to save Marek. Last night she had seemed so relieved to tell her story to him, glad to have assistance after all this time.

Evan wondered how she would react if they discovered that Marek wasn't here. If Devlon fled again to some far-off city somewhere, would she go too?

What if she went after him, disappeared, and he never saw her again? Even with the knowledge that she was engaged and a vampire, he still couldn't stop the yearning that overtook him whenever he thought of her. He couldn't risk losing her.

No, he would do everything in his power to make sure that this search of hers ended here, one way or another. If Marek were alive and they were reunited, then at least he would know that she was happy. That would have to be enough.

Evan finally stood, feeling better that he now had a purpose. He went to the office and grabbed his laptop. Taking one last look at the pub, he locked up and went home to get some rest before work that night.

***

For the first time in centuries, Marek's image did not haunt her dreams. Instead, it was Evan that invaded her mind.

Not the Evan that she had encountered several times over the last few days, warm human flesh, pliant and potent. She dreamt instead of Evan as a vampire. His skin had been the same flawless ivory as hers, his green eyes glowing metallically in the full moonlight, and his movements graceful and fluid as they strolled along the black sand beach, hand in hand.

The ocean air ruffled his black curls as Evan gazed down at her. Her heart did the same flip flop it had always done when Marek had looked at her with that same longing devotion.

Juliette tried to remember how he had come to be this way. When had he changed? How had he changed? And how were they walking so peacefully together along the edge of the sea without a care in the world?

Had the battle already taken place? Had they found Marek beyond help and beyond resurrection?

Had they defeated Devlon?

She stopped walking, her feet bare against the cool damp sand, the surf gently lapping at her toes as she curled them into the black grains glistening in the night. She shivered against his warm embrace as he wrapped his arms around her waist and pulled her against his solid frame... how was it that she was cold? She hadn't felt the elements against her skin the way a human would in so long she was

160

surprised at the sensations the deep-seated memory had caused.

Evan was clearly a vampire. How was it that his body radiated warmth against hers… Juliette gasped and jumped back as Evan's lips began to lower to meet hers. His puzzled expression and the hurt reflecting in his eyes hit her heart like a blow to the chest.

She looked at him… saw now for the first time the mortal blood pumping through his veins, his pulse beating strong in his neck, smelled the human bouquet of his skin and knew that her fear was coming to fruition. He was still human but was transitioning into a vampire quickly, right before her eyes.

Juliette sat up straight in the bed that Evan had only hours before occupied. She looked to her right where he had lain while unconscious, the indention still on the pillow from where his raven head had rested.

Was it possible? She had only given him enough of her blood to heal him, not nearly enough to turn him. But then again, she didn't know how much Tori had fed him when she'd interrupted her assault. Juliette flipped the blankets back and swung her feet to the floor, she needed to see him. Thank God the sun would be setting soon, and she could check on him and make sure that her dream was just that… a dream

***

    The pub was starting to get busy, the dinner rush well under way when Evan heard Trevor clear his throat and jerk his head towards the front door. Evan followed his nod to see Juliette walking towards the bar.

    The sight of her still took his breath away. He feared no amount of time with her would lessen his feelings for her.

    She looked amazing in skintight denim jeans, black knee-high boots, a plum sweater and black leather jacket. Her Hair flowed freely around her shoulders and her silver gaze smoldered beneath thick lashes, her cheeks slightly pink from the bite of the crisp night air. He pulled in a deep breath and walked to greet her, anxious to be near her.

    She leaned over the bar and cautiously reached her hand out to gently run her fingers through the hair on the back of his head, quietly searching for the lump she knew was there. She seemed to be looking him over very closely, concern shadowing her beautiful features.

    "How are you feeling Evan?"

    Her melodic voice and the sensations of her hand on his scalp engulfed him in scorching desire.

    "I'm feeling a lot better, thank you." He dropped his gaze from her eyes and searched her face, taking note of the flawless complexion and clear vibrant glow of her silver eyes… a sure giveaway of what she truly was.

    Now that he knew the truth, he wondered how he had missed it before. Although he knew she was a vampire now, his pulse still raced from her touch, and it didn't slow until she let her hand fall from the gentle exploration of his injury.

162

Just as he was noticing all the signs that she was a vampire, she was thoroughly examining him for any signs that he was in transition.

Her eyes traced his features looking for any sign of translucence in his skin tone; his eye color did not hold the metallic glow of a predator, and she could still feel the radiant warmth from his body. She heard his heartbeat increase as their eyes met and locked.

Their scrutiny of one another seemed to block out the rest of the pub. The continuous murmur of conversation from table to table, the clinking of cocktail glasses, the sound of forks scraping the ceramic dishware and the whir of the blender as April served her bar guests, all disappeared. It wasn't until the front door opened and a blast of cold air hit the couple, shattering their intimate moment, that they reluctantly moved away from each other. Mild embarrassment washed over her as she noticed that they were being watched by most of the customers as well as Evan's sister and best friend.

Juliette took a step away from the bar trying to put distance between them before they embarrassed themselves any further. It was clear that he was not transitioning, and there was no longer a need to remain in such close proximity to him.

"Could I bother you for a cup of coffee?" Juliette asked of Evan as he turned to fill an order that Trevor had handed him. April, having returned from delivering food to a table near the back, approached Juliette and pulled down a coffee cup.

"I can get that for you." Juliette noticed that April regarded her with open curiosity and genuine kindness.

"Thank you. You must be Evan's sister; you look very much alike." April smiled and handed Juliette the steaming cup of coffee.

"Yeah, I get that a lot. And you must be Juliette, Evan's new neighbor. Welcome to Chancellor. How do you like it here so far?" Juliette didn't expect April to know so much about her already and glanced quickly over at Evan. She wondered how much he had shared with his sister. Had he shared her history with anyone?

Evan came around the end of the bar and led Juliette to a seat near the taps where they could all keep her occupied as they worked. He placed a napkin under her coffee and then pulled the bar stool out for her to sit on.

As she took her seat, she smiled gratefully at him and turned to answer April's questions.

"The town is beautiful, small and.." she had been about to say peaceful but knowing that Devlon was stalking the forest and had turned this place into his own private hunting ground, she knew that was no longer true.

April was very observant. She caught Juliette's pause and had a good idea what was going through her head. Her heart-shaped face fell for a moment as she recalled what had happened to Charlie, and then almost instantly registered surprise as she recalled that Juliette had been at the pub the night she had found out about Charlie. She had been so distraught that she had not been formally introduced.

"I am so sorry; you were here last Sunday and I never had the chance to say hello!" Juliette let go of her warm coffee mug and placed her hand on April's arm,

"Please don't apologize. You had other things to occupy your thoughts. My warmest regards to your dear friend Charlie." Evan had been watching the exchange

164

between Juliette and April, taking notice of the way that Juliette cupped her hands around the hot mug before placing her hand on his sister's arm, much the same way she had before shaking his hand that first night they had met.

He recalled how cool her touch had been the night before as she had cared for his wounds, and how often she had placed her open palms near the fireplace to warm them. Was that how she concealed her cold vampire skin?

Trevor came to lean on the bar next to April and joined in the conversation; the three new friends seemed to get along well as they conversed without much urging from Evan. He decided to take a moment while they were entertaining Juliette to take a turn around the pub and make sure all his customers were taken care of.

April noticed that wherever Evan seemed to be in the room, he and Juliette were very much aware of one another, often locking eyes with each other. She wondered how involved they were and wandered over to ask Evan about their relationship when he returned from his rounds in the bar.

"She's very nice, and I like her a lot." Evan glanced down the bar at Juliette and Trevor, deep in conversation.

"Yeah, she's amazing." April leaned towards him as he poured a draft for a waiting customer,

"How amazing?" He noticed the meaningful gleam in her eye and what she was asking.

"She's engaged April, we're just friends." April's face registered the same amount of shock he had experienced upon learning she had a fiancé.

"What? Well… where is he then? Because with the way you two keep looking at each other, you would have

165

never known." Evan turned away from where Juliette and Trevor were sitting to lean towards his sister.

"I know! I am trying very hard to maintain boundaries, it's just..." he stopped and shook his head, unable to find the words that would express the depth of his feelings or the battle he waged every time she was near.

"She's here to find him. He disappeared a long time ago, taken by the same guy that we think took Charlie. She doesn't even know if he is still alive, but I promised to help her find out what happened to him."

He walked away and started to fill another customer's order, and April worked her way back towards where Trevor sat with Juliette.

April quietly digested the news that Evan had shared with her and felt such grief at Juliette's situation.

To have lost the man you loved and planned to marry, and to never give up the search for him, she didn't know that she could bear that kind of loss. Juliette was a strong woman, so much stronger than April thought she could ever be. Although they had only just met, April felt great admiration for her.

As the night went on, the bar crowd started to thin out as the dinner hour ended.

The foursome gathered at the end of the bar quietly conversing and getting to know each other. Juliette felt a kinship with these people... something she had felt with very few individuals throughout her lifetime.

It was an odd, yet welcomed feeling, almost like returning home after a long and arduous trip. She hadn't had a home to go to in centuries, she hadn't felt as if she belonged anywhere for just as long, but with that came the unwelcome quiver of fear.

166

Juliette needed to remember that anything that made you feel warm, and welcome could be stripped away from you in an instant. Nothing lasted forever. It was best not to establish roots lest they be torn from her again.

She looked around the bar and noticed that the last couple had just paid their tab and were walking out the door. Evan followed them out and locked the door behind them.

When he returned to the bar, he leaned down and pulled out a map similar to the one that Juliette had purchased at the gas station except it was already very worn from being opened and closed and had red markings scribbled on the front.

"Juliette, I think Trevor and April could be of some help finding Marek and Charlie. Do you mind if we share what we know with them?" She looked a little wary about this and leaned back, bracing herself for a difficult decision.

She didn't want to endanger Evan's family; they were very nice people and a strange sensation tugged at her heart as she thought about anything happening to any of them. But the truth was, Tori had already put Evan in danger, and she didn't seem likely to stop until she got what she wanted. Juliette couldn't be always with him, especially during the daylight hours. If they enlisted the help of April and Trevor, then he would never be alone, and they could cover a lot of ground during the day.

April noticed her hesitation and leaned forward to hold her hand. Juliette, not wanting to be rude and hurt the girl's feelings let her, inwardly cringing at how cold her skin must feel to her.

"Evan told me about your fiancé. I am so sorry for what you have been through. But let us help you, Juliette.

167

The least we can do is support each other while we search for the people that we have lost."

These humans were being so kind to her. She wasn't sure she deserved such compassion. She had done some horrible things in the past, letting her anger at a few individuals change her views on an entire race... a race she had once been a part of.

But the thought of continuing to search alone left her feeling shaken and depressed. It obviously hadn't done any good, trying to find Devlon on her own, as she was still searching. Juliette knew it was finally time to let someone help her. It was the right thing to do; it was time to ask for help.

Juliette stood on the beach, the sea breeze lifting her hair to swirl around her head in a mahogany cloud. She did nothing to keep it from whipping in her face, enjoying the feel of it caressing her cheeks.

It had been days since she had enlisted the help of Evan's family. She had done her best to explain what little she could about Devlon and the abduction of Marek, without including any details about them being vampires. Juliette and Evan seemed to have an unspoken agreement to leave that part out.

They had reviewed newspapers that Evan had thought to bring into the pub for information about the murders that had occurred in the forest. He had marked the locations of each attack on his map trying to create a search grid where they might locate Charlie.

They'd shared with April and Trevor what they had seen out at the lighthouse, leaving out the gory details of the amount of blood spatter. Evan also broached the possibility that Tori's disappearance had some connection with Devlon Colville. His gaze had held Juliette's as he tentatively tried to give them some idea as to what had happened to her.

April had admitted to calling the sheriff and filing a missing person's report after Tori hadn't shown up to work for the third night in a row. But as of that morning, they were no closer to knowing where she was. Until she was found, they were all working longer hours to cover her shifts. Between the town gossip they heard in the pub, the reports in the news and Juliette's nightly excursions in the forest, they were all doing what they could to gain more information on Devlon's whereabouts.

She was relieved to know that Evan wasn't being left alone during the early evening hours while she searched around town for clues. Tori's absence had seen to that.

Juliette hadn't been alone with him in what seemed like ages. They were both being very careful to not place themselves in any delicate situations where their more basic instincts could possibly take over. The struggle to stay away from him was emotionally draining, especially when he was so close. With Evan completely unaware, she was now keeping an eye on him every night to make sure he didn't have any more unwanted visits from the newly turned vamp.

As she strolled along the base of the cliff, Juliette filtered through the sound of the surf crashing on the beach to listen to the cool ocean breeze combing through the lush forest beyond the cliff. The sound of the tide moving away from the cove blended with that of the nocturnal orchestra of insects darting among the foliage and deer sifting through ferns searching for the sweet blackberries that grew freely here.

Juliette opened her senses beyond that of the nightly activity of the darkened wood, she listened for any movement in Evan's house, which was just up the cliff from where she now stood. He had taken a long shower and was now watching TV. She could hear the voices of the characters in the show he had been watching and noticed his breathing slow and steady as he drifted off to sleep.

She longed to be near him, to see his face, peaceful and at rest… to feel his warmth and know that he was okay. But she knew that being near him was putting them both in a very precarious situation. Even though they had agreed that they would remain friends and that he would honor her commitment to Marek, there was still this undercurrent of arousal that swept through her whenever he was near. She could see that he felt it too and was grateful that he was able to control his reaction to it so well.

She sighed deeply as she tried to clear her mind and focus on the surrounding area. She heard Ambrosia circling the perimeter and watched through her eyes as the dense forest opened to reveal the wide sandy inlet and the waves that swept up from the sea.

The moonlight shimmered down through the clouds casting spears of light onto the beach, creating pockets of shadows in the dunes and dips of the black sand.

The two walked in silence together, almost enjoying the serenity of the night and the cool feel of the sand beneath their bare feet.

Ambrosia kept her large head lowered to the ground, taking in the scents of the sea kelp and shells that had washed ashore when the tide had been high.

Juliette looked up towards the night sky and remembered a time when she had danced beneath the brilliant light of a moon very similar to this one. The smell of the sea foam disappeared, replaced by the potent memory of Marek's warm clean masculine scent of leather and spice that seemed to engulf her.

They had danced with no one else the entire evening, regardless of the disapproving glances from the other party goers and would be suitors.

Although they had made it clear that they wanted only each other, nothing formal had been announced yet as

171

Marek's father had been out of country and Juliette's father had been unable to make the arrangements for the union.

Marek was going to tell his father that she was the one he chose to marry and that had no intention of going forward with the betrothal that had already been arranged.

Marek had been properly courting her since their unforgettable encounter at the ball. However, the time that they were permitted by her parents didn't seem to be enough

They had maintained constant contact through written messages delivered secretly with the aid of Juliette's handmaid and Devlon. The town gossips made sure that all of polite society was aware of the events that had taken place at the ball the night they had met.

The story of how Marek bravely championed Juliette by standing between her and the man her father had carelessly chosen for her to marry.

The tale went on to portray Marek as a fearless knight that had saved her from a brutal beating by her cruel husband-to-be.

The Viscount Arnaud had escaped to his estate in the country, shamed by Marek's public rebuking. He had also, to Juliette's delight, withdrawn from the agreement with her father for her hand in marriage. Juliette was certain that it was only the fact that Marek was the future Duke of Brouillard that saved her from any retribution that her father may have decided to carry out.

Now the only thing standing in the way of them marrying was the betrothal that Devlon had warned Marek about. His father had been abroad and would be returning to the city soon. To that point, Marek had not yet been able to speak with him of his intent to marry Juliette.

172

Marek described his father as a fair man with nothing but pride and affection for his only son. But that didn't stop Juliette from worrying that the love that she and Marek shared, her father's title, and the small dowry that she had to offer, would be enough to allow the nuptials to take place.

She had voiced her fears to him that evening under the full moon's ghostly light. Marek lightly caressed her glorious shimmering tresses and pulled her gently against the length of his body, knowing that he only had a few moments hidden behind a cluster of blooming orange trees, the evening air heavy with the fragrant citrus. He nuzzled her neck and whispered in her ear:

"My heart will not be whole without you in my arms Juliette. You are the key to my happiness; my father cannot deny me the one person who completes me." He pulled back and looked intently into her silvery gaze, "Fear not my love, we will be wed. Even without the blessing of my family, I will not be without you."

It was this declaration that changed the course of their lives forever. Marek never doubted for a second that his father would not support this marriage. However, it was later learned through Devlon that he did not. The duke had heard of their courtship during his trip abroad and did not favor their union.

Devlon had delivered a missive to Marek, written by his father. In it was the declaration that he was betrothed to another and that his behavior at the ball, while the intent was honorable, had disgraced his family in the eyes of his future in-laws. His father's letter closed with a stern warning to end the relationship before causing further disgrace to his family as well as to Juliette.

Marek was stunned by his father's reaction to his relationship with Juliette and was greatly saddened by the letter. He didn't understand why the duke would force him to marry someone he did not love.

Suddenly his title, something he had always taken great pride in, paled in comparison to the vow he'd made to be with Juliette.

It sickened Juliette when she thought of all that he would lose by choosing her, and she begged him to reconsider, although her life without him would hardly be worth living. Marek refused to be without her, confident that in time, his father would come around.

They decided that they would meet with his father when he returned from his trip. If after that meeting, they were unable to change his mind on their marriage, then they would leave Paris and start a new life together.

A low growl from Ambrosia alerted Juliette to movement in the trees surrounding Evan's house. She looked towards the sky, curious as to how long she had been lost in thought and angry at herself for losing focus and putting Evan in danger.

They swiftly crossed the stretch of beach and were, in moments, soaring up the face of the cliff to land within yards of Evan's back porch.

Juliette remained crouched close to the earth, hidden in the ferns that grew wildly on the outskirts of the property, as her eyes quickly raked through the shadows that clung to the wood.

Ambrosia had taken mist form and was weaving through the tree's trying to locate which direction the intruder was approaching from.

174

Juliette heard branches snap to the east of the house and saw Ambrosia change course to track the noise.

It was Tori. Juliette was certain of it. Ambrosia would circle around behind the new vampire as Juliette met her head on, hopefully taking her by surprise, as neither she nor Devlon were aware of Ambrosia's existence.

Should Tori escape this night, she wanted Devlon to remain in the dark about her pet and communicated to Ambrosia to stay in mist form until she signaled otherwise.

Juliette had swiftly crept around a cluster of thin birch trees to see Tori standing in the thick of the forest. Her stance was rigid, feet slightly apart, and her hands were clenched into fists at her sides. She was completely unaware that she was being watched.

She almost pitied the girl as she took in the saddened longing expression carved into Tori's stone-like features. She gazed at Evan's house willing him to come to her.

Tori was so absorbed in trying to influence Evan that she didn't notice the low fog that had begun to churn at her feet and spread out along the ground away from where she was standing.

Juliette gasped. There was only one reason Tori should be able to conjure the elements and create the mist that was now creeping along the ground. All vampires could dissolve into mist, but none other than herself were able to create it!

Tori snapped out of her trance and hissed in Juliette's direction having heard her shocked intake of breath.

In an instant Tori was flying through the trees right at Juliette, claws extended, and fangs bared. Juliette braced

175

her feet on the damp forest floor and met her attack with a bone-jarring crash.

A look of shock registered in Tori's widened eyes as she realized that Juliette was much stronger than she was. With impressive speed Juliette swiveled the newborn around to slam her back against Juliette's chest, her arms locked around her and under her neck in a choke hold.

The outraged snarl that ripped through Tori's bared teeth was enough to wake anyone within a five-mile radius.

A light within the home flickered on as Evan raced to the door to investigate the noise.

Juliette heard the lock click as he turned the knob. Tori was now straining against her trying with all her new vampire strength to get at Evan as he emerged from the house.

"Stop moving before I rip your head from your body!" Juliette growled in her ear. Tori's bloodlust and infatuation had deafened her. She clawed at Juliette continuing to snarl and hiss.

Juliette saw the beam of Evan's flashlight strobe through the trees as he tried to see what was making the guttural animal noises outside his house.

Juliette silently ordered Ambrosia to take form and run through Evan's beam of light, hoping that seeing the great wolf would not only appease his curiosity but also make him go back into the house.

Evan gasped as he saw the blur of what had to be the biggest wolf he had ever seen. His heart began to hammer in his chest with fear as he quickly retreated into the house and locked the door. She could hear him scrambling for the phone as he called the sheriff to report what was lurking in the forest.

She had to get Tori out of here before the area was swarming with the sheriff's posse searching for her wolf. She ordered Ambrosia to stay out of sight, thankful that Tori had been too preoccupied in trying to break free that she hadn't seen Ambrosia distract Evan.

Juliette glanced behind her and gauged the distance between her and the edge of the cliff. If she could stun Tori for a moment and still her movements, she just might be able to reach the beach below. Without further hesitation, Juliette snapped Tori's head to the side and brutally sank her teeth into the cool flesh, savagely ripping at her neck.

Tori howled in pain and went rigid just long enough for Juliette to clasp her unyielding form against her chest and spring backwards, arching high above the moss-covered undergrowth and ferns.

The free fall had Tori scratching and scrambling at Juliette as she pivoted around in midair, bringing the snarling girl face to face with her as they descended towards the black sand beach below the cliff face.

They landed with an earth-shaking thud. Tori was on her back looking up towards the night sky while Juliette crouched on top of her, holding her to the ground with one hand as she used her other to brace for the impact.

The force of the fall knocked the wind from Tori. She gasped for air, not used to her vampire body. She acted as if she were still human and needed to breathe. Juliette leaned over the stunned girl, blood still glistening on her lips.

"I should kill you now and put you out of your misery." To her astonishment Tori's face crumbled and she began to sob.

"No! Please, don't hurt me, I'll stay away from him, I promise, just please d-don't kill me!" Juliette sat back on

177

her heels, keeping one arm firmly locked on Tori's already healing throat.

She probed the girl's emotions for anything that would show her if she spoke the truth. She was searching through painful flickering images of a dark figure beating her unmercifully. She tried desperately to see the face of this creature, knowing that it had to be Devlon. She was so focused on trying to catch a glimpse of his face that it took a moment for her to register that Tori was now laughing... a shrill demonic and disturbing laugh.

"You're too late you stupid bitch, he's already here! He's stronger than you!" Her laughter kept increasing in octave and was beginning to sound hysterical.

Juliette stared in confusion, her heart racing. Was she finally going to come face to face with Devlon after all these centuries of searching? Would he finally come out in the open just to save this girl?

Before she could move to a better defensive stance, she was suddenly thrown sideways. A great force had slammed into her, causing her to let loose of her hold on Tori and sent her rolling through the sand. She came to a stop on her hands and knees ready to spring at her attacker when she noticed that she was now alone in the cove. Nothing remained of Tori's presence on the beach other than the imprint of where she had been lying in the sand and the resounding laughter that followed a dark pungent cloud of mist that shot up towards the clouds and disappeared.

"You are weak!" His angry words echoed off the stone walls and stalagmites that adorned the interior of the cave.

"Useless!" The screaming persisted as Tori awoke with a start. The last thing that she remembered was being pinned down by that redheaded bitch and laughing and feeling Devlon's swift approach.

Suddenly she was struck in the face and yanked up off the damp floor by her hair.

"I found you, pathetic and alone! I showed you love; I enveloped you in my dark embrace and gave you the priceless gift of immortality and this is how you show me your gratitude? Stalking around in the shadows and sulking over that spineless sap you want as a lover? You've tried to change him, revealing your identity to that bitch Juliette?" Each statement was followed by a blow to her stomach.

Tori was blinded by the pain. Surely her ribs would crack from the beating, and it seemed like her hair was being ripped out by the roots. Yet as soon as the abuse halted the pain was already subsiding and her body healing.

Devlon let loose the grip he had on her hair and watched her crumble pathetically to the floor. She did not cry or sob or make excuses for her actions. He knelt and looked her in the face as she struggled to her feet. Her jaw was clenched with pride and a stubborn refusal to show weakness after his harsh insults.

He almost felt something close to admiration for the little slut. He may have finally chosen the right pawn to play this little game with after all.

He had disposed of that decrepit old man shortly after he had turned him… worthless bag of bones. He had done nothing but cry and whine about his dead wife and how he only wanted to be with her again. Well, that would never happen. An anchor and eternal life at the bottom of the bay had seen to that, a useful little trick that he had stumbled upon decades ago.

Abruptly he grabbed her by the neck and slammed her against the wall of the cavern. Her eyes did not show fear as they had the last time he had held her like this, instead, they shimmered with lust and hunger. The curling heat was again wafting up from her loins through her body to the pulse point at the back of her throat as her teeth lengthened to sharp needles. Devlon caressed her lips with his thumb and smiled as he saw how the desire and thirst affected her.

"Remember young one, I am your master now. That boy is nothing." He leaned in and purred next to her ear, allowing her to feel his breath against her skin and intensify the seduction.

"Let me show you how it is done. Drink from my veins, and I will share with you a passion unlike any you would ever experience with that human." Tori did not hesitate, he held her mind with his own and instructed her on how to execute the first bite without so much as a drop spilled.

The soft draw of that first torrent of his powerful blood was almost more pleasure than she could take.

Their blood sharing became a violent exchange of raw power as he dominated his new plaything. An eager pupil, she drank in his black thoughts, his raw hatred for Juliette, Marek, and anything mortal, even her precious Evan.

180

***

Evan entered the house from the back door into the kitchen. It seemed like it had been days since he had last been home, when it had only been a few hours that he and the Chancellor sheriff's office had been searching the woods outside his home for the great white wolf he had seen.

They had found nothing… not a tuft of hair, not a trampled fern or even a footprint that would lead them to where its den might be. The sheriff was beginning to think that everyone in this town was losing it.

The murders that had occurred, and the disappearance of Charlie and Tori, had the community in an uproar. They got at least ten calls a night about a noise someone had heard or a mysterious figure that they had seen, but nothing ever panned out. The recent events in the town were keeping the relatively small sheriff's office very busy.

Evan sank into the recliner and threw the lever back to raise his feet. He stretched and moaned feeling every muscle in his body pull. He was physically exhausted, but his mind was racing.

He knew what he had seen, and no one was going to convince him otherwise. He wondered if Juliette had encountered the wolf during her excursions in the forest searching for clues that would lead her to Marek. He shouldn't have thought of her; suddenly his mind was racing in a different direction.

It was just his luck to fall in love with the most beautiful woman he had ever laid eyes on, only to find out she was engaged, and a vampire.

Granted, her betrothed was missing and had been missing for some time. But he could tell by the way her face lit up when she spoke his name, that her love for the man was very much present and accounted for. How was he ever going to get past his feelings when they were going to be working so closely together to track down Devlon, Marek and Charlie?

He wondered if Marek was even alive still. What would happen when this was all over with, assuming that they survived, if it were discovered that Marek was dead? Would she turn to him for comfort? Would they be able to be together? She was a vampire; he was human. Evan didn't know how that could work out. He certainly was not interested in joining the world of the undead.

Evan lay sprawled out in the chair contemplating his future and how everything would play out. The moon was beginning to set in the cloud covered sky, casting a dreary glow on the mountainous landscape. It was going to rain again today. He was curious to see if Juliette would be able to leave the house with the clouds blocking the sunlight.

He wanted to see her desperately, to tell her about the wolf he had seen, but he didn't know if she would be asleep. The sun wouldn't be up for a few more hours as it was just past four in the morning. He had her cell phone number and had never used it.

Evan quickly dug his phone out of his pocket, eager to call her and possibly hear her voice. He scrolled through his contacts until he found her name and pressed the call button with shaky fingers.

The phone rang several times and her voicemail picked up with the automated voice requesting that he leave a message. His heart sank as he pressed the end call button.

Why was he letting himself get so worked up over her? She was in love with someone else. He feared that even if they found out Marek had been dead all along, she would want to be alone to mourn him, possibly even leave town.

Evan forced himself to stop thinking about her; it was only driving him crazy. He decided that he needed to get some sleep if he was going to get anything accomplished today. He would need to be at the pub in a few hours to take in the food delivery, but first he would need another shower. Hiking in the woods had left him covered in sweat and mud. He craved the feeling of the steaming water penetrating his sore muscles and headed to the bathroom. He didn't linger long in the shower knowing that the more time he spent showering, the less time he would have for sleep.

Evan turned off the shower and was reaching for a towel when he heard the phone ringing in the living room. Without first wrapping the towel around his waist, he bolted down the hall knowing that it must be Juliette returning his call.

Juliette was sitting cross-legged on her bed before a raging fire, having just finished feeding one last time before turning in. The battle on the beach had exhausted her, and it was obvious she was going to have to feed more often if she was going to have any chance of winning this war.

She heard the vibration of her cell phone on the bedside table and leaned forward to see who could possibly be calling her. Her breath caught in her throat as she saw Evan's number glowing on the small plastic screen.

Juliette picked up the phone as she stood and turned to face the flames in her fireplace, her emotions waging a war within her heart.

She wanted desperately to answer his call, to hear the warm timbre of his voice. But she knew that if she answered, with as tired as she was, she may not be able to resist the pull he had on her.

How was she going to control these raging emotions every time he called, every time he was near? The phone stopped moving in her palm, and the notification of a missed call blinked onto the screen.

A sudden wave of sadness washed over her, and she slowly bent to place the phone back onto the table. She sat on the edge of the bed trying desperately to think of Evan as nothing more than a friend... a very dear and trusted friend. She wondered what Marek would think of him if they ever had the opportunity to meet. He would see all the changes in her. She wondered if he would see the sadness when it came time to leave Chancellor. She was finally establishing roots. She had hoped that once this was over, she and Marek would be able to settle here for a time, but with her feelings for Evan growing by the day, that would be impossible.

She knew that Marek would not think less of her for how she felt about Evan. She would tell him, of that much, she was sure. She would never be dishonest about the things she had done. He would understand that she needed to remain close to Evan until he was safe from the threat of Tori. Suddenly a torrent of cold fear flooded her veins.

What if Evan had been calling because Tori was back? Had the police already left? What if something was wrong? Was he there alone? She whirled towards the heavily curtained window and cautiously pulled the linen aside. The sun would be up soon, but she feared for his safety.

Juliette pressed the call button on her phone, praying silently that he would answer, and all would be okay. The phone rang and rang and finally went to voicemail.

She looked at the clock. It was still early; she had time to make it to his house before the sun's ultraviolet rays would penetrate the cloud cover and hold her captive to the shadows.

Juliette dropped the phone on the bed and flew through the walls in a spray of mist. She wove through the trees and bushes following the curves and dips in the earth as she swiftly approached his house. The pressure in the atmosphere, churning throughout her ghostly shape, was building momentum as she plummeted through the forest and burst free in her human body outside his door. Without knocking she barreled through the back door to come face-to-face with a very naked Evan.

"Oh! Evan, I had no idea. I am so sorry." She swiveled away from him unable to get the image of him, standing there holding a towel, out of her mind. Hastily he wrapped the towel around his waist and secured it at the hip. He glanced down at his phone and could see that the call he missed had the current time stamped on it. How the hell did she get there so fast?

He noticed that she was in pajamas; she must have been getting ready to go to sleep too.

"I was worried, I thought maybe Tori had come here for you. Are you okay?" He tried to suppress a

186

chuckle. She was talking to him with her back to the room to avoid looking at him.

"Yes, I'm fine." He stepped to her and gently taking her arm, turned her towards him.

"I have a towel on now, it's okay." Juliette had never been so mortified. Granted she had seen him naked just a few days ago, but he had been passed out and that image was nothing compared to what she had just witnessed.

Everything about him exuded raw sexuality. His tall muscular frame, the expanse of his toned and firm chest, his tousled black hair still damp from his shower, and his unshaven jaw made her want to feel the rough hairs against her lips as he kissed her.

She took an abrupt step back as her thoughts took a dangerous turn, but he was quick and carefully grabbed her by the upper arms and pulled her back towards him.

Evan couldn't stop. He had been dreaming of holding her all night, regardless of her engagement, and he couldn't seem to control himself.

He couldn't stop touching her. He knew he needed to back away, put some clothes on, or better yet, take another shower... a cold one this time, but his body would not listen to him. She felt amazing in his arms. Again, her curves fit against his as though they were made for one another. They continued to lock eyes as he lowered his lips to hover above hers. She didn't pull away, and she didn't move a muscle, locked in his embrace.

Their breath mingled, their hearts pounded... not from the rush of passion as they had the last time he had held her close, but with the effort it took to hold back from kissing each other.

187

He gazed deeply into her eyes, trying to convey, with just a look, all the love and affection he felt for her. He could portray all of these things with just one kiss, but he had made a promise.

He would not make her feel shame again. She was not his to kiss.

His gentle touch and the unbreakable devotion that emanated from him had her clinging to him as she longed to feel his lips on her own.

Juliette could feel everything he felt. It stirred within her a flame that embraced her heart and enveloped her in a warmth she had not felt in centuries.

He ran his fingertips down the length of her hair, weaving his fingers through her long unruly tresses, pulling her waist tighter against his frame. She sucked in a breath and slid her hands around his back, glorying in the ripple of muscle and enflamed skin beneath her cool touch as she clasped his body to her own.

For a long moment they just stood there, locked in each other's arms, craving the feel of their lips meeting, but never giving in, until he softly leaned his forehead against hers and inhaled her glorious perfume.

Then he slowly began to pull away, but not before placing a chaste kiss upon her forehead.

She breathed in the intoxicating scent of his warm skin, noticing the clean fragrant aroma of soap and observing the droplets of water that clung to his fevered flesh. He had missed her call because he had been in the shower. There was no danger here aside from the vulnerable weakness that overwhelmed her every time he was near.

A tear escaped her lashes as he placed that tender kiss on her brow; how could they love each other so

188

deeply? She was bound to Marek, her heart belonged to him. But why then did these feelings for Evan continue to grow with each moment that passed?

Even if it turned out that Marek had not survived, she was a vampire… Evan a human. She could not condemn him to a life in eternal darkness by turning him. She now knew how Marek had felt when he had returned to her after becoming a vampire. He had tried to end their relationship knowing that he could not turn her just to keep her by his side for an eternity.

But Evan knew what she was, and he hadn't run, he still wanted her and was not afraid, even after all that he had been through.

She tilted her head back to look into his eyes, remaining in his arms, not wanting to break their embrace.

"What are we going to do?" she whispered. Evan didn't need any clarification; he knew what it was that she was asking.

She searched his eyes and saw an intense range of emotions there… love, yearning, and devotion. She wished he wouldn't look at her that way.

She was a monster. He clearly didn't remember what she had attempted in the lighthouse. Should she tell him now? She knew it was time to tell him everything, even things that might change the way he saw her.

She tried to back away, but his arms only tightened around her, unwilling to release her.

To his astonishment, she dissolved into a pool of vapor at his feet. The cool, honeyed mist that he had encountered on the pier swept up and around him, cooling his feverish skin and bathing him in moisture, like the gentle spray from a waterfall in the fragrant tropical rainforest.

189

She then drifted past him to the living room. By the time he had turned around, she was already in human form. She had placed a few yards between them, but that small distance seemed like miles as she longed to be held by him again. Nonetheless, she needed to keep her distance if she was going to be able to tell him that it had been her that had left him unconscious in the lighthouse. But before she could tell him, the look of disbelief and panic on his face caused her to pause.

"Evan... are you okay?" He stared, eyes wide, his arms remained positioned as if he were still holding her, frozen in place, unable to move. The knowledge that she was an eternal being, a vampire, a creature that survived off living blood, was a lot to handle. Seeing her disintegrate into vapor was pushing him over the edge of sanity. Vampire attacks, murders in the forest, Charlie missing, near death experiences, a giant white wolf, everything that he had experienced in the last few weeks was flashing through his mind in an endless cycle. His pulse was racing, blood pumping, he couldn't catch his breath.

"You... disappeared," he gasped, "you dissolved... what the hell was that?" Anxiety tore through him. She felt the terror take hold of him and felt his resolve crumbling.

"Evan, look at me, breathe. Please, I need you to slow your heart rate down. You're going to hyperventilate if you don't slow your breathing." He could barely hear her over the roaring in his ears and was starting to see black spots before his eyes. She was of no use on the other side of the room. Regardless of her inability to control her desire for him, he needed her now.

Juliette crossed the floor in an instant and embracing him, she sank to the carpet. Grasping his face

190

between her palms, she knelt nose to nose with him, locking eyes as she tried to coax him back to awareness.

"Evan. Evan… Evan" his name poured from her lips over and over again as she tried to reach him. His brain was rejecting the images that he was reliving; his subconscious was trying to shut down and repress the trauma that he had undergone.

Although she didn't want him to suffer and knew that this was his body's natural coping mechanism, she needed him to stay with her, to understand her. She hadn't realized until that moment how desperately she needed his acceptance, his guidance, his support, and his friendship. "Please Evan, stay with me…" Juliette whispered as she leaned her forehead against his. She tried to break through his mental barrier and sooth his racing thoughts.

Wrapping her arms around his frozen body, she slowly and deliberately focused all her energy onto her aura, warming it with every ration of compassion she could rally. She immersed her soul with love, desire, and adoration, breaking down every wall she had ever built around her heart to open herself up. The depth of emotion she was conjuring was so powerful it took all of her control to not choke on the sobs that rolled through her as she pushed these feelings through to Evan. Breathing deeply through bared teeth, Juliette trembled with the exertion of holding onto his mind as she immersed him in her love.

The flickering images that had moments ago drowned him in terror began to change color as if a film masked the hue of his dreams. Where there was once a deep and hostile crimson tainting his thoughts, there now glowed a shimmering and luminescent sunburst. The images of the nightmares he had faced over the last week were now replaced with memories of Juliette in his arms,

191

her soft hair tangled in his fists, his name on her lips as he trailed kisses down the column of her slender throat. His visions were now aglow in a brilliant golden radiance.

His arms came up to capture her, grasping at her, starved to feel her against him. Juliette felt the change in him down to her core. His lips sought hers, and she didn't have the strength to avoid his touch. The heat that erupted between them tore what was left of the armor around her heart away. His kiss was deep as he drank from her lips; she was lost to the passion that he had awakened in her. Nothing had ever felt so potent, and she wanted nothing more than to forget everything outside of his embrace. She was almost beyond reasoning when he abruptly released her from his kiss and cradled her head against his bare chest.

"Juliette, I am so sorry. I don't want to keep putting you in these situations. I know you're engaged; it seems I have no control over myself where you are concerned. I'm sorry for that." She wasn't sure how to react after what they had just experienced together.

"Please, don't apologize. After everything I have put you through, you should never apologize." She breathed in his scent one last time before pulling away to look into his eyes.

"I care for you a great deal, Evan; I think that much is obvious. And it hurts me more than you know to feel your suffering. I will do everything in my power to keep you from hurting again. Are you going to be, okay?" With her still wrapped firmly in his arms, it was hard to think about anything other than the feel of her body against his, but he still trembled slightly from the breakdown and exhaustion was catching up with him. She sensed this in him and helped him to his feet but remained in the circle of

192

his arms, not sure that he would be able to stand on his own.

"I'm not going to lie; seeing you turn into smoke almost kicked me over the edge. How did you turn it around? How did you bring me back?" She smiled affectionately and stood back confident that he was past the worst of it.

"Let's just say I can be very influential." Her attempt to make light of the situation was not lost on Evan, but he wasn't ready to let go of the feelings that she had shared with him during their connection.

"Juliette, what you shared with me, that was-"

"Please Evan…" She stepped back again, trying to distance herself now that she was sure he wasn't going to regress.

"I can't… *we* can't be together. Even if it weren't for Marek, you and I are from two very different worlds. You don't want to live this life. You have a family, a home, a future… these are things that I cannot have because of what I am. Continuing down this road would only hurt us both. I don't want to hurt you anymore." Evan had no idea that she was referring to the night in the lighthouse, and it seemed she was out of time to explain any further as she noticed the forest beyond the windows becoming bright and vibrant in the predawn light.

Juliette walked to Evan and reached out a hand beckoning him to her; he stepped cautiously to her and gently wrapped his arms around her waist pulling her against him once again. She rested her head on his smooth shoulder and whispered into his neck, "I must leave now. The sun will soon rise, and I must be home before it does. I have more to tell you, but it will have to wait until tonight." She leaned into his warm embrace as she placed a lingering

193

kiss on his rough unshaven cheek, before, once again, evaporating into a luminous argent mist that whirled around him, caressing his overheated skin in a damp wintry fog before plunging into the ceiling, leaving him standing alone in the middle of his living room. This time there was no panic, only a great sense of loss as she left him.

***

Trevor had just pulled up in his jeep outside of Evan's house when he noticed what appeared to be smoke drifting up from the cabin. He had hoped to speak with him about April before he had to be out on the boat this morning but had been worried that it was still too early.

Seeing the smoke rising above the cabin, Trevor was relieved to know that Evan was already awake and had a fire going in the fireplace. He reached over to the passenger seat and grabbed the hot thermos of coffee and bag of fresh breakfast pastries that he had brought along to soften the blow when he told his best friend that he was in love with his little sister.

The walk up from the drive didn't seem nearly long enough as the tension built in Trevor's gut. He was scared that with everything that was going on here in Chancellor, Evan would be too overwhelmed with what he was about to tell him. But he knew that if he found out some other way, or if Evan found out after something had already happened between them, there would be hell to pay.

Trevor stood there, with his arm raised to knock on the door, when it was suddenly jerked opened. Evan was standing in the entry buttoning his shirt as if dressing to leave in a hurry.

"Hey Trev, what are you doing here?" Evan was surprised to see his friend standing there. He had been trying to make it to Juliette's before the sun had risen so that she could explain what she had meant about having more to tell him. She had promised to fill him in later tonight, but he just couldn't wait. However, with Trevor there, it didn't seem that he had any other choice.

"I was hoping to talk to you about a few things; I brought breakfast." Trevor raised the fragrant bag of warm pastries to show Evan. He seemed preoccupied and kept looking past him, surveying the property as though he was looking for someone. Trevor hoped that food would entice him enough to let him in for a bit.

"Sure, smells great. Come on in." Evan stood aside allowing Trevor to enter the house, looking longingly down the road towards Juliette's property. It would be hard to maintain focus on what Trevor needed to discuss after what had just happened, but it wasn't often that Trevor dropped in like this, so whatever he needed, it must be important.

Reluctantly he closed the front door and followed his friend into the kitchen. He began to clear a spot on the dining room table for them to sit and talk when Trevor asked about the empty fireplace.

"I could have sworn I saw smoke from your fireplace outside…" Evan turned towards him quickly searching for an explanation for what Trevor had seen knowing that it must have been Juliette's ascent from his house that he had witnessed.

"Yeah, well, I had been trying to start a fire, but the wood was too wet and wouldn't light. You must have seen the smoke from the kindling I was trying to ignite... that's where I was going just now, to gather some dry wood before it rains, but it's not that big of a deal. What did you need to talk about?"

The guilt at how easy the lie came to his lips tore at him. He hated lying to his best friend, but it wasn't his secret to tell. He hoped that he could make it up to him by helping Trevor out with whatever he needed now. Trevor

196

turned from the fireplace and placed the thermos and bag on the now clean tabletop.

"You got any clean plates and coffee cups?" Evan entered the kitchen relieved to have the subject changed.

"Paper plates, okay? I hate doing dishes." Trevor chuckled at his friend's aversion to housekeeping.

"Good thing you have April to take care of you. If it weren't for her, you'd probably be eating off your newspapers." Trevor took a seat eyeing the pile of newspapers that had been relocated to the countertop.

"Yeah, she does take pretty good care of me. She's great." Evan set the plates and mugs down on the table and took a seat a cross from Trevor, giving him a meaningful look as he voiced his sentiment about his sister.

"Is that what you came here to talk about Trev, April?" Trevor placed his elbows on the table and leaned towards Evan, caught a little off guard and not sure how to respond.

"Has it been that transparent?" Trevor's heart skipped a beat at the thought that they had not been as discreet as he had thought. He hadn't even declared his feelings to her yet. Evan laughed and reached for the coffee to pour them both a steaming cup.

"I never thought I would see the day that Trevor Helms was nervous and lovesick over any girl, let alone my baby sister." The laughter in Evan's voice and the mischievous look in his eye as he handed his friend the steaming cup of coffee, finally allowing Trevor to release the breath he'd been holding for weeks, it seemed. He hadn't been able to breathe freely since the moment that he had realized his feelings for April. He had dreaded doing or saying anything that could jeopardize his relationship with her and Evan, they were his family.

"Thank God I can finally get this off my chest. Evan, this has been eating at me for a while. I wanted to tell you from the moment that I realized I cared for her, but I was trying to fight it. You have no idea what it's like to love someone that you really shouldn't."

Evan recognized the irony in his statement. They both loved women that they thought they couldn't have… except in Trevor's case, he had the ability to rectify the situation.

"Why shouldn't you? She's a great girl. You've known each other all your lives, and she's been in love with you since we were sixteen." Evan paused and smiled at a memory of a time when April had tried desperately to get Trevor to notice her, "Remember that summer she demanded to go with us on our annual trip to the Columbia River? She was determined to catch the biggest sturgeon because she thought that you might actually pay attention to her if she did." Evan laughed midstory, recalling how she had been scared half to death when she had finally hooked a fish after waiting all day with not a single bite.

"She hadn't caught anything, not even a nibble, but she didn't complain a bit. She was happy just to be on the same boat as you all day, and when she finally got a bite-" Trevor started laughing remembering the hysterics that had taken place after that.

"She was so excited until she got the fish in the boat, then she freaked out when it started squirming and flopping around. She screamed bloody murder, and began flailing about, knocking me into the freezing cold river, and then she threw the damn thing overboard!"

Evan and Trevor were both laughing loudly at the fond memory. She had only been fourteen at the time, and Trevor could still picture her, tall and gangly, her black curls unruly and frizzy framing her freckled face. She'd had braces and glasses and had burst into tears after that. No matter what Evan did, he couldn't cheer her up.

April had been mortified that she had pushed Trevor into the river when all she had been trying to do was impress him. It wasn't until Trevor had given her a very cold and wet hug and told her that he'd needed a bath anyways that she had finally smiled again.

As the laughter faded, Evan began to eat his breakfast and listened as Trevor began to retell just how long he had been trying to convince himself and April that they wouldn't work. All his stories of the womanizing, the way he shamelessly flirted with any girl who would flirt back… it had all been a ruse that he had tried to create to prove to everyone, including himself, that he wasn't falling head over heels in love with his best friend's little sister.

Evan leaned forward, bracing his elbows on the table as he held his coffee mug in both hands, and explained to Trevor that none of it had fooled him.

"I can't think of anyone better suited for April than you Trevor. You have my blessing or permission or whatever the hell it is that you are looking for here. Just know that as her big brother, I fully reserve the right to beat your ass if you hurt her. Deal?" Trevor wanted to laugh with relief but knew that, in his heart, he wouldn't feel good about this conversation until he had sworn an oath to his best friend to love April and care for her for as long as she would allow him to.

"She is everything to me Evan. I only regret not realizing it sooner; all these years that I have wasted. Trust me. I could never hurt her. You both mean so much to me. You're all the family that I have in this world. I won't jeopardize that for anything, and you have my word on that." Evan grinned and nodded, satisfied that at least one of them would be able to be with the woman they loved, and relieved that if anything were to happen to him within the next few weeks, April wouldn't be alone, and she would be cared for.

"Now why don't you tell me about what's going on between you and Juliette?" Evan's heart fluttered at just the sound of her name. He finished the bite of his Danish and took a long sip of his coffee as he leaned back in his chair, unsure of just how much to tell Trevor.

"She is amazing! I've never felt this way about anyone. I guess we both know what it's like to love someone we feel we can't have." Trevor leaned forward and reached for the thermos to refill their coffee.

"Yeah, I kind of figured there was something going on there. Do you really think that her fiancé is alive?" That was the question that had been circling in Evan's brain for the last week.

He thought back to this morning, and the uncontrollable infatuation that seemed to be growing between him and Juliette. They couldn't seem to keep their hands off each other. It pained his heart to know that this searing desire that engulfed them whenever they were near one another wouldn't matter at all once they found Marek, because she would go with him. But he loved her enough to know that he would let her go when their time was up.

He also knew her well enough, at this point, to know that the guilt she would suffer because of their feelings for each other would cause her an enormous amount of pain. She carried so much weight on her shoulders; she had been searching for Devlon and Marek for centuries, alone, with no one to talk to, no one to

200

confide in, and no one to help her, she didn't even know if Marek was going to be found alive.

If only there was a way to find out if Devlon still had Marek held prisoner. If there were a way for them to find out if he had survived, then he could eliminate that source of pain for her. She could finally grieve and move forward with her life, or it would once and for all give them the answer they needed to end what was happening between them. But it had been several days and there had been no new developments. Thankfully, there had been no more disappearances or deaths either, not since Devlon had recruited Tori.

It occurred to Evan that Tori was possibly the key. She had been wherever Devlon was hiding out. She would know if Marek were there, and she would also know if Charlie was being held captive there as well. He could try to reach out to her, maybe play along with her infatuation long enough to get the information he needed.

The only problem was trying to arrange the meeting without placing himself or anyone else in danger. He was confident, now that he knew what Tori was, he could handle her better. But Juliette would never go along with this plan, seeing as how Tori had almost killed him the last time.

He would have to make sure she met him somewhere away from town, somewhere out in the open where no one else could get hurt.

But how could he ensure his own safety without Juliette there? He hated the idea of keeping a secret from her and doing this behind her back, but he also knew that she would never go along with it. He would need to ask someone else for help. It occurred to him that Trevor might be able to assist him with this, but he would need to fill him in on a few things first, like the fact that they were dealing with vampires.

"Trevor, what would you say if I told you that Marek, Charlie, and Tori have all been taken by a very old vampire named Devlon?" Trevor stopped drinking his coffee mid-sip and looked at Evan over the rim of his coffee cup as if he were telling him that Santa Claus existed. He lowered the cup and paused, not knowing how to approach the subject that his friend was clearly insane.

"Does this have something to do with the mist that you saw on the wharf that night? April filled me in on it. You used to think that Juliette was somehow involved. Is she a vampire too?" Evan could hear the sarcasm in his questions and knew it sounded irrational. He would have to do better in his explanation and most likely tell him Juliette's secret to get him on board so that they could somehow capture and question Tori about Marek's whereabouts.

Evan began his explanation starting with the attack at the lighthouse and then told him about Tori attacking him in the pub. He seemed to have captured Trevor's interest and decided it would be best to just be honest about Juliette. He could trust Trevor with their secret.

He described to Trevor the pain of having his blood taken against his will, and how Juliette had saved him, and that he had vowed to return the favor by helping her end this battle once and for all.

"The key is Tori. If we could entice her to come out of hiding, trap her somehow and question her about Marek and Charlie and find out where Devlon is holing up, we could help her defeat him."

Trevor had taken in all that Evan had shared with him. He might have questioned his sanity had he not been

202

able to align these attacks to the times that he had disappeared. April had been worried about him and questioned why he had been lying to her.

Trevor had known Evan all his life, he would never shirk his responsibilities to his sister or his pub unless there were some life-threatening reasons. Trevor had also heard stories from the other townsfolk of a creature that was haunting the town.

They were calling it a shadow because that was all anyone had ever seen of it. The sheriff's office had just recently found another body in the forest, a fisherman who had been camping along the Chief riverbank. His neck had been savagely torn, and all the blood had been drained from his body. The same was said of the hiker who had been found earlier that week.

Evan watched as Trevor added all the facts up in his head and realized that although his story sounded ridiculous, it all added up.

"Wouldn't it be best if Juliette were there when we attempt to trap Tori, just in case she goes all psycho crazy vampire on you again?"

"You know how Tori obsessed over me before she turned? Well now that she is a vampire, that hasn't changed. I am counting on using that infatuation to learn what I need to from her. If Juliette were near, I'm afraid Tori would not come out of hiding." Trevor wasn't so sure that Tori's obsession over his friend was enough to keep them both from being killed when that feral bitch realized that they were just using her. They needed a backup, a way to protect themselves if this plan failed.

"Not to doubt your sexual prowess and all, but what do we have to protect ourselves if she doesn't buy it? How are we going to trap her? What kills these things?" Evan had already been contemplating a weapon that would destroy her if it came down to it. He had read about a stake through the heart, decapitating, and burning, but the only person that would truly know how to trap and take down a vampire was Juliette. After seeing her dissolve into mist, he wasn't even sure it would be possible to trap one, but again, that was something Juliette could answer.

"Let me speak with Juliette about that. She can tell me what we need to know about killing a vampire or at least incapacitating one. But I need your word that you won't tell anyone about this, especially April. She'll be safer if she doesn't know what's really going on here in Chancellor." Trevor agreed, but also knew that if she found out that they were hiding something, she would be pissed.

"I promise not to tell her as long as that's what's best for her, but if something happens that puts her life in jeopardy, I'm telling her."

"Agreed." Evan started to feel relieved now that Trevor was on board. He wouldn't tell Juliette just yet. He would wait until they had the information that they needed from Tori before breaking the news to her. He just hoped they could get what they needed from her without any consequences.

If Evan could remove Marek, Charlie, and Tori from the equation, then Juliette could fight Devlon with a clear mind and without distraction.

***

After Trevor left his house, Evan had to leave and go into work to take in the weekly food delivery. He had pushed all the plotting and scheming aside in order to concentrate on tracking the inventory and had just about finished up when April came into the office to help set up for lunch.

"Hey big brother, how are you today?" She hung her damp jacket on the hook behind the office door and shook the rain from her curls.

"I just finished updating the inventory. Is it coming down pretty hard out there?"

"It just started pouring. We'll probably have a busy day. I noticed a lot of boats coming back because the wind is starting to pick up. Should we open early?" Evan looked at his watch. They had another hour before they would normally open their doors, but with the weather taking a turn most of the captains would choose to come in to dock and wait out the storm.

"Yeah, might as well. I'll take care of the kitchen, you go set up the bar and put some coffee on, will you?"

Evan had spent most of the day in the kitchen preparing steaming bowls of chowder, burgers, and seafood boils. April handled the front of the house with the help of Trevor, who had come in not long after they had opened claiming that his charters had been cancelled due to the rain.

As April had predicted, the pub had remained busy until it became clear that the weather was not going to let up and the dinner hour began to roll around. The night kitchen staff had arrived and Evan was able to make his way to the front of the pub as the sun began to set behind the thick gray clouds that hung low over the wharf.

He had just poured himself a cup of coffee when Juliette walked in. She did not seem to be ruffled at all by the rainfall as she strolled in wearing a crimson trench coat over black leggings and a black turtleneck, soft red leather hiking boots, and her hair was pulled away from her face and hung in a thick braid down her back.

Evan came around the end of the bar to greet her as she approached. Juliette drank in the site of him. He smelled of food and sweat; his hair was disheveled, and his strong jawline, as always, was shadowed by the growth of a new beard. His denim jeans and black pub t-shirt hugged his well-muscled and lithe body, and it took every ounce of self-control to keep from wrapping her arms around him and pulling him close against her.

Instead, she briefly leaned into his embrace, placing her palms gently against his chest to keep him from being too close as he hugged her, then quickly dropped back, and looked up into his face trying to gauge his temperament after the way she had left him this morning.

April noticed how Juliette went straight into her brother's arms as soon as she entered the building and tried hard not to let the shock register on her face. She glanced at Trevor, who was pouring a beer, noticed his sly grin, and wondered if she was the only one that was not aware of how this relationship had gone from "just friends" to clearly something deeper.

Although they were restraining themselves, it was clear that there was an immense attraction between her brother and Juliette.

She finished ringing up her customer and began to make her way towards where Evan and Juliette were now sitting, heads bent close to one another, hands within mere inches of each other, trying desperately not to touch.

"Hey Juliette, how are you tonight? I love your coat." Evan stood to put some distance between him and Juliette; frustration burned within him as he yearned to completely forget that she was engaged and yank her over the bar and kiss her madly. Instead, he reluctantly turned to face his sister as Juliette spoke to her.

"Thank you, April. I am well, how are you?" April noticed the muscle in her brother's jaw clench and smiled inwardly at his discomfort. Trevor joined them as Evan rounded the end of the bar and made his way over to help a table that had just sat down.

The night wore on, business was steady enough that it was impossible to speak to Evan alone. They all made small talk with Juliette in between serving guests to ensure that she was never alone or left out. The conversation with April and Trevor was pleasant, but Juliette could not help noticing the way that Trevor was watching her every move as if looking for proof of something.

She wondered if she was just being paranoid at having revealed her secret to Evan, or if he had told Trevor. She would need to ask him when they had a moment alone together.

Throughout the night she found herself smiling at their playful banter and laughing at their antics behind the bar as they poured drafts and built cocktails. Juliette's silver gaze missed nothing, taking in every conversation they had with their patrons, who by all rights were really more than that. These people that came to the Waterfront Pub were more like family to her three new friends.

They spoke fondly of their parents and of the memories they all shared of their childhood. Most were

207

doing their best to embarrass Evan in front of the new woman in town.

Juliette experienced a sudden wave of affection take over where there had once been a feeling of great resentment towards all humans. These were good people… decent, honest, and hardworking.

Her eyes moved to where Evan was standing in front of the taps, speaking with his sister about changing a keg in back. His eyes rose to hers and they held. She saw the burning desire erupt in his gaze and felt the strong need to protect Evan and everyone he cared about.

It was astonishing to her that he was willing to turn his world upside down and face death to help her and save his town and the people in it. Juliette was now feeling the overpowering need to protect them all. It was then that she vowed to do everything in her power to make sure no harm came to anyone else in this town.

After a few hours, the dinner rush began to wind down, and the faint stirrings of panic began to well up inside of Juliette. She knew she had been given a small reprieve from relating the rest of her horror story to Evan but that was slowly coming to an end. She would need to tell him soon of what she had done to him in the lighthouse, and she feared that once she did, this newfound kinship she was developing with him, and his family would come to a quick and abrupt end.

Nevertheless, she knew that she could not involve Evan in this fight until he knew everything about her. He needed to have all the details before making the decision to endanger his life any more than he already had... for her.

The last of the Waterfronts guests had closed their tab and headed out into the cold and foggy night. Evan,

April, and Trevor began the evening chore of closing the pub. Juliette had offered to help, but Evan would not hear of it.

On his way back to the bar, Evan heard the front door open as a frigid gust of wind hit him. He turned to see who had entered and froze. Tori, dressed all in black, strolled into the pub. Her hair had been washed, and she was no longer the filthy mess that she had appeared to be the night that she'd attacked him.

Evan heard the surprised response from his sister as they took notice of who had entered the pub. He heard the scrape of the barstool as Juliette stood and the footsteps of her boots on the wood floor as she walked to stand by his side, but he could not move. The terror from the night she had attacked him came rushing back and paralyzed him. He couldn't call out a warning, he couldn't tell his sister and Trevor to run, and he couldn't shield Juliette from the evil that he knew lay just beneath the surface of Tori's smug little grin.

How on earth had he thought that he and Trevor could face her alone when just the site of her had him frozen with fear?

It wasn't until he felt Juliette's cool hand in his own and recalled that she was also a vampire, that some semblance of control returned to his body.

They had to get Tori out of here before anyone got hurt… but how?

Juliette spoke first, or so Evan thought. He heard her voice clear and strong, but when he looked at her, he could see that her lips were not moving. The words that she had spoken were in his head, she was feeding him the words telepathically.

209

Astonished that she had this ability as well, he quickly took her cue and voiced aloud the words that she had given him.

"Why are you here Tori? I would have thought you'd know better than to come back here after the things you have done..." Evan knew that they spoke of the attack, but the clever way she worded her question would lead April to assume he was referring to her recent termination from the pub due to her lack of attendance as well as her sexual advances on him.

He then heard Juliette's mental voice again, *"Good, stand strong Evan. The quicker we get her out of here, the safer your family will be. Don't let your fear of her weaken your resolve."*

He gripped her hand in his. Her words had reminded him that he had to protect his sister at all costs. His next words were his own.

"I think it would be best if you leave. You are no longer welcome here, and I don't think your new *employer* would appreciate you making a scene." He had hoped that the mention of Devlon would cause her to think twice. From everything that Juliette had told him, Devlon had remained in seclusion throughout this whole ordeal... his isolation making it easier for him to stay out of Juliette's reach. He was responsible for countless deaths, and Evan did not think that he would want his new protégée making problems for him in this new town.

His words did not have the intended impact on Tori. The smile faded from her lips, and anger glinted in her eyes as she let out a low snarl, and to Evan's surprise, she launched from where she had been standing and closed the distance between her and Juliette in the blink of an eye. A fierce gust of wind followed her approach and almost knocked Evan off his feet.

The shelves behind the bar began to shake violently, shot glasses and beer mugs crashed to the floor, bottles of liquor one by one began to explode spraying shards of glass and alcohol in every direction.

April screamed as Trevor yanked her back away from the blasts, shielding her with his own body.

Tori made her move towards Juliette.

Juliette didn't back down, even taking another step forward to place more distance between Tori and her friends, bringing her nose-to-nose with the new vampire.

She could feel Evan trying to pull her back, but he might as well have been pulling on a statue. Juliette did not budge instead; she placed a hand in front of Evan.

"Wait!" she commanded, "Stay back."

She met Tori's murderous glare with a low growl, too low for the humans to hear.

It seemed she had not been taught to control her abilities. She was bursting with fury, and if she did not control it, she would surely destroy this building and Evan and his family with it.

She wondered if Devlon had taught her anything about her new life as she recalled how she had ravaged Evan's throat searching for his vein to feed. Silently she spoke to Tori.

"Has he taught you nothing?" The confusion that briefly flickered through Tori's eyes was all the answer that Juliette needed.

Tori knew naught of what she had truly become… a vampire, yes. However, Devlon had apparently hidden the fact that Tori had been a witch before she turned, and now her powers were almost exploding from within her.

Juliette tried another approach. She cautiously took a step back and extended her hand to Tori while offering in a soft tone, "Let me help you." The rumbling of the shelves began to lessen as Tori tried to understand what Juliette was up to.

"Devlon turned you for a reason Tori... a decision he has never made before. Aren't you curious as to why he chose you?"

The anger returned to her eyes as a furious growl ripped through Tori's bared teeth.

"You're wrong. I'm not the first, but that sniveling old man was weak. Devlon says I am strong, maybe even stronger than you. That's why he sent me with a message."

The mention of the old man shocked Juliette causing her to take another step closer to Evan. Had she meant Charlie? Is that what had happened to him? She needed to keep the conversation going and get more information. What message could Devlon possibly have for her? Juliette pushed the burning curiosity away and focused on finding out where Charlie was being held. Knowing that what she said was going to need explaining to April and Trevor, Juliette pushed on.

"You are strong Tori, but don't be fooled into thinking that your powers surpass mine. I have been around for a very long time. You are new to this life and have much to learn. I can help you if you will let me. I can teach you to control your powers so that they cannot be used against you. I can help you through this without the viciousness that Devlon seems to use to get what he wants. You've seen what he is capable of. Just look at what he did to poor Charlie. Aren't you afraid you may see the same fate as him if you disappoint Devlon?"

212

The offer to teach her prickled at Tori's pride. Her posture stiffened and she raised her chin defiantly.

"I have more than my powers in my favor against a man like Devlon." Tori took a few more steps towards Juliette to close the gap once again between them, her hips swaying seductively with each step making it very clear what other abilities she used against Devlon.

"He may be a vampire and vicious, as you say. But in the end, he is still a man." She looked over at Evan, lust pulsating from every word as she spoke directly to him.

"Devlon does not fear my sexuality the way you did. He is a *real* man. He fulfills my desires in ways that you never could." Tori looked back at Juliette and arrogantly vowed.

"I will never find myself at the bottom of the bay, starving and alone, but you will if you don't back down. Devlon knows that you are after Marek's remains. He told me to tell you that he disposed of your lover centuries ago. There is nothing you can do to save him now; you've lost this battle. Give up or this town and everyone in it will be destroyed, including you."

The burst of pain, fury, and raw emotion that Juliette suffered upon hearing Marek's name spoken by this foul woman was more than she could contain.

The blast of power that Juliette thrust towards the new vampire was enough to slam her against the far wall of the pub, causing the neon lamp hanging next to the door to come crashing to the floor.

Another scream erupted from April as Tori thrust herself towards Juliette and dissolved into a swirling blur of black mist and icy wind that blew napkins and straws off the bar, knocked barstools and bar tops over, and caused more pictures and lights to shatter to the wood floor.

213

Trevor slammed April to the floor, covering her body with his own, shielding her from the destruction. Evan crouched next to Juliette, one arm guarding his eyes from the spraying glass that flew around the room until at last the whirling cloud blew through the door of the Waterfront Pub, leaving only the sound of April weeping and clinking glass behind.

Juliette stood in the center of the room, rooted to the floor and unable to move after Tori's departure. Shame, rage, and anguish threatened to crush her from every angle.

Evan slowly stood, shards of glass fell from his hair and shoulders making surreal chiming sounds as they cascaded to the ground. Trevor was still holding April, huddled on the floor against the bar, afraid the storm wasn't over.

The urge to flee the pub and never look back was overwhelming. The euphoria from earlier in the night vanished. Juliette had no desire to stay after hearing that Marek was gone. Her reason for fighting all these years had been dead, all along. In an instant her existence meant nothing.

Evan took in the sight of Juliette's white face, eyes wide, glistening with unshed tears, her lips trembling, shoulders wildly heaving; with each breath, a low growl building in her throat. He approached, her cautiously, at first, not sure how she would respond to his touch, but he could see that the pain was breaking her. He had to reach her before it consumed her.

"Juliette? Look at me." She didn't move. He knew something was building in the room again. Evan couldn't quite get a grasp on just what it was, but the pressure continued rising in the room, ready to blow the walls out and destroy the pub; but it was all centered around Juliette. Again, the walls began to shake, a rumbling began beneath the floorboards, and the debris began to vibrate and dance across the planks.

She was gathering some sort of invisible force to surround her. Suddenly he knew if he didn't stop her, she would be beyond his reach.

He tried to shake her, but she didn't move an inch. He moved his hands to the sides of her face, at first his hands were gentle, and then he gripped her fiercely, his nose mere inches from hers. An arctic wind was now whipping around the room throwing napkins in every direction.

"Juliette!" Her name ripped through his throat, trying to break through the noise that was quickly becoming deafening. He continued to hold her face in his hands, but she stared right through him, her anguish blinding her.

The pressure was reaching a peak, and Evan feared that there was nothing that could be done. He had to get through to her.

Suddenly, wrapping one arm around her stiff unyielding body and thrusting his other hand into her thick hair, gripping it in his fist, Evan slammed his body against Juliette and brought his lips down to crash against hers.

The passion, that always seemed to simmer just below the surface whenever they were near one another, erupted. It poured over them in great waves, finally breaking through her grief. Her lips finally moved beneath his responding to his touch. In an instant the wind stilled, and the napkins that had been furiously flying around the room froze in midair and began to drift quietly to the ground. The rumbling stopped, and Juliette crumpled against Evan's chest.

A piercing sound tore through the pub. The noise, having faded into silence, erupted again. The sound of a lone howl shattered the night air and breached the interior

216

of the pub, repeatedly. The wolf's grief-stricken cry reverberated through Juliette's body reminding her that her wolf needed her, and Evan needed her. She still had purpose.

Ambrosia's howls faded leaving the pub in silence, once again, broken only by Juliette's muffled sobs.

It took some time for Juliette's tears to subside. She clung to Evan as though he alone anchored her to some semblance of sanity. It wasn't until she heard April's hiccupping that she realized how much the events had upset the poor girl.

Juliette excused herself while Trevor and Evan worked to calm April. She thought it best to stay clear of April until she was no longer shaking with fear. Her terrified eyes followed Juliette as she exited the pub.

Once outside she paused and breathed in a shaky breath. The cool night air coming off the pier helped to calm her. She pulled in a dense fog bank to shield her from anyone who might be watching and signaled to Ambrosia to meet her at the end of the dock. After she had fed, she just stood at the end of the dock, next to her great wolf, gazing out over the water absently running her hands through Ambrosia's fur.

Ambrosia's presence was comforting. The bond she shared with her companion was a big part of the driving force she needed to keep going. She knew that now. But it had been Evan who had saved her, he had pulled her back from the precipice she had been ready to drop into, to escape the pain and loss that had incapacitated her.

Ambrosia nuzzled her palm and looked up, her wise silver eyes held Juliette's, and she knew that Ambrosia also experienced her pain. The tears began to fall again, and Juliette sank to the rough wooden planks and buried her face in the soft fur of Ambrosia's chest.

This was the scene that Evan came upon when he was finally able to make his way through the fog smothering the wharf.

She heard him pause and draw in a deep breath as he saw the great white wolf at her side. She instantly heard his heartbeat accelerate from fear until he realized that the wolf belonged to her. She lifted her tear-streaked face to meet his slow approach and smiled slightly at his astonished expression as he took in the sheer size of Ambrosia.

"I wasn't imagining it?" his gaze met hers as he voiced his question.

"No, you weren't, Evan. This is Ambrosia. She is my companion as well as my donor." She smiled fondly at Ambrosia and stroked her immense head. He moved forward another few feet. He wanted to touch her but wasn't sure if he should attempt it. Ambrosia stood and closed the distance between them. She placed her great muzzle in his hand and nudged him as a mortal dog would have when wanting attention.

"She likes you." Juliette stood and smiled warmly as Ambrosia attempted to put her friend at ease.

"She is amazing. You were there last night when I saw her… outside my house?"

"Yes, I was watching over you. I encountered Tori on your property and was trying to get you to go back into your house where it was safe. The very sight of you sent Tori into a frenzy, she is very dangerous Evan. You should not be alone until she is no longer a threat." Evan was astonished to hear that Juliette had been so close by the night before, and that she had fought with that psycho just to keep him safe.

He looked down at Ambrosia and took notice of the intelligence glowing behind the wolf's silver gaze. He also noticed that Juliette and Ambrosia had the same metallic sheen to their eyes.

"You both placed yourselves in danger to protect me? Juliette, I can't let you do that again." Ambrosia snorted and turned to sit next to Juliette. Evan could have sworn that he saw the giant wolf roll her eyes at his comment before taking a seat next to her mistress.

"Evan, Tori is newly turned, and she does not possess even half of the strength that I do. However, she was a witch before Devlon changed her. He will use her powers against us, and her, if she is not careful. The deal he is offering... I don't know if he will honor it. Last night he caught me off guard on the beach below the cliff face. He actually came out of hiding to rescue Tori. I didn't expect that, and now I know why. You must stay away from her."

Evan felt the guilt wash over him as he remembered his conversation with Trevor earlier that morning. He had thought that he could manipulate Tori and solve everything on his own. He had been so stupid.

"Juliette, I have to tell you something. You probably already figured it out, but I filled Trevor in on our situation this morning after you left. He showed up wanting to talk about April, and I thought that with his help, we could draw Tori out into the open and try to get her to give us information about Devlon, Marek, and Charlie." That explained why Trevor was looking at her differently this evening.

She understood why he would confide in his friend, and to be honest, she had half expected it when she had finally decided to tell him everything. It was his foolish

220

notion that they could take on a vampire without any assistance that angered her.

"Evan, you could get you and your friend killed trying something like that. You don't have any idea what her weaknesses are. I am glad you told me about this, but it scares me that you would even contemplate taking her on without me being there."

He closed the few feet that were between them and took her in his arms. Resting his forehead against hers, he breathed in her delicious perfume.

"I promise you that I won't ever try anything like that without you there. I just wanted so badly to give you some peace of mind when it came to..." he stopped talking, knowing that he couldn't say Marek's name without hurting her.

She knew why he paused, and her eyes dropped to the ground.

"I am sorry, Juliette. I can't even begin to know how you must be feeling right now." He pulled her chin up, forcing her to meet his gaze, and instantly felt the flare of lust that always flooded his body when they were together.

It was immediately followed with irritation that the flame would so easily erupt after all she'd been through tonight. He stepped back to place some distance between them before the flame could turn into a full-blown inferno of passion and unbridled emotion.

"I promised you that I would help you find him, what do you want to do now that you know..." he couldn't finish his statement. Instead, he tried another approach to ease her pain. "From what you have told me of Marek, he wouldn't want you wasting your life if he is no longer able to share it with you. He would want you to find happiness..." he stopped again; everything he was trying to

221

say just sounded so wrong. She was grieving, and he should allow her that and not put any pressure on her to find Charlie or to make a decision about them.

She knew what he was trying to get at and knew that what he said about Marek was true. Before she had a chance to respond they heard Trevor step out of the pub looking for them.

"Hey guys, you want to come back in so we can figure this out…" Trevor stopped speaking when he caught site of them through the fog. His amazement at seeing Ambrosia sitting calmly on the dock next to where Evan and Juliette stood was clearly written in his expression.

Evan looked down at Ambrosia and chuckled, knowing what must be going through his best friend's mind at seeing the huge wolf.

"Let's go inside; we can finish this later." He kissed her briefly on the cheek and held her hand as they began the short walk back to the pub. Juliette signaled for Ambrosia to follow.

April was sitting at a booth in the corner, a bottle of liquor next to an empty glass and a pile of used tissues scattered on the tabletop. Her tear-streaked face registered another wave of fear as she took in the sheer size of the wolf that walked in next to her brother. Evan stopped and turned towards Juliette,

"I already explained to April what just happened with Tori… and what you are…"

Juliette took a deep breath knowing that this was going to be one of the most difficult things she had ever done, opening up about what she was and everything that she had been through in her life. But it was necessary after the drama that had unfolded tonight.

She looked around the pub and noticed that all the tables had been righted and most of the damage cleaned up. There was nothing left to do except talk.

The foursome found themselves just staring at one another, not knowing where or how to start. Finally, Juliette took the lead, she began by first explaining the presence of her wolf.

"April, Trevor, this is Ambrosia. She is my donor."

"Donor?" April asked, her eyes never leaving Ambrosia. Juliette felt the tension in the room mounting and persuaded everyone to take a seat so that she could explain Ambrosia's place in all this.

Juliette quickly explained how Ambrosia had come to be her donor and how she and Marek had raised her from a small pup. Throughout the story, Ambrosia had slowly made her way over to where April sat and had placed her enormous head in April's lap. This seemed to ease the girl's discomfort, and she was now absently stroking the large wolf behind the ears as if she were the family pet.

Juliette was emotionally exhausted, but she knew that she could no longer hide what she was from all of them. She looked at Evan and their eyes met and held. He nodded to her, acknowledging that it was time to reveal everything.

She wanted to laugh and cry at the same time. She had been hiding what she was for centuries. She could finally come out of the shadows. She could finally confide in people. She had friends now and didn't have to be alone anymore... and yet she had never felt more alone than she did now. The knowledge that Marek was gone had almost killed her. She didn't know where to go from here, but she had made a vow earlier in the night that this town would be safe, and she had to make sure that Devlon kept his word.

223

She was uncertain about where to start with her story; she knew that the more she told them, the more she risked exposing her kind to humans. However, if they were to protect themselves, they would need to know everything.

Tori had made it clear that she wasn't afraid to show herself in a public setting. Juliette needed to let them know exactly what they were up against if Devlon chose not to honor his promise to leave the town alone, and it needed to happen tonight.

Evan reached across the table and grasped Juliette's hand in a gesture to show that he supported her. She took a ragged breath and began her story.

***

Marek and Juliette had escaped to a small hunting cabin in the Forêt de Roumare, a large, wooded area northwest of Paris.

Juliette's life had been in danger; several attempts to kidnap and harm her had been made shortly after they'd heard from Marek's father.

The attempts on her life caused them to flee before they had had a chance to plead with the duke to allow them to marry.

Marek had purchased the property before they left the city, not even Devlon had knowledge of their whereabouts.

The house was small and cozy, hidden in the lush forest, surrounded by beech trees and ferns. The Seine River lay to the east and provided fish, the forest was rich with game to hunt, and the grounds already had a garden that was over-grown with vegetables, herbs, and weeds. There was a small woodland hamlet to the north where Marek was able to barter for cloth, grains, livestock, and other necessities to help make their new home comfortable.

Although Juliette had been raised with servants, maids, and cooks, she had paid attention to how the household was maintained. She had learned to cook, make soap, and sew. She now had the freedom to read, garden, and make plans with Marek for their future and the things that they would see in the world.

The fact that they were not yet married changed nothing about the way they cared for one another. It was easy to forget that vows had never been made when Marek held Juliette at night. The soft glow from the fire burning in

225

the hearth cast shadows on the walls as they loved each other.

The days and nights that they spent together in the solitude of their own haven blended in a warm tapestry of tranquility, companionship, and passion. They had almost lost track of how long they had been in seclusion when Marek traveled to the nearest township to trade blankets and fragrant soaps that Juliette had crafted, for oil to fill their lamps

He had just finished loading the purchased supplies onto his horse when he was approached by the town blacksmith.

"Marek, may I have a word with you?" Bayard Duval was a large man, both in size and in stature. He kept a close eye on the happenings in and about the township to ensure that their peaceful way of life was not inhibited. Marek had made a point to apprise him of their situation once it had become clear that this was a man that they could trust.

Bayard did not care that Marek and Juliette were not yet married, he understood their reasons for fleeing the city and had aligned himself with their cause. He kept their secret and helped maintain the farce that they were man and wife to avoid any scandals their relationship might bring about with the other townspeople.

He was aware that they were in danger and had kept Marek informed of any news from Paris regarding his and Juliette's families. Until recently there had been no news to share.

"Bayard, you are looking well today. Have you news from Paris?" The grim expression on Bayard's face proved that his assumption was correct; he had news, and it was not good news.

226

"I traveled to Rouen the day before last for business. It was there that I learned of a curse that is plaguing the Coleville family. Within the last month an illness has taken over and killed everyone save the duke and your cousin." Marek felt the blood drain from his face, and icy dread claimed his heart. How had this happened?

"An illness you say?" Bayard grasped him by the shoulder, a fierce expression strained his large features.

"I know of no illness that infects only those of one lineage. There is something darker at work here Marek. There are rumors that your family has been cursed by the very devil himself, that he has possessed the banished son of the duke to kill those that would exile him and his dark bride." He paused; he could tell the news was taking a toll on Marek. Bayard whispered feverishly near his ear so that anyone walking by could not hear his words: *"I know these rumors to be false as I have seen you here in the village many times over the last month, and it would be impossible for you to be in more than one place at a time. Someone is murdering your family and placing the guilt at your feet."* Marek, finally able to draw breath, tried to clear his head. His hammering heart pounded furiously within his chest. He was grateful that Bayard had not released his hold on his shoulders as he surely would have crumpled to the ground.

Who would do such a thing? His family had never caused harm to anyone. His father was well respected in Paris and other than his departure with Juliette, scandal had never touched the Colevilles.

The fury that raced through his blood, as he thought of his tender and loving mother and his sweet innocent little sisters being murdered, gave Marek the strength he needed to shake off the panic and grief.

227

"Thank you, Bayard. You have been a good friend. I must get back to Juliette and prepare for my return to Paris." As he turned to mount his horse Bayard clasped him by the arm.

"Marek, I will keep an eye on Juliette to insure nothing happens while you are away. But the journey you are about to take is deadly, and I fear for your safe return. There is an old woman that is said to have great powers. She lives in a weathered stone house just west of the Seine in a swamp hidden from the road to Rouen by a thicket of dead beech trees. Visit her before you leave for Paris. She may be able to provide you with the protection you need to save you and your family." Marek nodded and swung up into his saddle to begin the short trip back to the cabin he shared with Juliette.

He argued with himself whether to visit the old woman or not. It seemed his family was cursed with enough dark magic at the moment. He didn't feel that it would be wise to invite more into this nightmare. He spurred his horse on, thundering down the trail that led him home, as images of his mother floated through his mind. Had he caused this? Had his leaving with Juliette created such animosity that someone had fated them to die? Was it the same murderous beast that had tried to harm Juliette? Was this a vendetta against him personally?

He didn't know what to believe, but he knew that he needed to find the fiend that was responsible for the murder of his mother and sisters and stop them before his father and cousin were killed.

As he approached the cabin, Juliette was standing in her herb garden, her hands covered in dirt, the weeds that she had pulled lay forgotten on the ground. Fear reflected in her beautiful silver eyes. She knew before he

228

even dismounted, having suffered his agony the moment he was within a few yards of her. He could never hide anything from her. Her empath abilities were always a source of amazement to him, but also another reason he loved her so dearly. She knew him as no other ever could.

She rushed to him as he dropped the reins and slid from his saddle. Ignoring the dirt encrusted under her nails, she clutched at his shirt as he wrapped his arms around her slim waist. They embraced, and the fear, the torment, and the fury that he felt took hold of her own emotions throwing her into a passionate frenzy. Tears ran down her cheeks as their lips met in a clash of desperation. The danger she felt was so close that she could taste it on his lips and feared that their beautiful time together had come to an end.

The night was slowly settling on the small cabin and a fire in the hearth simmered the stew that Juliette had prepared. A fresh loaf of bread cooled on the table near the fire. She watched Marek as he packed for his journey and tried to keep the tears at bay.

He told her what Bayard had learned and of his advice to go see the old woman before beginning his trip. He had already refused to go see her; he had also refused to allow Juliette to go with him. She had begged him to at least reconsider meeting the old woman. She feared that without whatever magic elixir she could provide, Marek would surely be killed, and she would never see him again. But he stubbornly refused.

After their meal, Juliette had tidied up the cabin and prepared for bed, dread of the next morning slowing her movements as she lay her nightgown on the bed. Marek had

229

seen the fear shimmering in her eyes all evening, and while he also was tormented at the thought of leaving her alone and possibly never seeing her again, he knew that he had to go to his family and that she could not go with him.

Marek approached her from behind as she stood with her back to the room. He could see her shoulders bow beneath the strain of his departure. He pushed her thick silken hair away from her shoulders, letting it cascade over her breasts, and bent to kiss the sweet soft skin at the nape of her neck.

She sighed at the warmth that flooded her skin where his lips touched her, dropping her chin to rest on her chest. His arms encircled her waist and pulled her back to lean into his strong embrace as his lips moved along her exposed back, traveling down her shoulder and back up to rain kisses on her neck, cheek, and ear. His warm breath created shivers that ran down the length of her arms and caused her breath to catch in her throat.

He turned her in his embrace bringing her around to meet his tortured gaze. Fear, desire, and desperation raged in his eyes as she looked up into his face. She took in the strong cut of his jaw, the straight line of his nose, and the way his nostrils flared with every breath that he took... his full lips parted and moist from his kisses, his dark hair fell in silken waves along his collar and lay in wild disarray on his brow. She took in every detail of his handsome face, carving it into her memory.

The firelight cast wavering shadows on the couple as they held onto one another, afraid to let go and see the night disappear without showing the true extent of their love for each other.

No words had ever been created that could define the strength of the bond they shared. There would be no

230

tear-swept goodbyes or tormented promises. He would leave her for the last time before the sun would rise and before the kindling of the fire had finally extinguished. But before that, he would remind her of how passionately he loved her.

Juliette lay in Marek's arms as she listened to his slow steady breathing. It had taken some time for her to slow his thoughts enough for him to drift off to sleep. This was something she had done for him in the past to help him rest when the stress of their situation kept sleep at bay. However, she hated using her gift to persuade him to rest on this last night they were to share. But she knew he needed his rest if he were to have all his wits about him on his journey. She also needed him asleep so that she could go and meet with the old woman before he awoke in the morning to leave.

She waited an hour before leaving, wanting to make certain that he would not wake up. She dressed in breaches and a dark silk shirt that she had taken from Marek and altered to fit her much smaller frame.

After tiptoeing out of the cabin, she sat on the stairs that led down to the garden and put on her black knee-high boots so that her footsteps did not disturb Marek. He would surely be displeased that she traveled through the woods in the middle of the night, alone, to meet a strange old woman. But she would deal with that when the time came. For now, she needed to know if there really were something that could be done to keep her love safe and alive.

She decided it would be best to walk and not make more noise saddling her horse. The path through the forest to the thicket was eerily lit by the light of the full moon overhead.

Juliette moved quickly through the forest, not wanting to linger in the dark any longer than necessary. She could hear creatures moving about in the trees, a twig snapped to her right, and she could hear what she thought was a low growl in the dark shadows that clung to the forest floor.

Her heartbeat hammered in her chest as she imagined what animals could possibly be beyond the tree-lined trail. She was somewhat relieved to see the shimmer of the Seine River beyond the slope of the narrow road. To her left was the thicket that Marek had described to her.

She paused before entering the tangled mass of dead beech trees, apprehensive at leaving the open trail. Finally, she stepped into the darkness. She felt as though she were being swallowed up by the forest, the cool light of the moon disappearing as she entered the wood. Juliette could feel the hairs on the back of her neck tingle as goose bumps traveled down her arms.

She swallowed the lump of fear that threatened to have her screaming in terror and running back to the safety of Marek's arms. She reminded herself that she had come this far, she would not turn back until she had what she needed to keep Marek alive.

Finally, after what seemed like hours of climbing through the twisted and snarled branches of the thicket, the trees opened to reveal a soft green marsh. The atmosphere seemed to change. The crisp night air was replaced by moist, balmy warmth. The cold hard ground of the forest was replaced by soft and spongy moss, lily pads floated in a small, serene pond, and fireflies twinkled in the mist that swirled about a small, thatched cottage.

The terror that had gripped her moments ago had somehow melted away. She now longed to take off her

232

boots and feel the silken moss beneath her bare feet, to dip her toes in the warmth of the pond, and twirl fearlessly as a child would among the magical glow of the fireflies.

But she resisted, knowing that she needed to finish her task here and return to Marek before he awoke.

She stood for a moment taking in the small cottage. Its clay walls and thatched roof gave it an almost fairytale feel. A warm light flooded the small front porch and illuminated the empty rustic rocking chair that swayed slightly in the warm night air. Smoke from a fire within floated up into the tranquil night sky. The fear that she should be feeling at approaching an unknown cottage in the middle of the night was nothing but a distant memory. It seemed that the cottage was beckoning her forward, inviting her to enter.

As she approached, the door swung slowly open. She paused in surprise but continued to step up onto the planked wooden deck, coming to stand in the open doorway.

The interior of the cabin was as magical as the exterior. The floor was covered in a soft mossy rug adorned with patches of tiny purple blooms. There were two twisted log columns holding up the thatched roof; ivy clung to the twisted branches within the pillars, and a great round table sat in the center of the room. The base of the table had been constructed of a large tree stump, the roots curving outwards supporting its immense size and weight.

The tabletop was a thick slab of knotted oak that looked like someone had taken a slice out of the tree; the polished rings gleamed in the golden firelight showing just how ancient the tree must have been.

Stools that resembled giant mushrooms gathered around the great stump, and a gnarled branch chandelier *hung from the ceiling, bejeweled with crystals hanging from twine that caused them to shimmer and twinkle in the firelight. There were potted ferns, flowers, and other herbs scattered around the gardened room that added to the floral fragrance of the cottage.*

Such an odd yet beautiful place. How had it come to be hidden in the depths of the Roumare Forest? As Juliette stepped into the cottage, she raised her hand to knock on the wooden door.

"Please do an old woman a favor and remove your boots before entering my home. We don't want to crush the pretty flowers now do we?" Juliette swung around to greet the voice that had come from outside the cabin. Her eyes widened in surprise as she noticed an old woman sitting in the rocker that had been empty moments ago, she was sure of it.

She was a tiny creature, her old, withered frame was enveloped in a soft, red, hooded cloak made from nettlecloth. Her face was kind, and clear blue eyes peered up at her from beneath the soft grey curls that escaped from her hooded cloak and hung to rest gently on her frail shoulders. Juliette knelt in front of the old woman.

"Madame, my name is Juliette, and I seek your help. It is said that you possess the ability to provide protection from illness and death, is that so?" The old woman stopped rocking in her chair and took in the desperation that gleamed in Juliette's odd silver eyes. She recognized that this gentle girl had abilities of her own but was oblivious of how to restrain them.

Juliette was unaware that she was casting her emotions out and away from her in a torrent of grief and fear. The strength with which she projected these emotions was the strongest the old woman had ever encountered and

234

would have been crippling had she not been able to keep them at bay.

She leaned forward in her chair and took both of Juliette's hands in her own. The old woman's hands trembled, and she felt an immediate kinship with the girl that she could not ignore. She decided, at that moment, that she would help this child, in more ways than one. She would give her the elixir she sought and offered to teach her how to control her gifts and use them to help her get through these turbulent times.

"Calm my child. You will exhaust me with your anxiety before we have a chance to become better acquainted. You may call me Claudette; but first, help an old woman from her chair so that I may make us some tea to soothe your worry."

Juliette slowly stood and helped Claudette to her feet. She was a slight little thing, and it barely took any effort from Juliette to help her up. Once standing, the old woman seemed to glide into the cottage as if her feet never touched the floor.

Juliette was as intrigued by Claudette as she was by this magical place. They didn't seem to belong to the outside world. It seemed that once she had left the path outside the hidden grove, she had entered another realm.

"You are quite right my dear; my world does not merge with where you came from. Time does not exist here. We can talk for hours, and the moon will still be in the same position it was in when you found my little haven." *Juliette kicked off her boots and entered the cottage, curious to know how Claudette had read her thoughts.*

"We are like-minded... I can hear your thoughts and you can hear mine. Had you not been gifted with such powers, you would not have found your way through the

235

thicket, and you would still be wandering around in the dark." Juliette came to stand in the middle of the room and noticed, that although she could hear Claudette speaking, her lips never moved.

The old woman's smiling eyes answered Juliette's astonished expression with a mischievous twinkle. Juliette opened her mouth to speak and stopped quickly when Claudette shook her head and tapped her temple just once.

"Use your mind my dear, this will be your first lesson." Juliette again opened her mouth to speak and caught herself. How was she going to do this? She didn't know how to project her thoughts.

"You just did sweet girl. You learn very quickly. Perhaps this won't take very long at all. It's a pity really. I was looking forward to spending time with you. It does get lonely on this side of the thicket."

Juliette was astonished at how they were communicating. If only Marek could hear her this way, they could still communicate even though he would be far away.

"He does hear you Juliette, but he doesn't perceive it as being your voice so much as your emotional influence. You are an empath, that much you are aware of. But I see an even deeper power within you. If you let me help you, I can show you how to expand your gifts and learn to master them, so they no longer control you."

Juliette didn't know what to say. She hadn't come here for this, and she really didn't know if that was something she was ready to take on. She'd been dealing with these "gifts" her entire life, and up until now, she had thought that she was controlling them quite well. She was torn. She yearned to find out what she was capable of, but she was here for Marek. She needed to do what she could to protect him.

236

Claudette flitted about the small room readying the table for tea and clucking her tongue in response to Juliette's thoughts. She made a mental note to teach Juliette the difference between telepathy and mental process so that her private thoughts could remain private in the presence of a like mind.

"Madame Claudette, I thank you for your offer, and while it intrigues me, I must stay focused on my reason for coming here. I need to find a way to protect someone I love very much. He is to leave for Paris at dawn. I fear death awaits him as it has already taken his mother and two young sisters. A plague, they say, is ravaging his family."

Claudette pulled the kettle from the fire and turned towards the table to pour them both a cup of herbal tea. She gestured for Juliette to sit, and although she hesitated, she eventually complied with the older woman's request.

"I have what you seek, but there are precautions that need to be taken. Nothing comes without a price my dear." Juliette didn't care what the price was. She was willing to pay it to keep Marek alive.

"Don't be so quick to accept until you have heard everything there is to know. It is not just you that will pay this price, but also the one you wish to protect." Claudette reached for Juliette and pulled her hand onto the table. Her weathered hands were soft and fragile as she placed two small silver vials into Juliette's upturned palm. The one vial had an intricate pattern of thorned vines carved into the silver and the other was plain with no adornment. They hung on a gleaming silver chain made of tiny silver leaves.

"This will keep him safe from injury, illness, and toxins. He needs but to drink them within hours of returning to Paris. It will stay in his system for 2 days and

2 nights." Claudette leaned forward and looked Juliette directly in the eye as she whispered the final instructions.

"He must drink the blood from the plain vial. Once the blood has been consumed, if anything should befall your beloved before the contents of the vial leaves his body, he will quickly heal. Should he be hurt beyond repair and his heart begin to falter, he need only drink the vial covered in vines to carry him over the threshold of death and back. Should he choose this fate, he will no longer be human, but a creature of the night and immortal." The blood drained from Juliette's face as this last bit of information sank in. Perhaps Marek was right, this was black magic, and it would be dangerous to court such things.

"Would he be himself if that were to happen?" She didn't speak the words out loud, afraid that the dread gripping her would cause her voice to waver.

Claudette responded telepathically, "His mind would be as it were however, his body would undergo some very extreme changes. He would never age, never grow old, and never die. He would need to feed on blood to maintain his immortality, preferably human or that of another immortal would suffice."

Juliette gasped.

"Another immortal? What you say suggests that there are more in this world?"

"There are many things in our realm, young Juliette, that you are unaware of, as is most of the world. Only a select few even know of my existence. My son, Bayard, must trust your man Marek very much to have advised him to come see me."

"Bayard is your son? "Juliette had met the gentle giant a few times when she had accompanied Marek into town. He had a quiet strength about him that drew others to

238

trust and depend on him. If Claudette were an empath as well, it made sense that Bayard would have the ability to soothe others and sway them to trust him. It took a strong person to manage those capabilities without using them for their own gain. She had great respect for Bayard.

"Yes, he inherited my gifts. Those, along with a long struggle to accept what his father has become, forced him to grow to be a very strong and capable man." Juliette noticed the sadness that had crept into Claudette's voice as she mentioned Bayard's father. Her gaze dropped to the pendant as it dangled from the chain on Juliette's hand.

"Is he....?" Claudette nodded in response to Juliette's unspoken questions.

"He became ill, and I was desperate to save him. I learned of this cure from a migrant coven of witches, but I was never warned about what would happen if his heart stopped beating while the immortal blood was still thriving within his body. It was too late when I gave it to him. He was too far gone, and his heart was not strong enough. Bayard was devastated. He was thirteen when we lost him- no longer a child, but not quite a man. We buried his father the day after he passed; when he rose from the grave that evening, it terrified the town where we had been living. He wandered through the streets, lost, and disoriented. He finally found his way home, and Bayard was the one who opened the door. He was elated. He didn't know how his father had survived, but he was standing before him, alive, heart beating in his chest... but he had turned. He was starving, he needed blood, and when Bayard threw his arms around his father, so overjoyed to see him, the hunger overtook him. He bit Bayard almost draining him completely." Juliette gasped at the image that Claudette had painted. How devastating that must have been.

239

Obviously, Bayard survived, but it must have been terrifying.

"Yes Juliette, I was petrified at first. That was the first time I had ever used my magic against another living being. I used every bit of my power to force him to release Bayard. His father was mortified at what he had done. He crumpled to the floor, holding Bayard's limp body in his arms. We thought we had lost him. His father insisted on using his own blood to heal him. I was torn. I wanted to save my son, of course, but the fear that he would turn into the creature that his father had become was immense." She paused in her story and sipped at her tea.

"I stayed by his side, checking his pulse, and monitoring his breathing for three days until he finally awoke. By then his father had left us. He was too afraid that he would hurt Bayard again, as was I. He sends letters, money, and from time to time, a vial of his blood to heal any ailments that we may have."

"He came to me once Bayard was grown, he was in control of his thirst and offered to change us. He said that he could teach us how to live so that we wouldn't ever have to grow old and die. We could all be together forever."

Juliette looked over Claudette's weathered features and wondered why she hadn't accepted his offer of immortality. To be with the man you love forever almost seemed like an easy decision to her. Claudette poured more tea for Juliette as she answered her unspoken question.

"I do love my husband, but to choose to become what he became... I couldn't do it. I could not live with myself if I were to hurt another human being... if I lost control of the thirst. The guilt that I bare for turning him into one of those creatures is enough to endure. When my

240

life is over, I pray that I am forgiven for that and can rest peacefully."

Juliette sat in silence for a few moments. What if things went terribly wrong after she had given Marek this vial? What if he turned? Would he forgive her? Could she forgive herself? She turned them in her palm, running her fingertips over the intricate carving, not certain she should even take it to give to him. The risk was too great... but what if she lost him? Could she bear to live the rest of her life without him? Tears filled her eyes and a lump rose in her chest just thinking about it. She would leave it up to him. She would at least take the vials to him, explain what they could do, and let him decide.

"Very wise decision my dear. You have a pure heart; I admire your good intentions and know that you will not force this upon your love." Juliette looked up and pushed her chair back. She needed time to be alone with her thoughts before she spoke with Marek.

"Thank you, Madame Claudette. My heart is heavy with the decisions that lay before us, but you have given me a glimmer of hope that I shall carry with me. I don't know when I will be back, but I will try to return." Claudette stood and came around to escort Juliette out onto the misty, warm porch, her mental voice sounded clear within Juliette's mind.

"Stay strong, young Juliette. I have much to teach you if you are willing to learn, but first see to your beloved. I wish him well on his journey."

Juliette left the cottage and headed towards the thicket, not really wanting to leave the safety and seclusion of the glen but knowing that she had to figure out how to explain this to Marek. He would be upset with her for going out in the middle of the night and putting herself in danger, *but it was too late to worry about that now. Right now, she needed to concentrate on how she was going to get him to at least consider taking the contents of the vials. She didn't want to think about what was really in them... vampire blood; that made it seem so much more sinister.*

The road back was colder than she remembered. A breeze had picked up and was whistling through the trees and kicking up leaves as she hurried along the path. The moon overhead seemed to follow her, and when the skin on the back of her neck began to stand up, she knew she was being followed.

She looked behind her and saw nothing, but still quickened her steps. She was almost to the clearing that led to the cabin when she heard hoofs on the road behind her. She swung around to see Marek coming up the road on horseback. His face looked ghostly pale in the moonlight and confused. How had she appeared out of thin air?

"Where did you go?" She stepped closer to him as he dropped down out of his saddle, gathered her in his arms and buried his face in her hair.

"I was so worried! I went looking for you and saw you as you disappeared into that crop of tangled beech trees. I tried to catch up to you, but I got disoriented. It seemed like I was lost for hours. The trees were clawing at me from every direction, and it felt like they were closing in on me, but I kept moving forward, and then I finally stumbled back out onto the road. The moon was in the same place, not a minute had passed, but I swear that I was in there for an eternity!" His eyes, clouded with fear, searched her face.

"Juliette, I was scared to death that something had happened to you. I tried to go around the back of the thicket to see if you had made it to the other side, but it just

242

goes on and on. I circled back around praying that you would find your way back to the road as I had. Are you okay?"

He pulled away from her and looked her over noticing the fine scratches on her ivory skin. He traced the line with his thumb and leaned his forehead against hers.

"Why did you go without me, Juliette? Had I known this was that important to you, I would have gone for you. Please don't ever scare me like that again." Juliette looked up into his handsome face and saw the worry etched onto his features. She knew at that moment that she had to convince him to take the vials. She couldn't let him go into this battle without the protection she knew she could provide.

"I had to see what she could offer. I had to know if there is a way to protect you. Marek, there is a way to save you, but it must be your decision. I cannot force you to do this." He looked down into her open palm and saw the silver bottles, then back into her face. Tears shimmered and spilled over her lashes as she plead with her eyes to at least consider what she was offering.

"Come, let's go inside, you're freezing. Once you are warm you can tell me." Juliette led them back into the small and cozy cabin. After removing her boots, she sat at the small table in front of the glowing fire as Marek built the flames back up to warm the interior of the small house.

He sat next to her and gathered her cold hands in his own trying to warm them. Dawn was only a few hours away, what time they had left was precious, and he knew that the vials she carried were of great importance to her.

"Tell me what can be done." Juliette described to him what she'd found at the interior of the thicket. He was amazed at what she had discovered. She shared with him

243

what she'd learned about her own abilities and how she was able to communicate with Claudette. She then went on to share with him the details of Bayard and his father.

The color drained from Marek's face as the realization of what she offered entailed. He looked again at the small flasks and held them up in the firelight to look closely at the engravings and he then inspected the plain silver bottle.

"This one holds the blood of a vampire?" Juliette took a deep breath, held it, and nodded.

"I have heard stories of such things, but never once did I think that these tales were real." He let the chain slide through his fingers and laid them on the table.

"Would you really want me to take such a chance, Juliette? Would you be able to love me as this creature if I were to change?" Juliette let out the pent-up breath that she had been holding, not certain what she wanted other than she wanted him to live.

"I will love you in any form Marek, but I cannot sway you to do this. As much as I want you to be safe and as much as it pains me to see you leave and face danger alone, this is something that I did not anticipate, and it is something that you must decide for yourself."

There were so many variables to weigh. This was not a decision to be made lightly. He lifted the vials again and let them dangle from the chain. The firelight glinted off the steel as he decided.

Juliette paused in her story and looked at the faces of the group as they took in every detail. They were thoroughly absorbed in her recounting of her human life with Marek. She could tell that they did not want her to

244

stop yet, but it was taking a toll on her bringing all of these memories to the surface.

Her voice had cracked several times throughout her tale, and only Evan's grasp on her hand had made it possible to push through. It was getting late, and she knew that the sun was going to be coming up in a few hours.

April was the first to speak, "Obviously he took it, or we wouldn't be sitting here listening to this amazing story..." her words trailed off and the air grew heavy with the words that they were all thinking.

Had Tori been telling the truth? Was Marek truly dead?

"I felt the truth in what she said. Marek is lost to me."

April's face fell, and Juliette could feel the pity rolling off her, but it mingled with another emotion she had not been expecting... admiration.

She had never really stopped to consider how remarkable her life had been up to this point. She had been too focused on her quest to get Marek back.

Seeing it from their perspective was something completely new to her, and it made her uneasy. Evan reached across the table, once again, and grabbed her hand. His expression was a mixture of awe and something else she couldn't quite decipher. She sensed sadness, but it went deeper than that.

His realization of just how deep her feelings for Marek were was heart wrenching. Both because it was clear that the centuries she had spent alone had clearly distorted the way that she viewed herself, if she thought of herself at all, and also because it cemented the fact that they were destined to be nothing more than friends. Even though

245

Marek was gone, she was grieving, and the urge to comfort her left no room for any other emotions.

He squeezed her hand and suggested they take a break to give Juliette some time to come to grips with everything she had learned tonight. It couldn't have been easy to relive these painful memories, let alone share them with people after all these years of secrecy and seclusion.

April rose and put the bottle of whisky back behind the bar and started a pot of coffee. Trevor followed her, stepping around to where Ambrosia lay on the floor, her silver gaze watching their movements, completely at ease in this new environment.

Juliette looked over at Evan and, again, felt the need to tell him about the lighthouse but squashed it knowing that this was not the right moment. They needed to be alone. Gauging the time, she wasn't sure it would happen tonight. There was still so much more to share with Trevor and April.

His eyes held hers, and he knew there was something she wanted to say, but he wasn't sure what was holding her back.

"Do you have any idea how remarkable you are?" Juliette pulled her hand out of his grasp as the guilt only grew from his words.

"There are things that you still don't know, Evan. I need to tell you, but I just can't yet, and I fear that once I do… your feelings will change. They should change." Evan's face did not register the confusion she had expected. Instead, he leaned forward and caressed her cheek with his fingertips.

"Nothing you could say… or do, for that matter, could change what you are to me, Juliette. Because I know that everything you have done, every decision you have made, has been selfless. You are driven by a need to save and protect others, but I wonder to what expense. When was the last time you thought about you?"

"I can't afford to think about me. Even now, knowing that Marek is gone... I have to make sure that Devlon leaves this town in peace, and I have to find Charlie." The sadness in her voice hit Evan hard. She wouldn't even take the time to grieve because she felt a duty to him to save his home and find his friend. He moved around the table to sit next to her and pulled her against him. She leaned into his embrace and rested her head against his shoulder savoring the warmth he offered.

"*We* will save the town, and *we* will find Charlie... together. You are not alone in this anymore, remember? We all have something to lose if Devlon doesn't leave. But you need to remember that you are not alone, and we will fight with you."

Juliette looked up and saw that April and Trevor stood behind Evan, holding hands, and saw the same resolve in their eyes. They were all in this together. They would face this together and fight this together ... they just needed a plan.

***

They quickly resumed their impromptu meeting to finish learning as much as they could about vampires before Juliette had to leave. They were intrigued by the powers that vampire blood possessed and were even more curious about what weaknesses they had.

Evan had done his research at some point and shared what he had learned when he had begun to suspect that vampires were the culprits of what was taking place here in Chancellor.

He seemed to know a lot about vampires. She was astonished to know how much he was able to find using the internet. If only that tool had been available to them when Marek had transitioned. Then they wouldn't have had to spend so much time apart as he searched for Bayard's father to learn more about the creature he had become and how to deal with his strength and control the blood lust.

Some of the theories that Evan had were built from fictional writings, and she had to explain what was true and what wasn't.

She had to explain that wearing silver crucifixes and carrying wooden stakes would do nothing to a vampire. Evan did mention an aversion to sunlight, but he wasn't aware that it was not the light that bothered them, but actually the ultraviolet light that burned them to death.

"Evan, that part about the sunlight is actually accurate. We can't be out in the sunlight because of the UV rays from the sun. Even on cloudy days I must stay inside as the UV rays penetrate cloud cover."

248

"So, wherever Charlie is, he has to be deep enough that the UV light can't burn him." Evan's statement drew Trevor's attention.

"There are only a few places in the bay that go to that depth, unless it's not the depth that is keeping him safe so much as the water clarity."

Juliette knew their optimism that Charlie was alive was one of the things that fueled them in this endeavor; and she hated to take that away from them, but she thought it best that they know there may be another fate that poor Charlie had succumbed to.

"Evan, you need to consider the possibility that Charlie didn't survive. I doubt that Devlon would take into consideration where to drop Charlie into the ocean so that he would survive." April sat forward.

"Tori said 'Eternity at the bottom of the bay'... wouldn't that mean that she knows he is alive down there, suffering?" Juliette hadn't considered that, and a flame of hope flickered to life.

"You're right. She may have slipped up, giving us more information than she had intended. Charlie and Devlon had to exchange blood for him to turn-the same goes for Tori. If they were turned within two days of one another, then Tori's bond with Devlon would let her know if Charlie was still alive."

"Bond with him?" April voiced the question out loud.

"Yes, sorry, I haven't explained that part yet. When a vampire exchanges blood with someone by mouth, they are psychically linked until their blood is no longer in their system. If Devlon dropped Charlie into the bay shortly before Tori fed from him, she would know if he survived for days, until Charlie's blood no longer ran through

Devlon's veins. It would be enough time for the sun to rise and set, enough time to know if the sun's rays would penetrate to his depth, enough time to know if he'd survived."

"That means if we find Charlie, he could possibly lead us to where they are hiding?"

"April, I don't know that we should try to find them after saving Charlie." Juliette's softy spoken statement caused them all to look at her in disbelief. Evan spoke first.

"Juliette, you already said that you aren't sure he will stay true to his word, that he will leave Chancellor and stop killing here. And even if he were to stop killing here, he would be killing somewhere else. We can't let that happen. I know you want to protect us, and you think stopping your plan to avenge Marek's death will do that… but there is a reason he turned Tori. There is a reason he wants her powers, and I don't think turning our backs is the right thing to do."

Juliette knew he was right, but she feared they didn't know the extent of the danger they were willing to place themselves in.

She looked at Trevor and April, took in their expressions, and saw the same determination in their eyes that she saw in Evan's and knew there would be no turning back now.

"Okay, but I must warn you, you have never been faced with anything like this before. This will be extremely dangerous for us all."

Evan and Juliette spent what was left of the night filling April and Trevor in on what they knew about Devlon.

Evan retold the events of the night that Tori had attacked him. April was horrified at what her brother had

250

been through, and Juliette could tell it only fueled her anger and determination to take them down.

Juliette explained the happenings of the night before in the forest outside of Evan's house and her encounter with Devlon.

"You have saved my brother on more than one occasion, Juliette. I can't thank you enough for that." April's gratitude brought with it another wave of shame. Juliette thought of her actions in the lighthouse, and she knew that she needed to tell them all the truth of what she had done. They all deserved to know what she had been capable of.

"There was another attack you haven't told them about Evan, the lighthouse." Her eyes were on the table in front of her, unable to make eye contact with the others as he told them of the attack that he assumed had been Devlon.

"What a monster!" April's response brought tears to Juliette's eyes.

"Yes, he is a monster. But that night, in the lighthouse... it wasn't him." Evan looked at her, confusion clouding his eyes.

"It had to be. Tori was human that night, I left her in the parking lot." Juliette raised her gaze to meet his, a single tear escaped as she finally revealed the truth.

"It wasn't Tori, Evan... it was me."

***

The silence was deafening, April's quick intake of breath was the only thing to be heard after Juliette's confession. The color ran from Evan's face, and he felt dazed by the flood of emotions that ran through him... anger, disbelief, betrayal, and fear. He searched for the words, not really sure what direction to take now that he knew the truth about that night.

He wasn't sure he wanted his family to see the display of anger he might not be able to reign in.

"Trevor, can you please take April home. I really think it best that Juliette and I have a moment alone." These words were spoken through clenched teeth, never once lifting his eyes to look at anyone.

Juliette could feel the range of emotions that Evan was experiencing, and it only increased the amount of guilt and shame she felt for what she had done. She looked at April and Trevor and could feel their fear of her as well. It was crippling.

It was also somewhat ironic. She had done everything in her power to keep humans away from her, to keep anyone from meaning anything to her for centuries. And now that she was finally breaking down those walls and allowing herself to care for someone else, she was devastated to lose them.

Juliette slowly stood and signaled to Ambrosia to follow her.

"There is no need for that Evan. I can sense what you are all feeling now. I am sorry that I didn't tell you sooner. I am sorry that I hurt you in the first place; I only

252

did it to try and keep you out of this. I needed you to know the whole truth before I let this go any further." She paused briefly, trying to speak around the lump that had formed in her throat. "You needed to be able to make a decision knowing all of the facts about what I am... I am a vampire first and foremost. I am not a good person... I've done many things throughout my life that I am not proud of, and I am sorry for involving you and your family in this mess. I can only hope that once I am gone Devlon will leave you and your town in peace."

Evan stood suddenly, furious because he knew that she was trying to say goodbye, and if he didn't speak up soon, she would be gone within seconds. Not caring that he had an audience, he reached for her, and roughly grabbing her shoulders, he looked into her eyes, hating the defeat that he saw there.

"You may be able to feel what I feel, Juliette, but you don't know what's driving those emotions. Don't you dare try to disappear, or dissolve, or whatever the hell it is you do before I say what I have to say! That night in the lighthouse, I felt so many things, most of them centered around you and your wellbeing. I was terrified that you had been hurt. I almost killed myself trying to get to you. You had so many opportunities to tell me, why did you wait? What reason had I given you not to trust me? The night that you saved me, in your bedroom, we talked all night. You even revealed yourself to me, and yet, you never said anything. And again, in my house this morning, why didn't you trust me enough to tell me then?" Anger made his voice shake.

Trevor and April were both standing now, eyes wide as they took in the fury that seethed from Evan. Never had they seen him so enraged.

253

Tears were openly pouring down Juliette's face as she saw the pain in Evan's green eyes. She was astounded by the things he was saying and feeling.

He was right, the thoughts behind his emotions had not been what she had presumed. His anger and betrayal were caused by the fact that she had not trusted him to see past what she had done and know that it had been an attempt to keep him safe.

His disbelief and fear were because he could finally see past the whimsical nature of what she was... no longer was she merely a beautiful swirl of sparkling argent mist, the enchanting creature with silver eyes and endless waves of glorious auburn hair.

Now he also saw the predator, the hunter, the dangerous creature hidden beneath her lovely features, and regardless of what that meant for him, he was still in love with her.

"Evan, I wanted to tell you the moment I revealed myself to you, but you were ill and needed to go home... and then after that, in your living room, but the sun was rising an-". Evan interrupted her, not needing to hear the rest.

His lips silenced her. He had promised he wouldn't kiss her, but the fact that she had trusted him, and that time had been the only reason she hadn't told him sooner, pushed aside all the self-control he had.

He buried his fingers in her braided hair and pulled her face to his, kissing her forehead, her eyelids and finally, again briefly, her lips.

"Juliette, nothing you could do will ever change the way that I feel about you. I am in love with you, and I am not going to rest until this is done and you have found peace."

254

His declaration, among all the other revelations that had occurred this night, left her shaken. There was so much to process and so little time. Juliette brought her hands to cradle Evan's face and looked deep into his eyes, searching for the truth of what he had just professed, and it was there... the passion, the love, the burning desire to make sure she was safe and taken care of. She saw all of the things that Marek had felt for her so long ago, before he had been taken from her.

Juliette found herself torn. She was mourning the loss of one love and yet rejoicing in the discovery of another. Her heart hurt. Marek was dead. The very thing that had been pushing her forward all these years was gone, and the loss was devastating. And yet Evan offered another chance at happiness. Could she really take it? Did she deserve it? So many things to consider, but the bane of her existence beckoned. The sun would be up soon, and she only had moments to get safely home.

Juliette pulled Evan to her, savoring the strength she felt in him and wishing that she could stay in his arms a bit longer. He felt her lift herself to place a kiss near his ear and heard her whispered words as she suddenly melted into vapor.

"I will return... to you." Her presence surged up and around him, bathing him in her refreshing mist as she swept up and through the rafters of the pub. Ambrosia must have followed because she was gone as well. He stood there for a moment, arms encircling empty air before he let them fall to his sides.

Evan turned to look at Trevor and April. The astonished looks on their faces at Juliette's departure was priceless. In other circumstances he would have found it hilarious. But he was too dazed to find humor now.

"Wow, when you said she would dissolve, you really meant it!" April looked up at the ceiling where Juliette had disappeared.

"Yeah, she has a habit of doing that." Evan sank back into the booth, exhaustion setting in. He yearned to follow her, to be with her, but he knew she needed to be alone for a while to sort through everything that had happened in the last twenty-four hours. This had been the longest night of his life.

Evan rested his head against the back of the booth and closed his eyes while he voiced his thoughts out loud. "We need to make some decisions in order to get through this."

April and Trevor looked at each other and then back at Evan. The astonishment of everything they had seen tonight, coupled with the revelation that Evan was in love with a vampire, was definitely something to discuss. And April feared that the decisions he was referring to meant him becoming a vampire as well.

Before she could voice her fears, Evan clarified his meaning.

"I think it best if we close the pub up for a while. I know we haven't done that since mom and dad died but keeping it open will only be a distraction and too dangerous. The last thing we need to do right now is endanger any of the towns people by inviting them here when Tori has made it clear that she would tear this place down in an instant."

April agreed. It wouldn't be the first time they had closed their doors to the public. She remembered, as a child, hanging a sign on the front door with her mother the week before Christmas.

The inheritance left to them by their parents was more than they would need in their lifetime, so closing the pub certainly wouldn't hurt them financially.

"You're right. We can simply say that we're mourning Charlie. It's not far from the truth. We all know once we find him, he won't be the same now that he is a vampire." Her words were pointedly phrased in case Evan had any crazy idea to join the world of the undead.

Neither Trevor nor Evan missed her meaning. April and Trevor stared at Evan waiting for some response, a promise that that was not even a possibility… they heard none.

"Evan! What are you thinking? Falling in love with someone you know is… is a monster?"

The instant the words were out, April regretted them. Juliette was not a monster; in fact, everything she had done since coming to Chancellor had been to keep her brother safe. But that didn't change the fact that April considered it a fate worse than death to become a vampire. Trevor sat across from Evan and reached for April's hand. Always the peacekeeper between the two, he tried to calm her down.

"April and I can see what she means to you Evan, and we see that despite what she is, she has a good heart. We will see this through, but what are your plans when it's all over? How can it possibly work between you two when you're not even the same species?"

"To be honest, I hadn't gotten that far yet. I only know that I have felt this undeniable pull towards her since the first time I saw her on the wharf. I don't even know what she is capable of right now. Having just found out that the man she has been searching for her entire life… is dead, she may not even want to be with me when this is done.

But it doesn't matter right now. What matters is getting Charlie back and making sure that Devlon and Tori can't hurt anyone else. We can figure out everything else later."

April didn't want to let the subject go, but she could see that her brother wouldn't discuss it any further.

"All right. But in the meantime, I don't think any of us should be alone. I think it best if we all stay with you, Evan, at the cabin. It will make meeting with Juliette easier too. We can come up with a plan to finish this there." She pulled Trevor to his feet.

"The sun is up now. Let's close the pub, and Trevor and I will go pack some clothes and meet you at your place." They all stood and began the preparations to close the pub until their town was, once again, the safe community they had all grown-up in.

***

As Juliette descended to the floor of her bedroom, she collapsed on the thick rug in front of the hearth. The torrent of emotions she had been holding at bay all evening came crashing down.

The pain was surreal, it surpassed anything she had ever experienced. Great wracking sobs she'd been smothering all night shook her, and the flow of tears could not be stemmed.

The walls of her home started to tremble, and the curtains swayed slightly. Juliette knew that she needed to regain some control of her emotions. The sun was quickly rising in the sky, and she couldn't allow any light to penetrate the cabin.

She felt Ambrosia at her side and heard her soft whimpering at her mistresses' agony. Her wolf had dropped to the floor in a crouching position near the fireplace, her tail and head hung low as she crawled towards Juliette on the rug. Slowly Ambrosia began to nuzzle Juliette, attempting to comfort her. Grasping at Ambrosia, Juliette buried her tear-soaked face in her soft fur, trying furiously to quench the onslaught of emotions.

Gradually the cabins trembles began to subside, and her sobs quieted. Juliette lay there spent, her head pillowed in Ambrosia's mane, as sleep finally took her. The great wolf curled around Juliette and gradually drifted off to sleep.

Juliette awoke to the patter of rain on the balcony outside. The moon had risen hours ago; she had slept much

259

longer than usual. She was still on the floor with Ambrosia. Typically, her wolf would have left by now to begin hunting, but it was clear that Ambrosia had known how much Juliette needed her now.

She sat up slowly noticing for the first time how Ambrosia had nestled around her, shielding her from the cold.

"Thank you love. You knew exactly what I needed." Juliette leaned into Ambrosia and stroked the white wolf behind the ears, letting out an affectionate sigh as Ambrosia licked the whole side of her face.

"I love you too." Juliette stood and shrugged out of her jacket, which she still wore and pulled her phone out of the pocket as she lay it on the foot of the bed.

She powered it on to check the time. It was a quarter after eight, and she had missed a text from Evan,

"We are at my place. I am here for you when you're ready. I miss you." His sentiment brought a brief smile to her face. She missed him too. What did this mean? She didn't have time to dwell on that thought, she was already late meeting up with him.

"I am going to take a quick shower, and then I'll need to go over to Evan's place. Why don't you head out and find something to eat?" Ambrosia stood and stretched, then seemed to pause and look back at Juliette, unsure she should leave her alone.

"I'll be okay love. Come meet me when you're done hunting." Ambrosia dropped her large head in acknowledgment and then trotted towards the French doors, dissolving into mist as she disappeared out into the wet night.

After Ambrosia had left, Juliette headed into the bathroom hoping that a hot shower would help clarify the jumble of feelings in her head.

She really was at a loss as to what to do. Aside from finding Charlie and trying to rid the world of Devlon once and for all, the rest of her life was a mystery. What would she do now that Marek was truly gone? Where would she go? Could she make a home here in Chancellor, with Evan? Should she continue trying to find out more about her witch lineage? Was there even a point to that anymore?

So many questions pouring through her mind and not a single resolution. Perhaps she should push all of that aside for now and concentrate on saving Charlie and ridding this town of Devlon. Then, when this was once again a peaceful little fishing village, she could contemplate her future.

She turned on the water and stripped down, throwing her clothes in the hamper. She realized that her outfit from the night before was a little extravagant compared to what the other people in the pub had been wearing. She decided that she would try to blend in more and draw less attention to herself.

As she stepped into the hot spray of water, she tried to keep her thoughts on what they needed to do in order to find Charlie, but Marek kept making his way into her head. It dawned on her that she had never had a chance to say goodbye. Marek had tried, before he left to save his family and then again after his transition, but she wouldn't hear of it.

She had waited well over a year for him to return to her once he had come to grips with his new immortality and how to control his new hunger for blood. She has spent that lonely year with Claudette, spending day and night trying to get a handle on her witch abilities so that when they were reunited, she was also more in control of herself.

Back then, he talked often of leaving her so that she could go on to live a normal human life but could never bring himself to do it. She was far from normal. As it was, her powers were growing daily. It was only when she had been discovered as a witch that he finally made the decision to change her to save her.

She had never been able to thank him for everything he had ever done for her, for everything that he had given up for her. She felt a pang in her heart as she thought about how she had failed him. She had promised him, as he burned alive, that they would be together again.

Juliette sank to her knees on the tile floor of her shower and sat there trying hard to remember the things that Marek had told her the morning he had ridden off to save his father.

They lay intertwined in their small bed, the fire in the hearth now just a pile of glowing embers. The sun was turning the night sky purple in the east and was beginning to rise above the horizon.

Juliette's head rested on Marek's bare chest. She listened to the rhythm of his heartbeat and the slow intake of breath, wondering if this were the last time she would be held in his arms while he was still human.

His hand combed through the soft locks at the nape of her neck causing gooseflesh to cascade down her arms, glorying in the feel of her body pressed to his.

"I will hold this moment in my heart forever love." *he whispered into the top of her head, breathing in her fragrant chestnut hair. Juliette sat back to lean on her elbow and look down into his handsome face.*

"No goodbyes Marek. You will return to me, and no matter what form you are in, I will love you still." He closed his eyes against the fear he saw in her face, despite her confident words. He sat up and gathered her face in his hands, kissed her slowly and rested his forehead against hers.

"Promise me Juliette... promise me that if I cannot come back to you, if I don't make it home, please don't waste your life grieving me. I need to know that you will go on living, that you will go on to find love again. There is so much fire in you, I couldn't bear it if you were to let that fire die because I am no longer at your side. Please promise me this Juliette." She tried to pull away, shaking her head in denial of his words, but Marek pulled her closer, crushing her to his chest.

"Please Juliette, live. For me, for us... live!" The words tore from him, filled with agony and desperation. She could feel the mounting fear emanating from him and knew that without this promise he would likely lose the upcoming battle because of his fear for her.

"I promise Marek. I'll promise you anything you ask, just promise me that you will come to me, even if you are changed." He savagely kissed her again... this kiss filled with all the love they carried for one another, the fire in the hearth burst to a roaring flame as Juliette's emotions ran wild.

Marek gathered her close and loved her one last time, their uncertain future looming ahead of them. But for now, she was his, in his arms, and her fire burned brighter than it ever had.

The water had turned cold. Juliette still sat on the floor of the shower, not noticing the chill that now penetrated the bathroom. She didn't hear the bathroom door open and only faintly registered the presence of someone else in the room. It was only when Evan turned off the water and scooped her up off the floor that she realized she was shivering uncontrollably.

He wrapped her in a thick towel and sat on the edge of her bed, slowly rocking her in his arms and holding her close until the shivering subsided. She hadn't said a word, just continued to stare blindly ahead while her tears slowly fell.

"I promised," she finally said. The words were so faint that Evan almost missed them. He got up and turned, placing her on the bed and kneeling in front of her. The worry Evan felt creased his brow as he looked into her face. Her eyes were closed, her lips quivering as she spoke again.

"I promised", her voice broke as Evan leaned forward, cupping her face in his hands.

"What did you promise Juliette?" His thumb wiped away a tear as she slowly opened her eyes, the silver sheen enhanced from her weeping.

"I promised Marek… to live, to love again. I never thought that the day would come… when I would need to honor that promise. I never thought he would ever truly be gone. I never knew there would exist another man that would make me feel the way he did… but you do." Evan could see how this was tearing her apart… the obligation to fulfill a promise and the devotion to her first love clashing. The yearning to love again and the longing to mourn the love lost… was too much for her to endure.

264

At a loss for words, Evan pulled her back into his lap on the floor and cradled her to his chest. She clung to him, burying her face in his neck, and feeling her heart stir with the strength of his embrace.

Perhaps this was the path her life was supposed to take. Before she had lost Marek, she had always been a firm believer that everything in life happened for a reason. She had pushed aside that belief once his family had been taken from him, unable to have faith in an existence that could be so cruel to someone as good as Marek.

She wondered if Marek had found peace, and if there was a life beyond this world for creatures like her. She voiced her questions out loud. Evan pulled her tighter.

"Yes," he said. "I do believe that. The man that you describe him to be was a good and honest man. I have faith, that wherever we go when our time on earth is over, that place would not refuse him." He pulled back to look into her eyes. "You have to believe he watches over you now and has seen all the good you have done trying to save him. You are good, Juliette." He searched her face, taking in the raw pain he saw there, and wishing he could take it away. But only time would allow her to heal.

"I know it hurts… this loss. I wish I could take the pain away, but I know it will take some time before you are ready to move on. I just want you to know that I am here, and I'm not going anywhere. Take as much time as you need Juliette; just don't forget that I'm not immortal…" She shivered as he pushed her wet hair back over her shoulder.

"Don't let this amazing life he has given you be in vain. Keep the promise you made to him, live…" She smiled through her tears and knew that what Evan said had to be true.

Marek would be watching over her, and although she'd failed in her promise to save him, she would not fail in her promise to keep living.

"I have been mourning Marek since the moment he was taken from me. I never thought I would ever be able to see past that pain, but you… you have healed me with your warmth and your strength. Your love has helped put the pieces of my heart back together. You have helped me find closure." She paused briefly, tracing the planes of his face with her eyes. "Thank you for that."

***

They walked hand in hand down the beach towards Evan's house. She had dressed in loose fitting jeans rolled at the bottom and a large soft beige sweater. Her hair hung loose, curling down her back, and her feet were bare in the sand as they strolled along in the moonlight. Evan thought she had never looked more beautiful.

He was still in awe of the things she was beginning to share with him. When they left her cabin and had begun to head out into the rain, he stared in wonder as Juliette closed her eyes and tilted her face up towards the sky. The rain clouds slowly began to drift apart letting the moonlight filter through, and the rain disappeared, leaving behind a soft floating mist that hovered above the ground, receding only where she stepped. The night had gone from being quite chilly to a balmy warmth that was not common for the Oregon coast.

"Did you do that?" Evan asked in amazement.

Juliette explained that before she had turned, she had been a powerful witch. After spending so much time honing her abilities, she had been scared that once she had become a vampire, she would lose that part of herself.

But her powers had only become stronger, and she had the ability to control the elements, create fire, banish rain, and change the temperature whenever she wished, among other things.

In time, they found that Marek could acquire some of her abilities when they shared blood. It would only last a short time, until her blood no longer ran through his veins. Evan wondered aloud if the same was true of a human that shared her blood.

Juliette stopped walking and pulled him around so that she could look into his face.

"The only time we could have tested that theory, I was too busy trying to keep you alive and keep you from finding out what I am. It's too dangerous to try again. I don't want to risk turning you. A little of my blood will heal you, too much will poison you." He could see she hadn't even contemplated the idea of turning him and seemed almost afraid at the idea.

He wasn't quite sure himself how he felt about it. It stung a little to think that she wouldn't want to, and at the same time, he wanted to laugh at the absurdity of that feeling. He didn't want to be a vampire. His stomach churned at the idea of having to drink blood to survive, but there was still a piece of him that yearned to be with her always. To avoid confronting his own mixed feelings on the subject, Evan questioned Devlon's reason for choosing Tori.

"Is that why he changed her? So, he could have her powers?"

"I believe so, yes." She turned and stared out at the ocean,

"He is still not as strong as me, but I am outnumbered now that he has her. If I went up against him…" She didn't finish her sentence.

"But you aren't outnumbered, you have us." Juliette fought the urge to laugh bitterly at his suggestion that they bettered her odds in a battle against Devlon. She didn't want to insult him.

"Two vampires with powers, against one and three humans, does not even the playing field, Evan. And I can't involve Ambrosia. I have been very careful to keep her existence from Devlon. If he found out about her, I fear that he would not stop until he had her. I can't allow that."

Evan mulled over what she had said. It sounded like she was against trying to take Devlon and Tori down. Where did that leave them?

"So, if a fight against them is out of the question, what is the plan?" Juliette faced him again and took both of his hands in hers,

"We find Charlie, and we help him decide what he wants to do with this new life he's been given, and we sit tight and hope that Devlon and Tori stay true to their word and leave Chancellor."

Evan couldn't argue that the task of finding Charlie was priority. But it had never occurred to him that once they found him, they would have some challenges to face as far as helping him deal with the changes he had been through.

"I knew Charlie well... before he was taken. He was sick, and he knew his time was coming. He was ready for it, Juliette. He wanted to be with his wife again, he was ready to pass on. The idea that he will never die will devastate him."

"Then he will need to make the decision to greet the sun. It will be painful, but it will be an end."

Juliette gently released one of his hands and continued walking down the beach. They didn't say anything else, both lost in their own thoughts as they listened to the waves crash on the sand and fizzle back into the sea.

Evan knew it would be hard to see his old friend in pain, but perhaps Charlie wouldn't care. He seemed to be quite ill the last time they were together, but at peace that his end was nearing.

He wondered if Charlie was in pain now, had he been in pain when he was turned? What was involved with becoming a vampire? Again, his thoughts turned to the possibility of no longer being human. What was wrong with him?

"How does one change Juliette?" He felt her body grow suddenly tense, but she kept walking, wishing she could leave that part of the conversation behind.

"Why do you want to know?" Evan's mind raced through the many reasons he wanted to know, wondering which was the best answer to give.

"Does it hurt? Did Charlie… and Tori suffer?" She walked on but looked up into his worried expression. She could see there was more behind his question; his heart was racing, and he trembled, but she decided he should know, whatever his reasons were.

"You must have vampire blood in your system for the transition to take place. But it goes beyond that. To simply have the blood in your system is not enough, you must be very close to death and have a sudden burst of adrenaline. The adrenaline would keep your heart beating long enough for the vampire blood to carry you over the threshold of death and back. It is painful. Your body essentially dies and is shocked back to life. It would feel very similar to what your doctors use to save a patient whose heart stops beating, I believe you call them defibrillators? However, the pain is much more severe, excruciatingly so."

His blood ran cold, and he felt furious for what Charlie had suffered at the hands of Devlon. The old man had been through enough in his lifetime without having to experience that as well.

"Is he suffering now?"

270

Juliette stopped walking again and pulled Evan to her, wrapping her arms around his waist, she let her head fall back so that she could look into his eyes.

"We will find him Evan, but when we do, I must be the only one within reach. He will be starving, and his hunger may cause him to attack. I am the only one that he can't kill, I heal very quickly, and my blood will get him past his thirst much faster than human blood. I don't know what he is going through right now. The pain of starvation is unbearable, but the pain of hurting one of you would be much worse. He might never get past that guilt. Remember that please. When we find him, I will need you and the others to stay far away."

Evan hated agreeing to this. If she thought that seeing her hurt would be any easier just because she healed fast, she was wrong. But he couldn't risk letting April or Trevor near Charlie, and once they learned of the danger, they likely would feel the same way about him.

"All right. We'll stay back, but we aren't going to be completely unarmed. I think you should know that while you were sleeping today, we came up with some defenses that might help. Come on, I'll show you."

Juliette let him pull her along towards the old wooden staircase that led up from the beach. They quickly reached the cliff-top and through the darkness she could see Trevor standing precariously on a ladder outside Evan's cabin, securing something to the outer beams. April clung to the ladder, trying to keep it from toppling over. Ambrosia lay on the porch, her great head resting on her paws watching every movement her humans made. As they approached, Trevor looked over and greeted them with his boyish grin.

271

"Almost done, just one more wire to connect and we're all set!" Juliette followed the wire he was referring to with her eyes and noticed every few yards there were very large purple bulbs secured behind silver screens aimed away from the house. They seemed to extend all the way around the roof. Evan gestured to the work Trevor was completing and explained what it was.

"We've installed ultraviolet flood lights. They only illuminate the area outside the house. You'll be safe inside. There are more on the roof facing up, so it will be impossible for any vampire to get inside once they are on. We also have portable hand-held lights to take with us when we are away from the house." Juliette was stunned at their ingenuity and also suddenly fearful of their creation.

"Have you tested it yet?" She anxiously looked over at Ambrosia.

"No, not yet. We haven't really figured out how to do that," Trevor answered as he finally climbed down from the ladder.

"I guess we'll just have to hope for the best," April chimed in looking up at Trevor's handiwork.

"There is one way..." Juliette began to offer, but Evan cut her off.

"Absolutely not!" She turned and reassuringly placed her hand on his arm.

"I wasn't volunteering to walk into the lights, Evan. There is another way, it won't hurt me, I promise." His expression relaxed, and he stepped back to allow her entrance into the house. Juliette signaled for Ambrosia to follow, and everyone filed into the cabin.

They all stood a few yards back from the doorway in the middle of Evan's living room as Trevor flipped the

272

switch that changed the dark shadow of trees into an eerie violet forest.

There was nowhere to hide beyond the cabin walls... not one single fern or tree that wasn't touched by the strange purple light. It was a good thing there weren't any neighbors nearby. They would surely have the sheriff knocking on their door.

"Okay", Trevor breathed, "Ready when you are." The back door was still open giving Juliette a clear shot out into the light. She looked over at Evan and held his gaze as she used her thumb nail to slice her upturned palm. She saw the anger glint in his eyes as a pool of blood quickly filled her hand.

"You promised!" He bellowed. Juliette looked down into her hand.

"Look, it's already healed. It didn't hurt a bit." Evan stopped short, surprised that what she said was true. The slice in her palm was no longer there; all that was left was the small puddle of blood that Juliette was staring intently at.

April gasped as she witnessed the pool of blood slowly begin to bubble in Juliette's open hand. Steam seemed to rise from the boiling blood, creating a swirl of red mist hovering in the air until her hand was completely empty.

Juliette leaned forward and gently blew on the strange crimson cloud causing it to drift out into the night, swirling and churning through the open door and out over the porch.

As soon as the violet light touched each microscopic bead they ignited, bursting into flashes of searing flames that lit the porch, turning the night into day. The blast was instant and deafening. The flare was so

273

intense that they all jumped back, shielding their eyes from the blinding light, until the last drop of blood had been incinerated and the night was, once again, illuminated only by the strange violet bulbs.

Evan hadn't expected the lights to have that effect. It was much too dangerous to have Juliette or Ambrosia anywhere near this house while those lights were on.

He grabbed Juliette by the waist and pulled her behind him, shielding her from the lights.

"Trevor, shut it down." He turned and looked into Juliette's face, she seemed just as shaken as he was.

"Did you know that was going to happen?" Evan demanded.

"I've never witnessed it firsthand, but I knew that my blood reacts violently to the sun." Trevor turned the lights off, and the night outside went dark.

"It's fine, Evan. Ambrosia and I are okay as long as we are inside. It's important to me that you are all safe, and this is the only way."

"No," he said, shaking his head. "I can't put you at risk like that." He turned to Trevor and April.

"I'm taking her home." Juliette felt bewildered. It had been so long since someone had treated her like this, she wasn't sure how she felt about it.

"No, you aren't." She tried to keep her voice from rising. The agitation in the room was increasing, and it was getting hard to control her own emotions. Juliette took a deep calming breath.

"We need to start working on a plan to find Charlie. That's what's important right now." Evan opened his mouth to argue, but she stopped him.

"Evan, every moment we stand here arguing, poor Charlie is down there, alone, drowning in the dark,

274

suffering. Please, let me help you find him." April finally took a step towards Evan and Juliette and placed a hand on her brother's arm.

"She's right Evan. Please. Calm down." She couldn't remember a time she had ever seen her brother so worked up.

Juliette's presence seemed to breathe life back into her brother. After their parents died, Evan had withdrawn, just living life day to day, numbly going through the motions, never truly living… until now. The fact that this particular woman was a vampire was an increasing concern to April. But Juliette was their only hope of saving Charlie, and they needed her here.

April gestured to the window coverings she had hung earlier that day.

"I bought thick curtains that will block the light from coming in the house. Juliette and Ambrosia are safe in here. We all are. Please let's just find Charlie. I can't stand the thought of him suffering another minute."

Juliette noticed the changes in the room for the first time. Every window was now concealed behind thick, dark green curtains that would keep the light out. Once the back door was closed, there would be no danger of the light being reflected into the house. She was, once again, at ease. She looked over at April.

"Thank you for doing that. It was very thoughtful of you." April's pale cheeks flushed, and she shrugged as if it were nothing. But in doing so, Juliette noticed that April wouldn't make eye contact with her. Perhaps she was uncomfortable with what she was now that she had had a chance to think about it. She would need to speak with Evan and see if it would be best that she keep her distance from April. She was a very sweet girl, and Juliette didn't want to make her feel uneasy.

Trevor closed and locked the back door, pulled the curtains closed, and turned the violet lights back on. As he did this he spoke over his shoulder to the group.

"I have mapped out Cerulean Bay and have circled the deepest pockets. That's most likely where Devlon would have dropped Charlie so that the sunlight didn't kill him." Evan took Juliette by the hand and led her to the kitchen where a large map lay open on the countertop. There were eight places circled, and they were spaced a great distance apart. It would take some time to search each location unless they got lucky and found Charlie within the first few attempts.

Evan pointed to a site near the lighthouse.

"This isn't far from the beach where he was taken. We might be off base here, but it's our hope that Devlon dropped him near where he was taken." It was a good place to start, but Juliette feared it wouldn't be that easy.

"I think we should also consider the thought that he may have had Charlie for a few days before deciding to dispose of him. He disappeared three days before Tori disappeared. If he isn't close to the beach, we may need to widen our search." Trevor looked over the map trying to figure out where else he might be.

"Juliette, you said you have been following this guy for a while. What type of places has he hidden in before? That might give us a better idea of where else to look." Juliette turned the map on the counter and surveyed it trying to see where he might be hiding.

"Any place dark, hidden from the light. He's been known to hide in crypts, but I've already checked the cemetery and there was no trace of him or any other

276

vampires. Aside from that he has chosen abandoned places, or somewhere very difficult if not impossible for humans to get to."

April was sitting on a bar stool opposite the kitchen, leaning on the counter, her chin propped on her hands, when she suddenly sat up straight.

"What about the Clandestine Cliffs north of town, that would be the perfect place for him to hide out." April eagerly stood and came around the counter to point it out to Juliette on the map.

"The cliffs are very jagged and riddled with caves. Some of them are only accessible from under water. They get their name because most of the caves in the cliffs have never been searched. It's too dangerous, and there are warning signs posted all over so that no daredevils get themselves killed being stupid." Juliette looked towards Evan to see if he agreed. He was nodding and had begun tracing the cliffs with a highlighter.

"I tracked him to those cliffs. I lost his trail at the drop off, and it never occurred to me that he might be hiding inside the cliffs." Juliette was astonished that he had been so close.

There were three circles west of the cliffs marking deep pockets in the bay. He numbered the three sites and set the marker down.

"This is where we start. We already have the scuba gear ready. All that's left to do is rig the boat with the lights." He looked at Trevor as he said this.

"I can handle the lights tomorrow morning. We should be good to go tomorrow night if the weather cooperates."

Juliette didn't like the idea of them being down in the water with a starving vampire.

"Evan, we talked about this. None of you can go down there. If any one of you encounter Charlie before I find him, he would kill you. He wouldn't be able to control it. The thirst would take over."

Evan clearly was not liking the idea of her going alone.

"No, you going by yourself is not an option. Are you a trained diver? Trevor and I have been down there dozens of times. We have to do this together."

"It's too dangerous Evan. You have no idea what he has turned into now that he is starving. Imagine the worst zombie movie ever created, now give the corpse immeasurable strength and the ability to survive underwater. He is weak by vampire standards and unable to surface on his own, but compared to a human, he would ravage you in an instant. You already know what that feels like. Would you subject Trevor to that feeling?" Juliette clasped both of his hands in hers, willing him to understand just how treacherous this plan of his was.

"I am a vampire. I won't even need the scuba gear. I can survive in the most extreme depths of the ocean without oxygen. It can be uncomfortable, but not debilitating. I will heal if he bites me, in fact, that's what he will need to do to regain his strength fully and his sanity. Once he has fed, I will bring him up, and you will all be safe. He will be Charlie again. He won't want to hurt any of you."

She stepped closer to him, wrapping her arms around his waist, pulling him against her and looking up into his unyielding expression.

"This is the only way, Evan. To give Charlie the peace he deserves, this is how it must be."

278

"I don't like it," he growled, placing his face in her hair, and breathing deeply.

How was he supposed to protect her when he was a weak, defenseless human? It was brief moments like this that he wished he were a vampire so that they could do this side by side, together, so that he would know she was okay.

"I know. I wish there were another way, but there isn't." He pulled back almost shouting that there was, but he knew better than to suggest his previous thought out loud and in front of his sister.

"Alright." He conceded for now. He would address the idea of her changing him later when they were alone. He knew it was an insane idea, but it was the only way he could guarantee that she was safe, and it would allow them to be together without any barriers in the way. April had Trevor to watch over her now.

He had been watching them all day. It was obvious that they were perfect for each other. Evan knew that Trevor would make sure April was happy and safe.

They spent the remainder of the evening preparing for the trip out on the boat.

Trevor put together more lights that they would be able to mount on the boat in case they were attacked while they were out in the open. April baked some frozen pizzas for them to eat and packed food for their trip while Evan packed up the first aid kit, fire extinguisher, and any other safety essentials they may need while they were gone.

Juliette sat near Ambrosia on the rug in front of Evan's fireplace, gently stroking the wolf's coat as she watched them busy at their tasks. Evan had refused to let her help with anything. She wondered if there was a place

279

she could go within the house to discreetly feed. Going outside with the lights on was obviously out of the question.

She glanced at April and didn't want to voice the question out loud for fear of upsetting her. She reached out to Evan's mind and hoped she didn't startle him again.

"Is there someplace that I might be alone for a moment? I haven't yet had a chance to feed..." Evan quickly looked up from taking inventory of the first-aid kit, and his eyes met hers across the room. She smiled tentatively, feeling a bit embarrassed for having to ask. She wasn't accustomed to being in someone else's home and unable to take care of her needs at will.

Evan glanced at Trevor and April. Satisfied that they were both busy with their own projects, he looked back at Juliette and jerked his head in the direction of the hallway that led to the rest of the cabin.

Juliette stood and Ambrosia stayed close by her side as they followed Evan down the hall.

Trevor took notice of them leaving and tried to gauge April's feelings on Juliette's and her brother's departure. She was frowning at the hallway, clearly not happy about them being alone together.

"He's in love with her April. He doesn't care what she is." He whispered in her direction. April swung around to look at him like he had lost his mind too.

"But it's impossible for them to be together. Don't they get that?" Trevor stood and came around the counter and gingerly took her face in his hands.

"I don't think they care..." Before she could respond he lowered his head and kissed her softly. April froze. What was he doing? Here? In Evan's house? Trevor pulled back briefly to give her a chance to pull away if she

280

wanted to, she didn't. *To hell with it,* she thought. If he can have a torrid love affair with his vampire, then he couldn't keep her from Trevor.

April launched herself at Trevor. She had dreamed of kissing him since she was an awkward preteen. It took him by surprise, but he just held on and enjoyed the feeling of her in his arms. The kiss was everything she had wanted it to be... and more. She couldn't believe this was finally happening.

April finally pulled back and rested her forehead against his collar bone.

"We should probably talk to Evan about this before we let things go too far..." Trevor placed a feather light kiss on the top of her raven head and chuckled.

"I already did. He gave me his blessing, you're all mine." April gasped and yanked back to give Trevor a playful punch in the shoulder.

"His '*blessing*'? What is that all about? This isn't the dark ages, Trevor Helms!"

He laughed again, "What does it matter? He knows that I am crazy about you, and he's okay with it. We can be together. He wants us to be happy. Shouldn't we want that for him, too, no matter how he chooses to find his happiness?"

April knew what he was hinting at, and the scowl returned to her freckled face.

"I'm sorry Trevor, I just can't get on board with my brother becoming a creature of the undead because he finally found love. Juliette is wonderful. I can't deny that. But I can't stand by and watch him throw his humanity away. It's unnatural. Mom and Dad would freak!"

Trevor pulled her close and nuzzled her ear.

281

"Let's not think about that until we have a reason to believe that is his intention. Alright?"

"Fine," she grumbled into his shoulder. She would let it go for now, but once Charlie was found and the other vampires had left town, they were going to sit down and have a heart to heart... *all* of them.

Evan took Juliette by the hand and guided her down the hall that led to the bedrooms. At the end of the hallway the house split, the master bedroom was to the left and the other bedrooms had their own wing to the right.

He opened the double doors outside the master and indicated for her to go in.

"This is my room. Make yourself at home."

She walked to the foot of his bed and took in the furnishings. His bed was a king size four poster, the pine dresser and chest of drawers matched, and it was surprisingly tidy compared to how the rest of the house had been days before. In fact, Juliette recalled that the whole house had been picked up.

"April helped me clean up a little when they got here this morning with their bags. She said she refused to stay in a bachelor pad." Evan had obviously noticed her scrutiny of the room. She walked over to the fireplace and picked up the baseball that had been sitting on the mantel.

"Your lucky ball. It found its way back to you..." Evan chuckled and walked towards her, reaching for the ball as she placed it in his upturned palm.

"You nearly scared me to death you know. I thought I was losing my mind. I kept seeing a beautiful girl in clouds of silver mist, who somehow had my ball that I saw roll into the bay… I think April was ready to have me committed." Juliette smiled weakly at the memory.

"I'm sorry, Evan. I tried to keep my distance so that you would be safe. I never intended for any of this to happen the way it did." Evan placed the baseball back on the mantle and pulled her into his arms.

"And now? How do you feel now?" She met his gaze as he voiced the questions.

"I'm scared… I don't know that I can endure another loss." Evan knew exactly how she felt. He pulled her to him and held her.

"I'm not going anywhere." She rested her head on his shoulder and held onto him. His warmth momentarily pushed all her fears aside.

Her gaze settled on an acoustic guitar that rested against the wall in the corner of his room.

"Do you play?" He glanced over his shoulder to see that she was referring to his guitar.

"I used to." She heard the sadness in his words. She hadn't heard that tone since the night on the wharf when she overheard him talking to his parents. She pulled back, her eyes searching his face, seeing the pain etched on his features.

"You miss them terribly, don't you?" He was taken aback by her question. He knew she must have been on the dock the night that he had lost the ball, but he hadn't realized she had overheard him talking to himself.

"They died a few years ago. Their boat was caught in a storm, and it capsized. They were never found." Juliette could see the agony in his expression and tried to smooth it away with her hand.

"I'm sorry Evan." The whispered words held so much emotion. They stared into each other's eyes for a moment before she stood on tip toes and placed her lips on his. It was the first time that she had initiated the kiss. His heart swelled; all sadness forgotten in that moment.

He crushed her to his chest, lifting her up from the floor, wishing there were a way to get even closer to her. Their kiss turned passionate. She gripped his shoulders holding herself tightly against him as she was swept away on a tide of pure ecstasy. To be able to freely express her feelings for him felt surreal. She moaned into his mouth reveling in the way he possessed every nerve in her body to respond to his.

She felt his hands in her hair, on her face, cherishing every inch of her. His lips left hers to travel the length of her neck to sprinkle feather-light kisses along her shoulder and collarbone where the collar of her sweater dipped to reveal smooth flawless perfection.

He was lost in the feel of her. Her skin was velvet warmth against his overheated body. He felt the tremors shower through her as he worked his way back up to her ear.

"I love you", he whispered, almost too low for anyone to hear… but she did. She slowly pulled back to look into his eyes again. The impassioned fire he had ignited inside of her still lapped at her heart. She loved him too, and she finally allowed herself to accept that. Tears filled her eyes as the pleasure overtook her.

"I love you Evan." He blinked in astonishment. He hadn't expected to hear her say the words back to him but couldn't stop himself from expressing how he felt about her.

The immense joy of hearing those words brought him to his knees. He pulled her down on the floor with him. They knelt face to face, unable to release each other. Her hands drew his face to hers while her eyes held his. Once again, she leaned into his arms to kiss him, softer this time.

A warm blaze erupted in the hearth beside them, igniting the logs within as she drew back to softly whisper, "I have been fighting it, but you have cast a spell over me Evan, a spell that I couldn't shake. And now… I don't want to." She kissed him again, once on the lips, his jaw, his eyelids, and his forehead.

He breathed in the fragrance of her. She smelled again of the wooded forest after a fresh spring rain. Despite all that they had been through and everything that they would soon face, Evan had never been happier. He loved the way she felt in his arms, as though she had always been there and would always be. He would move heaven and earth to keep her.

"Will you play for me?" Evan hadn't had the urge to play in years, but now, with this newfound happiness, all he wanted was to please her. He reached around her and took the guitar in his hands. After shifting his position, he began to tune the instrument.

She slowly rose and closed the doors that led to his bedroom and while he tuned the guitar, with his back to her, she went to Ambrosia.

The large wolf rolled onto her back in a submissive position as Juliette knelt quietly by her side and bent to feed.

When she was done, Ambrosia stood and went to lay on the floor next to Evan. She rested her head on her paws, watching the fire.

Evan had known what she was doing while he prepared to play for her. He longed to turn and see how it was done but wanted to give her the privacy that she deserved.

Juliette was grateful that he had given her a moment to see to her needs and, once again, took her place on the carpet in front of Evan as he strummed the first chords of the song, he had chosen to play for her.

He plucked at the strings, and the music poured through the room. She closed her eyes and rocked to the rhythm he was creating. His voice slowly joined the chords and carried such emotion.

The words he sang were full of desperation, loss, passion and so many more feelings. They wrapped around Juliette causing gooseflesh to raise on her arms and tears to glisten on her lashes. The smooth tenor of his voice was a perfect complement to his extraordinary talent with the guitar.

He watched her as he sang. He could see that his music touched her, and it felt great to share this part of himself with her. He missed the feel of the guitar strings on his fingers and the sensation of singing along to the music. It had been too long.

He thought back on the last time that he had played. He had sung of love, passion, and eternal devotion. It occurred to him, that he hadn't had the slightest idea of what the words had meant... until now. She had brought to life emotions that he had never experienced before. She had brought him back from the pit of despair that he had fallen into after the death of his parents.

He owed her so much, and he didn't care how long it took. If it took him all of eternity, he would spend every day of the rest of his life showing her just how precious she was to him.

April had just taken the pizzas out of the oven and placed them on the counter when she heard the music coming from the bedroom.

She gasped and looked at Trevor as he was putting the finishing touches on the flood lights. They hadn't been able to get Evan to play in years. Trevor smiled at her; his eyes twinkling mischievously, and she knew what he was thinking. Juliette was bringing him back.

In the past, Evan had played at the pub every night. He had a natural gift, and he put the crowd under his spell in ways she had never seen.

Once her parents had passed away, he stopped playing to concentrate on keeping the bar running. Business slowed a bit, but the loyalty of their customers kept them in business despite no longer having Evan on stage to entertain them.

April leaned against the counter and listened to her brother play. Trevor could see the trembling of her chin and knew how she was feeling.

He put the tools down and came into the kitchen to wrap her in his arms.

As soon as he touched her, the tears let loose, and she began to sob into his shoulder.

Evan was playing again, and it brought back so many memories... images of their father showing Evan how to play the guitar as a young boy, and of April and her mother writing songs together for Evan to sing. The pain and the joy of hearing his music again was incredible, and had Trevor not been there to hold her, she surely would have crumpled to the floor.

Trevor continued to embrace her, gently swaying to the pulse of Evan's music as she cried. Her tears had subsided a bit and now all he heard was her soft sniffles.

He rubbed her shoulders as she calmed down. There weren't any words for him to say. He knew the impact that hearing Evan play had had on her. He himself had to fight back the tears a time or two.

His friend was finally finding his way back. He had Juliette to thank for that. He just prayed that however their blossoming relationship turned out, his friend found lasting happiness. Even if it meant that April would have to cope with him changing, he would be there to help her through it.

Evan and Juliette came walking hand in hand back into the kitchen just as April and Trevor were slicing the pizza and preparing a salad.

"Do you eat food Juliette?" April asked without looking up, unable to make eye contact with anyone in case they noticed that her eyes were still red from crying.

Juliette could smell the pizza. It smelled good, but only because it brought back memories of her human years... the way the smell of pine trees might make someone fondly remember Christmas.

"I have no use for food. It doesn't give me strength like it does you. I can still eat it, but I haven't in a very long time." She again noticed that April wasn't looking at her. She could sense a great deal of pain in her right now and worried that she was causing her anguish.

"Would you like to try it? It's only frozen pizza and a Caesar salad, but you are more than welcome to join us." April finally looked up, and Juliette could see that she had been crying. The hopeful look of her expression eased some of the worry in Juliette. April wanted her to stay, so she wasn't afraid of her... but then what was bothering her?

288

"I would love to. Thank you." Evan gave Juliette's waist a little squeeze as he left her to make their plates.

"Why don't you have a seat at the table. Do you want anything to drink?"

Juliette wasn't sure how to respond. She didn't know what her preferences were, given it had been so long since she had consumed anything other than blood.

"I'll have whatever you are having. Thank you." She pulled out a chair and sat. She watched as Evan entered the kitchen and playfully ruffled April's hair. It seemed he could tell she was upset as well, and he was trying to reassure her.

Evan looked down at his little sister as she dished the pizza out to everyone's plates and wondered if she had heard him playing the guitar. That would explain her gloomy mood.

She attempted to keep her eyes down on her work, but he poked her in the ribs right where he knew she was most ticklish, and she erupted into giggles. The sound was contagious.

Trevor came up behind April and held her while Evan continued his assault on her. They were all laughing hysterically now, and Juliette couldn't help but laugh as well.

She had never experienced this before, this levity and lighthearted behavior. Even when Marek had been alive, their lives had been so full of fear and struggle that even the good times were never like this.

She suddenly felt very lucky to be here and to share in this time with them. She would need to thank April for sharing her family with her. Maybe then she would know they were just as important to her, and that she would never let anything happen to them.

Evan helped April up off the kitchen floor where she had collapsed trying to get away from him and Trevor. Still laughing, he turned and glanced at Juliette over the counter. She was leaning on her elbows, completely enthralled with what they were doing and had the most gorgeous smile on her face.

He had never seen her light up this way before. Her smile beamed and her eyes sparkled; she laughed with them, and the sound was intoxicating. He could listen to her laugh for the rest of his life and never tire of it.

He brought their plates over to the table, and as he placed hers in front of her, he leaned down and kissed her softly, then nuzzled her ear causing another eruption of laughter from her. He was falling in love with her all over again.

April and Trevor followed Evan and gave each other knowing smiles as they noticed Evan's gesture of affection towards Juliette. April recalled Trevor's words when she saw her brother kissing Juliette and decided he was right. For now, he was happy. She would worry about his choices later.

They sat at the dinner table, an unlikely picture of a happy family... the two siblings that had grown up in this house, their lifelong best friend, and the vampire girl with her vampire wolf. As unconventional as it was, it worked for them. And for the rest of the night, they simply enjoyed each other's company and basked in their newfound loves.

The laughter continued as they watched Juliette try frozen pizza for the first time. The expression on her face spoke volumes of how sensitive her vampire taste buds were. She gracefully swallowed the small bite that she had taken and then politely offered the rest to Evan.

Trevor then attempted to entice Ambrosia with a piece, but the giant wolf simply snorted, turned her nose up at the offering, and went to lay in front of the fireplace again.

The lighthearted atmosphere finally had everyone at ease and as they were all finishing their meals, they each began to yawn. The long day and night without any sleep was finally catching up to them. It was nearing midnight when April announced that she was going to turn in.

Trevor helped her to her feet and walked with her towards the end of the hall.

"Do you want to lie down with me?" She kept her eyes on the floor, still too nervous with their new relationship to be so bold.

"You wouldn't mind?" He didn't want to push things too far, and he could tell how tired she was.

"It would be nice to have someone next to me. With everything that's going on, I don't really want to be alone."

Trevor clasped her to him and guided her to the door of the bedroom she had slept in while growing up. He opened the door and led her in quietly closing the door behind them.

Juliette and Evan cleared the table after Trevor and April had gone to bed.

"Have they always been a couple?" Juliette asked, seeing the slight grin on Evan's face as he watched Trevor follow his sister out of the kitchen.

"It's a new development, one she has been wishing for ever since she was a young girl. She's good for him. I'm glad they will have each other." The way he said that sounded like he wouldn't be around to be there for her

291

himself. Juliette looked at him trying to see what he meant by that.

But he just kept his head down as he put the remaining pizza in the refrigerator.

"I think she was bothered by something tonight. I hope it's not my presence." That finally caused Evan to look up. The last thing he wanted was for Juliette to think that she was the cause of his sister's sadness.

He turned and cupped her face in his hands, bringing his face down to hers so that they were looking into each other's eyes.

"It's not you, okay? She's just worried about what I want to do with my life now that I've fallen in love with you." Juliette wasn't quite sure what he meant.

"I don't understand. What exactly have you said you want now that we've met?" Evan sighed heavily; he had hoped to avoid this conversation until he knew for sure what he wanted.

"I haven't said anything. That's what's bothering her. I haven't decided about what I want, and she thinks the answer should be easy." Juliette still needed some clarification.

"The answer to what decision Evan?" She felt that she already knew but needed to hear it from him.

"Whether or not I can be with you… forever." She closed her eyes and leaned into his embrace, burying her face in his neck. It *was* about her. If she had been any other girl that he had fallen for, this wouldn't even be an issue. April had a very real reason to worry.

This love was so new. The idea of spending eternity with Evan was very compelling but at the same time terrifying. She had hoped that they would have more time to explore the subject.

Evan was worried about her reaction to his honesty. He began to feel the twinge of rejection. Juliette felt that emotion sweep over him and hated that she was the cause of it.

"Evan no! Please don't feel like that. I just thought we had more time to consider it. It's not that I don't love you, it's that I love you enough to not want to take anything away from your life. Do you know that Marek waited years before he would turn me? He wanted to give me the chance to find another human to love... someone who could marry me, give me children and everything else he thought I should have. It wasn't until my life was in jeopardy that he finally gave in. Had he not, I would have died a very long time ago."

Evan held her close to him, wondering about the things that she had never experienced because of what she had become and wondered if he would miss any of those things. He had never really considered the idea of a family other than the one he already had.

He had learned, when his parents died, that anything good in life could be taken away in an instant. He didn't think he could bear that sort of loss if it involved children of his own.

But Juliette was different. She couldn't die; she would never leave this world and that made it safe to love her. He shared these thoughts with her, wanting to be as honest as he could.

"But in time, you would still have to watch age take your sister… and your friend. Loss is a part of life that we cannot escape… no matter how immortal you are." She was speaking of losing Marek. He had been immortal, and still she had lost him.

"Let's not talk about this right now. We have time. There is no reason we have to decide tonight. Let's just enjoy this time together, okay?"

He leaned down to place a soft kiss on her lips and closing his eyes, leaned his head against hers and just held her. They stood that way, not moving, for what seemed like an eternity.

Juliette slowly ran her hands up Evan's back, feeling the muscles beneath his t-shirt. He quivered.

"I should probably go so that you can get some sleep," she whispered. Not moving his head away from hers, he gently shook it in denial.

"Stay with me," he said softly. The flutter of anticipation those words caused was glorious. Every nerve in her body responded to his invitation.

Silently she commanded Ambrosia to stay and began to walk backwards towards the hallway, pulling Evan with her.

They entered his bedroom unable to release their hold on one another. He kicked the door shut behind him and they found themselves standing again in front of the fire.

He looked down at her, the hunger he felt mirrored in her eyes. Evan gently swept a strand of hair away from her face and touched his lips to hers. The kiss was just as tender as the last time they had stood in this very spot.

Her mouth yielded to his, conveying the tenderness of her love for him. Juliette ran her hands up his back again, this time pushing his t-shirt up and over his head.

Evan tossed it to the floor and closed his eyes at the sensations she was creating in him as she explored his chest

294

and belly with her hands and her lips. His skin glowed in the firelight, and she wanted to weep at the beauty of him.

She swept feather light kisses down the base of his throat and felt him shudder. He ran his fingers through her hair and cupped her head as she rained kisses on his neck, pausing briefly at his pulse point.

"Will you bind me to you?" Juliette gently pulled back to look at him.

"Evan... it's not safe," she whispered. "You will be able to feel everything that I feel, both physically and emotionally. It isn't something that just goes away. It will linger for days." He kissed her again,

"I want to experience how I make you feel. I want to be as close to you as I can, and this is the only way. I'm not afraid. I want to know what it feels like to be a part of you." There was not a trace of fear in his eyes, only longing.

She kissed him, deeper this time. He pulled her to him, melding their bodies together. He wrapped his hands around her waist and slowly began to lift her sweater from her.

She wore a pink silk camisole that was translucent in the flickering light of the fire.

He swept her glorious, thick, fragrant hair to the side and kissed her neck, nipped at her ear, and worked his way down her jaw back to her sweet lips.

She moaned... the need for him building within her to the point of becoming unbearable. Juliette wanted him and wanted Evan to feel her desire for him. She cradled his neck in one hand to steady him as she kissed him one last time before making her way back to his throat.

She felt her fangs begin to lengthen, she waited until they were as sharp as needles to avoid hurting him.

With her other hand she trailed her fingers down his arm, causing shivers to rain across his skin. She wove her fingers through his, holding his hand as she carefully descended into his neck.

Evan moaned, but not in pain. The feeling of giving her his blood freely was more pleasurable than he could have ever imagined. It pulled through his body causing a rush of endorphins to explode. He felt a warming euphoric numbness spreading throughout his limbs until she finally withdrew.

Juliette kept her face down waiting for her teeth to retract, but Evan tipped her chin up and kissed her severely, tasting his own blood on her lips.

Her teeth were still sharp, and she tried to pull back to avoid hurting him, but he deepened the kiss. In an effort to keep him from being injured by her teeth, she inadvertently cut her own lip before her fangs finally retracted. Her blood flowed freely for a moment, giving him the chance to bind to her.

The moment her blood touched his tongue, he began to feel like he was floating. He felt Juliette in his arms, he felt her body responding to him, but somewhere he got lost in the sensation of skin on skin. He didn't know where he left off and she began.

She felt him begin to quiver from the intensity of the binding and gently led him to the bed. When Evan felt the mattress against his leg, he used it to anchor himself and slowly regained control of his body.

He lowered Juliette to the soft feather-down quilt and covered her body with his own. The weight of him pressing her into the bed was sensational.

Evan pulled her camisole over her head and feasted his eyes on her magnificent body before delving in and kissing every inch of her.

Juliette arched off the bed trying to press herself closer to him, to his hands, his mouth, his scorching body. Slowly, layer by layer, their clothes disappeared until they lay skin to skin.

The fire cast shadows on their bodies as they merged into one. Evan was almost undone by the powerful feeling of being one with Juliette, both in mind and in body.

They moved together in a timeless rhythm, touching, and exploring until they had worked each other into a frenzy.

Juliette felt his lips on her skin and her skin on his lips. Evan felt her hands pressing him to her and felt the taut muscles of his body through her fingertips as they rode towards the final explosion.

The last wave of pleasure tore through them at the same time. Juliette pulled his lips down to crash against hers, muffling their cries as they rode through the flood of ecstasy together.

Finally, breathless, Evan lay next to Juliette, their limbs intertwined. He placed a soft kiss on her bare shoulder and pulled the blanket up to cover them.

He looked down into her upturned face, her eyes closed, a dreamy expression settled on her lips. He leaned in to kiss her and whispered, "I love you." Just at the exact moment she said the same. Juliette opened her eyes and smiled.

"We are bound together. We feel what the other does. I feel your love for me. Do you feel mine for you?"

Evan searched her eyes, their silver depths alive with happiness.

"I do, it feels amazing. You are a drug to me Juliette. I will never be able to get enough of you. I will never let you go; I am yours... forever."

***

Juliette awoke in Evans arms, her head pillowed on his chest. She lay there unmoving, savoring the feeling of complete contentment. Evan, sensing that she was awake, softly traced his fingertips up and down her arm and kissed the top of her head.

"Good morning... or should I say good evening?" His chuckle rumbled deep in his chest, and Juliette propped her head up on her elbow so that she could see his face.

His hair was tousled from sleep, and the dusting of facial hair that she had come to love covered his jaw. Her feeling of serenity washed over him, and he was amazed at the intensity of it.

Being able to experience every emotion as she did would never grow old. He wished they would always be bound together, that it didn't have to end.

Binding herself to him had been one of the most sensual experiences she had ever had. She felt as if she had known him for years instead of weeks.

Evan had merged his spirit with hers and given her his heart. There was no going back now.

"I love you Evan." He smiled in response, and she heard his heart rate increase. Had they not been bound to one another; it still would have been quite obvious how those words affected him.

He leaned up to kiss her and whispered against her lips, "I love you."

Suddenly a knock at the door reminded them of the fact that they were not alone in the house.

"Hey, the sun just set. April is making sandwiches to take with us. We're ready to go when you are." They heard Trevor's footsteps retreating as he made his way back to the kitchen.

Juliette was sad to see this moment come to an end, but they had to save Charlie. The poor man had been left in the ocean's depths far too long.

Evan sat up and pulled her up into his arms for one last kiss before rolling out of bed and pulling on his jeans.

"I guess we better head out soon." Juliette shared his sudden mounting nervousness and stood pulling the sheet to wrap around her and looked up into his worried face.

"What's bothering you?" Evan sighed heavily and ran his fingers through his hair in frustration.

"I don't want you going down there alone. I know you are more than capable, and my fear is ridiculous... I just can't stand the idea of being away from you." She smiled tentatively.

"But you won't be away from me. We are bound, remember? We'll be able to communicate better than if we were talking on the phone. Try it. Reach out to me with your mind." Evan hesitated not sure how to do what she was asking, then he heard her voice in his head.

"*Tell me you love me again. I never grow tired of hearing it.*" Without even giving it much thought, he answered with his mind,

"*And I will never tire of saying it...*" Just simply thinking the words and thinking of her was all it took. The smile that lit her face was astounding. She had heard him.

"*See,*" she responded silently, "*I am just a thought away. You will know everything that is happening as it happens. It will be alright Evan. We'll do this together.*"

"*Thank you for sharing this with me.*" The soundless conversation was something he could get used to.

300

He wondered how far of a distance they would be able to keep it up."

She spoke out loud to answer his question as she gathered her clothes and began to dress.

"It depends on how often we bind together. The more often we do it, the longer of a distance we can go. But with you being human, we don't want to get carried away. You want to be able to choose your fate, not have it thrust upon you."

Evan wasn't so sure about that. It almost seemed easier to have the choice taken out of his hands. On the outside she made being a vampire look glamorous, but he knew that there had been centuries of suffering. He knew that better now, after being able to see into her mind.

She was glad he was able to see every aspect of what she was now. Perhaps that would help him make a more informed decision when it came to his own mortality.

"Let's not keep your sister and Trevor waiting. I still have to stop at my place and change clothes." They left the bedroom and went to meet the others in the kitchen.

It was decided that Juliette would travel home in her unique way and change, then come back and pick them up in her SUV.

Trevor briefly turned the lights off so that it was safe for Ambrosia and Juliette to leave. Once she signaled to Evan that they were far enough away, they turned them back on.

"I didn't hear your phone ring..." Trevor stated looking at Evan as he flipped the switch causing the outside to turn the strange violet hue once again.

"How did you know she was home?" April glanced curiously at her brother wondering the same thing.

301

Evan didn't want to go into too much detail about what had happened with Juliette. The memory was too sacred for him to share flippantly with anyone else.

"Do you remember when she talked about Devlon and Charlie being bound to each other because they had shared blood?" April's face scrunched up in disgust.

"Ew! Evan, you didn't! So gross!" Trevor was trying not to laugh at April's expression. She just kept shaking her head, not wanting to hear anymore.

"It was only a small amount, and to be honest, I don't remember that part much at all. But now we can communicate with our thoughts. Just until it's no longer in my system. It will really help being able to talk to each other while she's down there looking for Charlie." Trevor laughed and slapped Evan on the shoulder as he went to start piling their gear next to the front door.

"Cool man, like walkie talkies." April glowered at her brother as she began packing the cooler with food and drinks.

"April, it's fine. It didn't hurt, really." She stood, arms hanging loosely at her sides, as she searched for the right words to describe to her big brother how she just didn't get it. She didn't understand how he could be so nonchalant about swallowing someone else's blood. Just the thought of it grossed her out. But then she remembered Trevor's advice in her head; let it go until Charlie is safe.

She sucked in a deep breath, closed her eyes, and tried to shrug it off.

"I'm letting it go…" Then she turned on her heels and followed Trevor with an armful of towels, leaving Evan standing there dumfounded at his sister's newfound ability to hold her tongue.

302

***

It wasn't long before Juliette arrived back at the cabin with her large SUV. Trevor and April shared the backseat with Ambrosia since the cargo space was loaded down with all the equipment they were going to need on the boat.

They had scuba gear just in case the guys needed to assist in any way. Juliette was against it, but Evan said it was better to have it just in case.

There were towels for when she and Charlie returned to the surface, and a first aid kit if any of the humans were injured.

Evan had been about to tell April that Juliette could simply heal them with her blood but thought better of it.

They also had a few fire extinguishers, the ultraviolet lamp to attach to the boat and the handheld light as well.

Once they reached the dock, they all helped unload the gear onto Trevor's boat, *The Fish N' Ships*. After all of the equipment had been stowed away, Juliette commanded Ambrosia to stay below deck so that she wouldn't be seen by anyone, and Trevor took them out of the harbor and into the bay.

The darkness was calm, a few clouds scattered in the sky letting the moonlight filter through. The night still had a bite to it, and Juliette was not looking forward to getting into the cold water.

Evan mounted the ultraviolet light to the boat while Juliette changed into the wetsuit that April had brought along for her to wear. It was lucky they were close to the

303

same size. Although Juliette didn't need the regulator or the tank, the wetsuit, mask and flippers would be useful.

While April helped her change into the scuba gear, she wondered aloud about the vampire ability to change into mist.

"Can all vampires disappear into mist?" Juliette looked over her shoulder as April pulled the zipper up on the back of the wetsuit.

"Yes, but it takes a lot of concentration and strength. Charlie is starving and won't have the ability to escape his bindings without help. And I doubt Devlon would have taught him how to do it. He wouldn't have been able to hold him prisoner if he had taught him how to dissipate."

April looked down at the flippers in her hands, not sure how to ask her next question without being offensive. Juliette, sensing her hesitation, placed her hand on April's arm, a gesture of friendship and comfort.

"Ask me anything, April. I want no secrets between us." April looked up and saw the sincerity glimmering in Juliette's unusual eyes.

"I just wondered how a vampire is captured or... killed, when all you have to do is simply disappear?" Juliette knew that her question was voiced out of fear that they may never be free of Devlon and hoped to ease her anxiety.

"As I said, it takes much concentration to dissipate. If our attention lies elsewhere, and we are able to be weakened, it would be possible. There are also talismans, stones with carvings, that once enchanted, prevent us from being able to use our powers." Juliette could feel the relief pour over April at the knowledge that vampires were not completely indestructible. They exited the cabin arm in arm

304

and joined the men on deck as they navigated the nighttime waters of Cerulean Bay.

As the boat approached the first deep pocket off the Clandestine Cliffs, April kept her eyes on the fish finder hoping to see a cluster that might be Charlie. Unfortunately, this time of night the sea was teaming with Marine life, and it was impossible to decipher what was a fish and what could have been Charlie.

April turned to Juliette to ask about the fish being a possible source of food for Charlie when she noticed her standing in Evan's arms. They were looking longingly into each other's eyes, not saying a word.

She wondered what was going on until she remembered that they could now communicate telepathically. April had never seen her brother act this way with anyone. It melted her heart and at the same time terrified her. If only Juliette was human. She really did like her. What was not to like? She was thoughtful, gracious, and fearless. It was obvious that she loved her brother very much and would stop at nothing to keep him safe.

Finally, Trevor's bellowing voice broke the spell that had entrapped Juliette and Evan.

"We're over the first site. It's not a trench, but the seafloor does slope down pretty steep and then curve back up. Do you want to take a light down with you? The visibility isn't going to be great, but that might help." Juliette let loose of Evan's hand and sat on the railing of the boat to pull on her flippers.

"No, thank you. I will be able to see clearly enough with the dive mask. The dark doesn't impair my vision, and I'll need both of my hands free if I am going to be able to help Charlie."

She pulled her hair back into a ponytail and was beginning to put the mask on when Evan dropped to his knees in front of her.

"This is killing me," his mind said to hers.

"Promise me you'll stay in contact. I will go crazy if I don't hear from you."

Juliette traced the planes of his face with her fingertips and leaned in to place her lips against his.

"I promise." She pulled the mask on and used Evan to push off and roll backwards into the black water. She bobbed on the surface long enough to wave at April and Trevor who stood by Evan as he leaned over the side of the boat longing to go with her.

Juliette dove straight down to the seabed and hovered there looking towards the slope that Trevor had told her about. He was right about the visibility. The current was coming at the cliff face from an angle, pulling silt and other debris out of the bay back into the open sea.

Her vampire eyes made it possible to see a much greater distance than a human would have been able too, but there were still areas in the distance she was blind to. That made her uneasy.

Juliette tasted the current trying to catch any scent of Charlie, but there was none. She began to glide swiftly through the blue water, her eyes scanning the ocean floor for any shape that might be a body.

She was a little frightened at what she might find. She had never encountered a vampire in Charlie's state before and really didn't know what to expect.

As soon as the thought entered her mind, she instantly regretted it. She could feel Evan's mounting impatience and her train of thought had not helped.

"It's okay love, all is well. Please try to relax." She heard his mental voice grumble in response.

She laughed inwardly at his over protectiveness and continued to survey the ocean floor. She had made quick work of it and was nearing the upward slant that marked the end of this pocket. Charlie wasn't here. She quickly surfaced, bursting from the water. She dissipated into mist and flew across the waves to drop gracefully onto the deck of the boat.

She startled April who yelped and almost knocked Trevor overboard.

"Oh! Sorry Trevor, I have a bad habit of doing that don't I?" April laughed in embarrassment and clutched Trevor's arm to keep him from toppling over.

"It's my fault. I should have announced myself." Juliette apologized as she was pulling the mask off and ringing the seawater from her hair.

Evan was at her side in an instant.

"I'm sorry Evan. He wasn't there. We should move on to the next location."

It didn't take them long to reach the next location and drop anchor.

The clouds were starting to move in, and Juliette hoped that they could find Charlie before the weather took a turn for the worse. She already had her hands full keeping communication open with Evan and using all of her senses to find Charlie. That made it impossible to be able to control the weather as well.

"This time it will be a deep crevice. Its only about fifty yards long, but its deep and narrow," Trevor explained, as he leaned over glancing at his anchor line. The water was beginning to get rough, and he hoped it would hold their position while she was under.

She pulled the mask back on and felt a chill run down her spine, they must be close to Charlie. She could possibly be sensing his unrest.

She looked up at Evan before dropping overboard, and they locked eyes.

"*I feel it too,*" he said. "*Please be careful.*" She hit the water just as his thoughts touched her mind.

The water seemed colder now. And the current tried to push her in the opposite direction of where she needed to be. She began her descent and saw the gash in the sea floor.

"*I'm at the crevice. I'm going to skim along the top first.*" Evan again cautioned her. Something was brewing up on the surface. The wind was picking up and waves were angrily tossing the boat around which only increased his concern for her.

Juliette was now hovering over the gorge peering down into its depths. The rocks were covered in brightly colored starfish and sea anemone. The bright colors did little to ease the apprehension she felt. There were deep crags in the walls that made it hard to see in parts of the already darkened ravine. She was about halfway along the gorge when something white caught her eye.

Juliette held her position and looked closer. At first, she thought she might have imagined it, or that it had been light reflecting off a fish, but just as she was about to move on, the flash of white appeared again.

From beneath the overhang of the cliff, on the floor of the gorge, a boney white hand was slowly grasping at the sea water.

"*Evan...I've found him.*" She was unable to suppress the fear that carried her words to him. Evan reached out to her mind almost immediately.

"*Don't move; I'm coming down!*"

"*No! Evan, from what I can see, he is in a bad state. If you were to come down here, he would kill you. Stay where you are. Please. I can't help him and worry about you too; please stay there.*"

She felt his increased frustration. Satisfied that he was heeding her command, she began the descent into the gorge.

***

Juliette used the wall opposite where Charlie was positioned to get down to his depth. Until she knew what she was getting into, staying out of his reach was the safest place for her.

As she reached the overhang that had concealed him, her entire body turned to ice.

Charlie was a skeletal corpse; his skin was pulled taught over bone revealing every joint that held his emaciated body together. His eyes were sunken into his skull, the lids were pulled back making them bulge wildly, his teeth were exposed, and his fangs snapped in her direction. His leg was anchored to the sea floor with an enormous iron anchor that looked ancient.

This was one of the most terrifying things Juliette had ever encountered, and it was at the hands of Devlon, yet again.

Juliette thought it might be best to let him feed from her wrist. She just hoped that she could get close enough without him ravaging her.

Before she pushed away from the rocky seawall, she reached out to Evan.

"I will try to keep up communications with you, but I am going to need to control the current to safely maneuver and get him blood without this getting out of control. Please stay calm if I don't respond right away." Evan reluctantly agreed, anxiety crackling between them like static electricity.

Juliette prepared herself mentally and eyed Charlie. He floated above the seabed, his hands still clawing at the water between them, his eyes were blind, mindless, and

310

fixed on her face. She could feel that the hunger in him was excruciating. She concentrated on pushing the current up and out of the gorge so as not to be pushed towards him. Then, using a divers' knife that Evan had equipped her with, she sliced her wrist and began to move closer to him, trying to choreograph her movements to avoid getting snared by his claws.

The moment he tasted her blood in the water disaster struck. Charlie's corpse began to thrash widely, swift frantic movement almost too fast for her to keep track of. Juliette tried to drop back to avoid his hands, but she suddenly heard Evan's mental voice scream out a warning to Trevor. Something was happening on the surface. Her concentration broke and she lost her grip on the motion of the tide. The sea was not on her side and the current pushed her right into Charlie's grasp.

She felt the sharp bones of his fingers sink into the muscle of her arms as he pulled her to him. Charlie savagely lurched for her throat, and Juliette quickly jerked her head to the side presenting him with her shoulder. His teeth tore through the fiber of the wet suit as if it were tissue paper. She felt the searing pain of his fangs tearing her neck and shoulder to ribbons. She screamed in agony, but her vocal cords were silenced by the seawater.

More shouts could be heard from the world above, but Juliette was trapped in Charlie's talons and unable to surface. In the middle of the attack, Juliette felt a violent punch to her abdomen that caused her to gain some distance between her and Charlie.

Before she had time to wonder what had happened, she was suddenly blinded by a searing blow to the back of her skull. Confusion quickly gave way to terror as she realized that the blows she was taking was actually an attack on Evan.

Juliette felt a panic tear through her that she hadn't experienced since watching Marek being burned alive. She needed to get to Evan now!

Charlie was still clutching at her, trying to pull her back to his teeth. She could see that what blood he had managed to get from her was already helping restore his body, but she didn't have time to continue feeding him. Evan needed her.

She used a burst of strength to dislodge herself from Charlie's arms and thrust herself up towards the surface.

In seconds she burst from the rioting waves and located the fishing boat that was now being tossed around in the angry whitecaps. She flashed across the surface in her mist form and dropped onto the deck of Trevor's boat, only this time there was no one to startle.

April lay unconscious near the steering wheel, and Trevor was sprawled out on the bottom of the boat near the anchor line that had been cut. Evan was gone.

Juliette ran to April who was beginning to come around. After checking her pulse and making sure she had no serious injuries, she helped her sit upright and rest against the side of the boat as she called out to Ambrosia. Soon the great wolf was at her side.

"Stay with April while I wake Trevor, love. I need to make sure they are okay before I go after Evan."

Ambrosia whined uneasily and did as she was told. Juliette was grateful that she had listened to her instructions to stay below deck despite what had happened here. Had Devlon learned of her existence, she would be facing a very different fight.

Trevor came to shortly after Juliette knelt by his side. He had a knot beginning to form on the back of his head from where he had been hit, and it throbbed.

"Is April okay?" Juliette could feel the panic and hear it in Trevor's voice as she helped him climb to his feet.

"She's alright. What happened?"

Trevor staggered over to where April sat holding her head. The waves continued to slam into the side of the boat making it hard to stay upright.

April answered, her voice filled with dread. "They came at us so fast Juliette! We didn't even have a chance to get to the violet light... they broke it, and they took Evan!" Juliette glanced over her shoulder where Ambrosia was now skirting around broken purple glass that littered the bottom of the boat, sniffing at the scent that had been left behind.

"Oh my god! What happened to your shoulder?" April's eyes were wide as she stared at the open wound that was still healing under the shredded wetsuit.

"Don't worry about me. I must go after them. Are you and Trevor going to be okay if I leave you here?"

Trevor pulled April to her feet and steadied her with his arm around her waist. She had never seen him so serious; he was terrified for his friend.

"We'll be fine; just go get him. Please Juliette, bring him back to us." She looked back and forth between their faces, heavy with worry and sick with fear. She nodded.

"Put some lifejackets on and try to anchor the boat again. I don't know how bad this storm is going to get, but Ambrosia will be here with you."

313

April's tear-streaked face was the last thing that Juliette saw as she erupted into mist and flew into the turbulent night sky.

She hovered above the boat for a moment trying to use her connection with Evan to determine his whereabouts. Lightning flashed across the sky and thunder rumbled all around her. Trying desperately not to lose focus, Juliette homed in on Evan's mind. She was catching only flickers of images. He seemed to be unconscious, and she was not able to hear his thoughts or feel his emotions, probably from the blow to the back of his head that Juliette had experienced.

Thankfully, his subconscious was still linked to her, and she was able to discover their path and see where they were.

They had taken Evan up the great face of the cliffs and disappeared into one of the many caves that riddled the giant limestone wall.

Juliette soared to the entrance of the cave that matched the last image she had seen flash through Evan's mind.

She paused outside and listened for any movement within the hollow opening… she heard none. Regaining human form, Juliette clung to the cliff side and peered within the narrow passage. It went deep underground and opened to reveal a large chasm that dropped about twenty meters down touching ocean water. Juliette could hear the sea lapping at the rock base within the cave and prayed that Evan was safe.

She cautiously entered the mouth of the tunnel that would lead her to where they held Evan, knowing they had intended for her to follow, and that she must surely be walking into a trap. As she inched along the rough, rocky walls, she finally heard Evan's mind.

"They have the hand-held light Juliette. Don't come in here." He was alive! The relief that swept through her was short-lived as he registered his condition with her.

He was on his knees against the cave wall, his hands were tied behind his back and secured to his feet with nylon rope they had taken from the boat. His mouth had been gagged with cloth, and he was covered in a foul-smelling black sticky substance. Her blood ran cold as it dawned on her what it was.

Devlon had doused Evan in vampire blood and held the ultraviolet light, ready to use it at any moment.

She saw the sadistic grin that spread across Devlon's smug face as he took notice that Evan was now awake.

"I hear your girlfriend. Have you shared your fate with her yet?" Evan snarled at Devlon around the cloth in his mouth. He only laughed in response.

"Tori my dear, you never shared with me how amusing this one is." Evan glanced at Tori who was standing directly to his left.

Juliette noticed that she looked ashen and frail. Devlon had been feeding from her a great deal, it seemed. He had depleted her strength to gain her powers. Tori kept her eyes downcast, seemingly beaten down and defeated.

Juliette attempted to reach out to her. The connection was weak, but the moment their minds touched Tori twitched towards the mouth of the cave.

"Tori, please. I can see what he has done to you. Help me... help Evan. He is covered in vampire blood. If Devlon uses that light on him, he will burn to death."

315

Her response was barely a whisper. *"I can't, I have nothing left in me... I should have listened to you."* Suddenly Devlon's bellowing voice caused Tori to jump.

"Stop that! I will not permit such insolence girl. Shall I remind you what happens when I am displeased?" Devlon raised his hand and lightly twitched a finger in Tori's direction. She was abruptly snatched off her feet and hurtled through the air. Devlon captured her brutally by the neck and brought her throat to his growing fangs.

Mercilessly he tore at her flesh, bleeding her dry. Then, with a flick of his wrist and a fresh burst of power, he sent Tori crashing against the far wall. She slammed into the rock and crumpled to the ground, curled into a fetus position, she lay there quivering.

Despite the danger of the light, Juliette flew into a rage and erupted into a funnel of mist that swept down to stand between Tori, Evan and Devlon.

"Devlon stop! I have followed you, as you clearly wanted, leave the girl alone." Meeting Devlon face to face for the first time in centuries, after all that he had done to her, was surreal.

There was so much she wanted to say, and so much fury seething within her, yet she pushed it all aside. She could feel the power growing in him after taking Tori's blood. She needed to stay focused and figure out how to get Evan and Tori out of here safely.

"Ah, Juliette. Finally, we see one another again. I suppose it's about time. I have grown quite tired of this little cat and mouse game we have been playing. I had hoped you would finally give up now that you have found a new plaything." His eyes touched briefly on Evan.

"But then I see you trying to bring that decaying old man up from the bottom of the ocean and can only assume

316

it is so that he can lead you to me. So rather than letting you go through all the trouble, I decided to extend an invitation to you." Having him clarify why he ambushed Evan did not ease the anger that coursed through her.

"You misunderstood my reasons for finding Charlie. We were attempting to put an end to his misery. I get no enjoyment from the suffering of others." Devlon began to walk around the pool that lay between them. He was dressed all in black, still favoring the fashion that was in style when they had been human. He wore tight black pants with knee-high, polished black boots and a billowing black button-down shirt. He looked slightly older than the last time she had seen him, with silver highlighting his black hair and crow's feet appearing when he grinned, somehow making him appear even more arrogant.

He read her scrutiny of him, "Yes, I have aged since we last met. My dear cousin denied me his immortality, his own flesh and blood... yet clearly, he had no issue sharing that gift with you." He practically spat the words at her, dripping with resentment and disgust. Bringing Marek up only intensified the pure rage that was building within her.

"You were the very reason he became immortal. Had you not murdered his entire family, he never would have gone to such great lengths to save them. You are absolute evil Devlon, Marek had a pure heart. He was smart to keep this from you." He stopped walking to glare at her, fury glinting in his black eyes.

"And yet he failed! Here I stand... alive and more powerful than he ever was, while he is nothing but an annoying and very distant memory."

The emotions that his words caused tore through Juliette; she snarled. Bright flashes of lightning illuminated the interior of the cavern, and the black churning water

317

rolling in from the ocean turned a bright silvery blue as deafening thunder followed. Her rage was mounting causing the weather outside to worsen. She heard Evan in her mind.

"He's goading you Juliette, don't let him, breathe… calm down." She noticed for the first time that the water within the tide pool had begun to boil with the rage that was coursing through her. She was losing control of her emotions, and it was impacting the environment. The cave walls had begun to tremble causing pebbles to dance across the floor and dust to fall from the ceiling.

She concentrated on her breathing as Evan had instructed, her breath hissing through her clenched teeth. Tori finally sat up to look in wonder as the dust fell around her, until Juliette finally gained some control and it ceased.

"Had I known you were a witch as well, I would have orchestrated our little meeting much sooner. It seems that you have a great deal more power than my little enchantress over there. Join me, Juliette. I am much more your equal than this boy will ever be." The idea that she would ever join him after all he had done to Marek and to her was insane. Somewhere in his quest for power, he had clearly lost his mind.

"Your obsession has twisted your mind Devlon. I have no desire to spend even one more minute in your company, least of all an eternity. This ends tonight. You will finally meet the fate that you earned so many years ago, you murderous bastard!"

He sneered, his eyes sparkling with excitement at her challenge.

Juliette tried once again to reach Tori.

318

"It's now or never Tori, help me end him so that you can be free of him." Tori crouched next to Evan, looking from Juliette and back to Devlon weighing her options.

Devlon glanced momentarily in her direction, a brow raised at her audacity to re-enter the conversation with Juliette. He raised his hand again to thrust another wave of power at Tori, but Juliette launched herself across the pool and slammed into Devlon causing him to lose his grasp on the lamp.

He howled in rage as they fell to the rough floor. A snarl tore through Juliette as she dove for his throat with her fangs. She would drain him of all his powers and end him, but before she could tear into his skin, he caught her neck in his fist, holding her back.

"You shouldn't have done that. Now you will die regardless of how precious your blood is to me." Devlon reached his free hand out to grab the lamp, but it was not where it had fallen.

In his confusion, his grip on Juliette faltered and she slapped his hand away, pinning it to the rock floor of the cave.

With her other hand Juliette gripped Devlon's hair and snapped his head back to expose his throat. She pulled back to allow her fangs to reach their full length and heaved forward to impale Devlon and drain him.

The moment her fangs penetrated his artery the cave walls began to shake violently. Large boulders and stalactites began to fall to the floor shattering into pieces. Juliette wavered, if one of those hit Evan he would be crushed.

No sooner had the thought crossed her mind than a large stalactite impaled Juliette's shoulder, pinning her to the floor. She screamed in pain, releasing Devlon.

319

Evan's scream echoed in the cave. Feeling Juliette being impaled, he fell to the floor.

Devlon rolled out from under her and sprang to his feet. He began to stalk Tori who now held the ultraviolet light.

"Give that to me you little fool!" Juliette could see Tori fumbling for the switch, trying desperately to turn it on. Her fear of Devlon made her clumsy, and the tears that filled her eyes blinded her.

Before Tori could figure out how to use it, Devlon used his power to cast a large rock at her, hitting her in the ribs. She fell beneath its weight and dropped the light. She quickly scrambled to her feet and tried to reach the lamp again, but Devlon already had it in his hand.

Juliette tried again and again to dislodge the stalactite from her shoulder with her powers but as soon as the rock began to move in her flesh, the pain caused her to lose her grasp on it. Dissipating was impossible.

Devlon turned his head to look at her over his shoulder. A sinister grin pulled his thin lips back to reveal his fangs.

"Prepare yourself Juliette and watch another one of your lovers *burn*!" Devlon brought the lamp up, aiming it in Evan's direction,

"NO!" Her scream never even caused him to pause. He flipped the switch and a beam of purple light shot towards Evan."

Juliette stared in horror as the room filled with a blinding light that burned her eyes. The blast that filled the cave was deafening. The aftershock of the explosion freed Juliette from the spike and hurled her roughly against the far wall. Beams of piercing white light shot out in every direction, reflecting off the cave walls. Juliette had to close

320

her eyes against the brightness and heard her own screams echoing after the explosion.

Once the silence penetrated her mind, she pushed herself onto her hands and knees and looked to where Evan had been laying.

To her astonishment Evan was still there, unconscious, but alive. Her eyes surveyed the cave to see that Tori was nowhere to be found. Had she thrown herself in front of the ultraviolet beam? Juliette didn't have time to explore it further; Devlon was walking quickly to where Evan lay unconscious on the floor.

The look on his face was of pure determination and rage.

"Well, that was disappointing. I had such high hopes for that little slut. I guess we will have to go with plan B."

He reached down and yanked Evan up off the cave floor by his hair. Devlon looked at Juliette, his eyes bore into hers, challenging her, he hissed,

"I think he should be awake for this don't you?" Devlon looked down at Evan and forced his way into his mind causing him to awaken to the nightmare taking place.

Juliette, desperate to get him away from Evan, pulled a torrent of water from the inner pool. The upsurge soared across the cave towards Devlon, but he saw it coming and deflected it back to her. The force of the wall of water propelled her backwards to crash into the cave wall once again before pulling her into the now turbulent sea. She surfaced within seconds to see Devlon holding her divers' knife to Evan's throat. She must have dropped it during their struggle.

Evan's eyes, full of fear and remorse, met hers. His thoughts reached out to her.

321

"I love you Juliette." No sooner had Evan's thought crossed over to Juliette than she heard Devlon's horrifying words.

"It ends here!" He snapped Evan's head back exposing his throat, and using her blade, he sliced Evan's throat from ear to ear.

"Evan!" The scream hadn't even left her lips before she saw his blood flooding the cave floor. He would be dead in moments.

"Save your lover or follow me, the choice is yours." Devlon threw both Evan and the knife to the ground, burst into a turbulent black cloud, and soared from the cave.

***

Juliette was at Evan's side in seconds. She picked up the knife that Devlon had dropped and cut her wrist. In her haste to draw her own blood, she nearly severed her own hand. Her blood poured from her wrist over the slash in Evan's throat, and the wounds slowly healed. She heard his heart falter and knew that with the amount of blood he had lost, he didn't have long.

She needed to make the decision... turn him or let him die.

Juliette knew that she couldn't make the choice alone. Although the last thing she wanted was to lose Evan, he had a family that had every right to decide his fate for him.

Juliette stood, pulled Evan over her shoulder, and carried him to the mouth of the cave. She could hear the wind howling through the chambers of stone as she stepped out into the pelting rain.

She looked down gauging the waters depth beneath the raging waves. She feared that if she couldn't calm the current, it would slam her and Evan into the cliff face.

She pulled in a deep breath and tried with all her might to calm her emotions and the raging sea. She thought of Evan and of his love for her... she thought of the tender way he had held her that morning and of the warmth in his strong embrace.

Juliette felt the wind lessen and looked back down to the cliff base. To her relief the waters had calmed enough for her to jump, and Trevor's boat was just outside the cave circling at the bottom of the cliff. The explosion must have alerted them to their location.

Juliette pulled Evan from her shoulder and hugged him to her chest, supporting his weight as she stepped out over the edge.

They dropped like a stone, the ocean spray whipping around them as they descended towards the water. They plunged into the icy waves. Juliette immediately grasped the current with her mind and used it to thrust them back up to break through the surface, just yards away from the boat.

"Evan!" April's scream carried all the emotion that Juliette had been trying to hold at bay.

Juliette pushed Evan towards the boat, lifting him up to Trevor who bent over the side of the boat to retrieve his unconscious body

She was climbing aboard as Trevor lay Evan on the wet floorboards.

Trevor and April dropped to their knees on either side of Evan. He was soaking wet and his pale ashen complexion stark against the dark towels that April was wrapping around him.

"What happened?" Tears were now openly pouring down Juliette's face.

"Devlon cut his throat. I healed the wound... but he's lost too much blood. April, you need to decide... or he will die."

April's head snapped up to lock eyes with Juliette. Her chin began to quiver, and she burst into great wracking sobs that shook her small frame.

Juliette placed a hand on her shoulder trying to comfort her through her own pain.

"There isn't much time April, every second we wait, the more he slips away. What is your choice?"

324

"You mean, let him die or…" She couldn't bring herself to say it. Juliette simply nodded not trusting her voice to speak again. She didn't want to influence April's decision with her own emotions.

Trevor clasped April's hand where it rested on Evan's chest. He said nothing, just nodded once.

April took a deep shuddering breath and turned to Juliette.

"Save him, I don't care how, just don't let my brother die! Please!" Juliette was spurred into action the moment April gave her permission.

"I need to reach him mentally; he has my blood in his system but that isn't enough. I need to generate a burst of adrenaline in him for the transition to work. I need to concentrate."

Juliette moved behind Evan and pulled his head into her lap. Placing both hands on either side of his face, she closed her eyes and attempted to bore her way into his subconscious.

His mind was a thick cobweb of darkness. It was dense and hard to break through. Finally reaching the inner core where his spirit hovered weakly, Juliette reached out.

"Evan, come back to me. April and Trevor are here, they are holding your hand. Do you feel them?" His mind tentatively touched hers. She could feel indecision there. Something else was holding on from the other side, something that was causing him to consider letting go, to disappear into oblivion.

She couldn't see what it was from her perspective, but suddenly she felt the pure white joy burst forth from Evan.

His parents were there, just on the other side of heaven, holding on to his soul by a thin silver thread. The

325

elation that she felt from him tore at her heart. How could she steal him away from this? Her own selfishness aside, April and Trevor would be destroyed if she let him slip out of her fingers.

Juliette softly whispered Evan's name, again. He reached back towards her and hovered there, somewhere between two worlds. She felt his whisper in her heart, she felt once more the burst of love from him as he was being pulled away. She was losing her grip on him.

Juliette felt a sob escape from deep within her chest.

"No! Please Evan, don't leave me… I can't lose you too." She heard the anguish in her voice as she spoke her thoughts out loud. She was frozen in the darkened space of Evan's mind as she watched him drift further and further away from her. She tried to follow but came up against an invisible barrier that separated them. She sobbed his name once more, as she felt him slipping further and further into the dark abyss.

So lost in her own grief, she didn't notice the commotion that was occurring on the boat. She didn't hear the gasp from April as she heard Juliette beg Evan not to leave her. She didn't hear her demand that Trevor bring her the first aid kit. She wasn't aware that Trevor had cut Evan's shirt away from his body, she didn't notice the storm that was now bearing down on the tiny boat causing it to slam into the rocky cliff.

All she could do was float inside Evan's deteriorating mind and watch as he began to recede from her world to join his parents in the afterlife.

"Now!" April's scream finally broke through Juliette's fading connection with Evan's mind. She opened her eyes just in time to see April plunge something into Evan's chest.

326

Within an instant his body jerked, and a spasm tore through him causing his spine to bend backwards, lifting him up from the floorboards. His soul came slamming back with such force that it sent Juliette crashing to the floor of the boat. She felt the same shock of adrenaline surge through her body while Evan again arched his back, his feet pushing against the deck, a grotesque snarl escaped from deep in his throat.

April and Trevor backed up against the side of the boat, Ambrosia placed herself between the humans and Evan, watching cautiously as he began to change. Juliette lay next to him writhing in pain as the transition incapacitated them both.

April saw her brother twisting and bending in unnatural ways but couldn't avert her eyes. It wasn't until his head snapped back and another terrifying snarl erupted from him that she saw that his teeth were changing. Dagger-sharp fangs thrust from his jaw, and his eyes bulged beneath the strain of the transformation. His eyes had taken on a metallic green sheen, his skin grew pale and translucent, and his veins, visible through his skin, shone vibrant blue as the adrenaline mixed with the vampire blood flowing through his body. It seemed to move through him, throbbing and pulsating until his skin was as smooth and as flawless as alabaster.

Finally, the spasms subsided, and he lay curled on his side, panting and clutching at the wood on the bottom of the boat.

Juliette could feel his essence brighter than it had ever been. The pain was gone and now all that followed was disorientation. He was unaccustomed to this new body and feelings.

327

She pulled herself up onto her knees and crawled over to him. Gently she pushed his hair back off his brow and looked into his face.

"Evan?" He locked eyes with her and reached up to cup her face with his hands.

The small gesture sent sensations shooting through his body that he had never felt before. His mind screamed in fear, unsure if it was pain or pleasure that rolled through him. There were no words to express these new feelings.

Juliette felt the panic take hold of him and wrapped her arms around him. The feel of her skin on him caused another shockwave of sensations to tear through him. He attempted to jerk away from her, but she held on clasping him to her.

Her voice rang through his mind.

"Breathe Evan, I know this is disorienting, but I need you to calm yourself. Look at me." He tried to do as she said, sucking in a deep breath. He could smell the salt in the air, taste the brine of the sea and then the scent of blood assaulted his senses. He jerked again in the direction of Trevor and April, trying to get to the source of the delicious aroma. Juliette clamped her arms around him as he thrashed within her unrelenting grasp.

"No, Evan... look at me. Feel me against you, listen to my voice, concentrate on me." She brought his face around to look into his eyes, now the color of metallic emeralds. His gaze searched her face; she heard his heartbeat flutter as he began to feel the love that she poured over him.

Her mind continued to whisper to him as she brought her lips to his.

"Do you feel it Evan, my love for you?" Lost in the sweet soft current that ran from her lips to his, he sighed

328

into her kiss. His body relaxed in her embrace and his arms came up to hold her to him. He felt the warmth of her adoration filling his heart, and nothing else existed outside of their bond.

"Good, I need you to feed, Evan." She instructed him with her mind. His lips traveled down the smooth column of her ivory throat until he reached the spot where her pulse leapt from the pleasure of his touch.

"Let your fangs grow, feel them lengthen..." She could sense the change in him as his arousal gave way to hunger. She felt the brief twinge of his fangs as he began to feed. She felt the euphoric warmth that showered over her as he pulled her blood from her veins. His mind gasped at the pleasure he felt from the bond they shared. The desire, the love, the sated hunger washed over them as he finally withdrew from her and kissed her once more before pulling back to look into her impassioned face.

He remembered everything that had happened. He had been ready to leave this all behind to be with his parents. But now, as he looked at Juliette and felt the warmth of her love, he couldn't find it in him to mourn his inability to cross over.

He sat up slowly, feeling the rolling and pitching of the boat subsiding. He wondered why that was. Had Juliette's turmoil for his safety been the cause of the storm all along?

The wind and waves had calmed, and a clean fresh rain began to fall. Evan was lost in the feeling of the cool moisture on his new skin. He looked around and held a hand out to capture the rain in his upturned palm.

It was then that he saw his little sister, huddled in the corner of the boat, wrapped in Trevor's arms, looking at him as if she were afraid of him.

329

The sight of them tore at his heart, but he was also lost in the amazement of what his new eyesight revealed to him. He saw every glint of light reflected back to him. The gleam of the rain that had fallen caused every surface to glow with a silver radiance.

Evan turned, reaching out to April. Her eyes flickered to Juliette, unsure if it was safe for her to go near her brother.

Juliette sensed only longing for family, his hunger was under control now that he had her blood coursing through his veins.

She nodded giving April the sign that it was okay to go near him. April approached cautiously holding fiercely to Trevor's hand and reached out her fingertips to touch Evan's palm. He wrapped his fingers around hers and pulled her and Trevor into his strong embrace.

Juliette stood back, tears overflowing as she watched her new family rejoice in the moment. Evan was alive, and it didn't matter what he had become, they were together, and everyone was okay.

Her heart swelled for a moment until she recalled the one that didn't make it out... Tori.

Evan pulled back slightly at this thought and looked over his shoulder at Juliette.

"What happened?" he asked, a little startled at how smooth and refined his voice now sounded.

Juliette slowly walked over and knelt to embrace Ambrosia, so very thankful that she had not been in the middle of all that had happened.

She looked at Evan, April, and Trevor, all three had their eyes on her... waiting. Her voice shook as she tried to control the tears that refused to stop.

330

"Tori sacrificed herself to save you. Devlon had doused your body in vampire blood and was going to turn the violet light on you, she must have thrown herself in front of you. She didn't survive."

April looked up into her brother's face, seeing clearly just how close she had come to losing him tonight.

"Evan, we almost lost you. Had it not been for Juliette... I can't even begin to imagine how very different we would all be feeling right now."

Juliette came to kneel beside April.

"It wasn't me who saved him April..." She looked down at April's closed hand, still gripping a cylindrical object in her fist.

April opened her hand, palm up, to reveal an epinephrine pen. She handed it to Juliette.

"I heard you begging him not to leave you. I thought that maybe you couldn't reach him, and I remembered you saying he needed adrenaline to complete the transition." She sheepishly looked up at Juliette.

"I have severe allergies and I carry my epinephrine pen with me everywhere... I thought it might help." Juliette gathered April in her arms and gave her a warm hug. Thanks to her quick thinking, she had brought Evan back from the brink of death and saved his life.

There was a new feeling of wonderment on the boat as they all tried to get used to Evan in his new form. Juliette wished they could be alone so she could help him deal with the changes, but she understood his need to be with his sister after everything he had just been through.

Evan was trying to remain focused on the conversation, but his new body was distracting. He recalled feeling similar sensations when he had been recovering after Tori had attacked him. It seemed like a lifetime ago

331

that he had sat with Juliette on her balcony and learned that vampires were here in his hometown, and now... he was one of them.

Juliette read his thoughts and reached out to squeeze his hand reassuringly. He wasn't feeling remorse at his transition, but it didn't feel real just yet.

His thoughts were interrupted when Trevor asked what had happened to Devlon.

Juliette's gaze stayed on Evan as she spoke.

"He told me to choose... follow him or save Evan. The choice was easy." Juliette sighed as she pulled her fingers through Ambrosia's fur. Evan stood and closed the distance between them and pulled her into his arms. She had let go of centuries of building hatred to save him, but that choice may prove to be dangerous for her now that Devlon had escaped.

"He mentioned that your blood is very valuable to him because of your powers. I wouldn't put it past him to come after you at some point." She remembered him saying that, but at the time, she had been so caught up in saving Evan it hadn't registered.

"He might come back, and if he does, we will face him together. But I refuse to chase him any longer. I don't believe that Marek would want me to continue living my life fueled with revenge." Juliette paused and looked up into Evan's smoldering gaze. "I have you now to build a life with. I choose to be happy for the first time in my life. But first, we need to save Charlie." Evan turned to look into the depths of the water, a somber expression settled on his handsome face.

"I can help you now." Juliette tried to object.

"Evan, you have been through so much tonight, you don't need to do this, get some rest." He pulled her tighter against him.

"I don't need rest. I need to be with you." Juliette shook her head, out of habit, still wanting to protect him. She tried to dissuade him from going. But all Evan had to do was point out the shredded wetsuit she still wore, and his point was made. It would be easier with his help.

Evan did decide to use a wetsuit and diving equipment, just because he wasn't used to the abilities his new vampire body possessed.

They geared up for the final dive, and Trevor threw his last anchor overboard as they approached Charlie's location. April drove the boat, still looking shaken from all that had happened and scared that seeing Charlie would add to the nightmares she would surely have after tonight.

Once the anchor had caught on the seabed, she turned the boat off and joined Trevor on deck to watch Juliette and Evan splash into the water.

They made it to the bottom quickly, and Juliette was relieved to see that Charlie was in much better shape after taking her blood. He was almost back to his original form... still very thin, but he had his wits about him, and she could see the relief that washed over his features as he saw Evan with her.

He was in control of himself, and they would be able to bring him up without feeding him underwater. Evan descended to the anchor Charlie was latched to that bound him to the ocean floor and wasted no time in breaking the chain with his newfound strength.

They each supported one of Charlie's arms and carried him up to the surface. Once their heads broke the surface and April could see that Charlie was not a monster, she erupted in applause.

Her levity was contagious as they got Charlie loaded onto the boat and wrapped him in warm towels. Juliette still cautioned April and Trevor to keep their distance as she could still feel Charlie's hunger. Although he had no intentions of hurting his young friends, he followed her lead and agreed it would be best.

Juliette brought Ambrosia to sit before the frail old man to introduce herself to him.

"Charlie, my name is Juliette, and this is Ambrosia. She is my donor. Unlike Devlon, I have never killed a human, I've never had it in me to hurt someone in order to take their blood. I raised Ambrosia to become my donor. I know you are very thirsty and to keep the others safe, I think it best that you feed. Would you like me to show you how?"

Charlie's eyes grew wide as he took in the size of Juliette's companion, and he felt great admiration towards her for not being the monster that Devlon had been, but he could not do it. Ever so slowly he shook his head as he clutched the towels to his chest.

"I can't do it. I know doing that will make me live forever, and I don't want that. I've spent days down there wondering if this is my final punishment for all of the wrong I did in my life. I thought for sure that I would never see my Millie again... please tell me there is a way that I might end this?" Juliette squatted down in front of Charlie and grasped his hands in hers. Evan came to stand behind her and placed his hand on her shoulder.

Charlie looked up at Evan who no longer wore the scuba equipment, and his eyes flared in surprise.

334

"No! Oh son, not you too!" Charlie could see the transformation that Evan had gone through and mourned for his young friend.

"It's okay Charlie. I'm happy." He looked from Evan's face down at his hand resting gently on Juliette's shoulder and the loving look the two exchanged.

"I can see that you are. I'm happy for you then boy. But I can't do this. I was ready for the end when that monster ruined everything. Thank the good lord you kids found me. Now, just help me move on. I'm ready."

Juliette squeezed his hands.

"Charlie, if this is what you want, you'll need to wait for the sun to come up. We can't be exposed to the sunlight, and it will end this for you, but I must warn you, it will be painful." The gentle soul that he was didn't want this pretty girl worried about such things.

"Dear, after what I have just been through, it will be a blessing." Juliette gave his hand one more affectionate squeeze and stood so that Evan could have some time with his friend.

She turned to Trevor and said, "Let's go home."

***

Charlie, Evan, April, and Trevor sat out on the porch speaking of the old days and waiting for the sunrise. It had been a very long night. To Juliette it seemed like ages ago that they had packed up the SUV and driven to the docks together.

She sat cross legged in front of the fireplace looking into the flickering flames, entranced by their beauty, while stroking Ambrosia's head.

"He's going to be okay now... right Juliette?" April's voice broke into her thoughts. She looked up at her, April had come inside to make another pot of coffee to keep the cold at bay while they sat outside. Juliette smiled reassuringly.

"It will take him some time to get used to this new life, and he may need to spend some time away from you until he gets a grasp on his thirst, but he will be fine." She looked down at Ambrosia, thankful that Evan would have an option for feeding until they could find a donor for him as well.

"How close were we? To losing him I mean?" Juliette closed her eyes against the memories of Evan's spirit being pulled away, and of their parents hovering somewhere in the darkness. That was a story best shared by Evan. He would want to relay to April everything that he had experienced.

Juliette could see his memories and knew that he recalled every moment spent in the presence of his parent's souls. At first, she'd feared he would be angry that he had been yanked back, but in his mind, it had been the closure that he had needed all of these years.

336

"Give Evan some time, he recalls everything that happened. He should be the one to share it." April respected her for guarding Evan's secrets.

"For what it's worth, I'm glad that he found you. You've brought him back to life in more ways than one. We will always be grateful for that." The way she said 'we' made Juliette smile.

"You know, he is very happy that you and Trevor are together now. I don't mind sharing that, because I know it's something he would have told you himself if you were to ask." April grinned at her and blushed a little.

"Will you stay here with us now that Devlon is gone?" Juliette didn't have time to comment. The back door opened, and Evan came into the family room.

"The sun is going to be up soon. It's time." She could see the mixture of pain and relief in his eyes. She felt that he was already mourning his friend but also happy that he would finally be at peace.

Juliette stood and went to Evan, sinking into his embrace. He never tired of holding her.

"I'll go explain to him how to dissipate. It will make it much easier for him." Evan and April followed Juliette out onto the porch. April went to stand with Charlie, facing out into the woods, her arm threaded through his. She rested her head briefly on his shoulder.

Charlie turned towards Juliette as she approached,

"Charlie, it's almost time. I want to make this as easy as possible for you." He looked into her pretty face and was glad that she was here to help him through this.

"I'm all ears sweetheart." She nodded in understanding.

"We have the ability to dissipate. We can change into mist and travel that way if we are strong enough. You

337

are, at the moment, because you have my blood in your system. If you do this, when the sun rises, your passing will be less painful. Do you want to try it?"

"Yes, I think I will. Thank you." Charlie took one last look at his young friends. They had been there for him so many times over the years, and he didn't have the words to tell them how grateful he was for their kindheartedness.

He went to them, one by one, hugging them and thanking each one for a moment that their kindness had touched him.

"April my dear, thank you for your cheerful smile every morning when you would bring a cold, old man a nice hot cup of coffee. I will always cherish watching the sunrise with you." He briefly kissed her tearstained cheek and moved on to Trevor.

"Thank you, son, for sitting with me on the docks every now and then and sharing your fishing adventures with me. Not many people around this town gave old Charlie the time of day but you always took the time to swap fish tales with me. I will be eternally grateful for that." Trevor gave Charlie a long hug and moved aside so that Evan could say his goodbyes.

"Evan my boy, I think you've finally found that sweet young thing that will keep you warm at night. Treat her well and always be grateful for the gifts that life brings you. You shared your family with me when mine was gone. You gave me warmth, you gave me friendship, you gave me hope. Thank you, for every moment of kindness, it made my time on this Earth worth living." He hugged Evan and then turned to Juliette.

"I'm sorry about what I did to you down there. I wasn't myself. I will be forever in your debt for saving me

338

from this life." His eyes went to Evan, and he continued, "Take good care of him, he's a good lad."

Juliette nodded as she felt tears sliding down her cheeks. She was touched by Charlie's words, experiencing the grief that was felt by all of them had caused her voice to tremble as she explained to Charlie how to dissipate.

"Take a deep breath Charlie and concentrate on the feel of the wind against your skin, feel the weight of your body begin to fall away and let the breeze carry you." Holding Juliette's hand, he turned towards the pink horizon and lifted his face towards the sky.

Taking several deep breaths as she had instructed, Charlie slowly began to dissolve into a brilliant argent mist. He floated gently in the crisp morning air, the soft light of dawn glinting off of each glittering dewdrop until he surged upwards riding the breeze, and then swept back down and around them all, bathing them in the radiant bliss and freedom that he felt at that moment before soaring off into the sunrise and beyond into the heavens. As he reached the altitude where the sun kissed the horizon, a brilliant flash of light and a deep rumbling thunder rolled through the forest.

Evan's eyes were on the sky.

"Goodbye old friend," he whispered.

Evan felt Juliette's hand in his own and looked down into her exquisite features.

"Thank you for helping him through this." He couldn't get used to the new tone of his voice. The smooth tenor flowed effortlessly despite the emotion that should have caused it to tremble. She felt his sadness and longed to comfort him, but the sun was rising, and they needed to find shelter.

"Come, let's go inside." She tugged his arm and led him back into the cabin. April and Trevor followed.

"What now?" April softly voiced as she pushed the door closed and secured the curtains to block out the light.

Having Juliette's blood in his system gave Evan a sample of her empath abilities, and he heard the fear in his sister's question. He knew she was afraid he would leave now that he was no longer human. He would love nothing more than to stay right here with Juliette and try to live as normal of a life as he could. Would it be possible?

He knew Juliette could hear his thoughts and turned to her for an answer.

"If we are going to stay here, we are going to need to get you a donor. Ambrosia will be able to sustain us for a time, but as you discover more of your abilities, you will need more blood to be able to endure them without becoming weak." Evan looked at Ambrosia and thought about having two large wolves in the house.

"We might need a bigger place." Evan's humor lightened the mood in the house, and they all laughed. Trevor sat at the table as April made her way to the kitchen to reheat some of the pizza from the night before.

"So, you're going to stick around buddy?" Evan moved to sit across from Trevor and pulled Juliette into his lap.

"I won't be able to be around forever. I think the people in town will think it a little strange when I don't get any older." April's face fell as the realization hit her. She looked grief-stricken as she came around the end of the counter.

"How long do we have?" Juliette wanted nothing more than to put April at ease, but the truth of it was, they wouldn't be able to stay much longer than five years at most. April's face drained of color at this information.

340

Evan quickly stood and went to her, her eyes filling with tears.

"That doesn't mean you'll never see me again; it just means that I can't be seen by anyone else. I could stay close by, or you and Trevor could go with us... we could travel." He tried to make it sound fun, but the thought of leaving her and the pub was more painful than he had imagined it would be.

Juliette felt a pang of remorse for having let them become entangled in her war with Devlon. Had she disposed of Devlon years ago, Evan wouldn't be faced with these decisions.

April sniffed, wiped her tears away and tried to imagine what life would be like to leave Chancellor.

"I have always pictured living my life here Evan, running the pub and raising a family." Her eyes went to Trevor, and he smiled affectionately at her.

"I know you would have picked this path even had your life not been in danger, but it's not a choice that I can make for mine." She looked up at her big brother feeling like she was losing him all over again. Evan hugged her to his chest, careful to be gentle with her now that he was so much stronger.

"I will always be a phone call away if you need anything. I will be here as soon as I can." He turned to see Trevor looking up at them. "And I had better be invited to the wedding!" That caused April to finally smile through her tears. Trevor stood to take her from Evan and pulled her close. He looked at Evan over the top of her raven head.

"Next week sounds good to me."

341

**

April had thought that Trevor was kidding, but it didn't take her long to see that he couldn't have been more serious.

Evan was glad she would be taken care of and that she now had something to distract her from everything that had happened over the last few weeks.

They decided to wait until it was clear that Devlon was indeed gone from Chancellor. But despite Trevor's rather casual marriage proposal, April couldn't have been happier about planning a wedding.

Her brother wasn't going anywhere any time soon. He was alive and happy, the town would once again be peaceful, and she was going to marry the only man she had ever loved.

April and Trevor left not long after that. And Juliette and Evan were left alone to explore their own future together.

"Are you tired?" Juliette searched his face for any sign of fatigue after all that he had been through.

"Not in the least." They stood, once again in his bedroom, another warm fire casting shadows against the far wall.

"How do you feel?" He tried to find the words that could describe everything that was going on inside of him now that he was a vampire, when he realized that he didn't need to. She could already see the thoughts that were running through his mind.

342

He had never been more content. From the moment he'd laid eyes on Juliette, he'd had the uncontrollable urge to touch her, hold her and protect her.

So much had happened in such a short amount of time. It was hard to believe that their first encounter on the docks had only been a few weeks ago.

His feelings for her had developed in ways he hadn't thought possible. And now, being able to feel her love in return, it was surreal.

"You've awakened me, Juliette. After my parents died, I was on autopilot... scared to feel anything for anyone. But the moment I met you, everything changed. You made me want to live again, you gave me something to fight for. I will be eternally grateful for everything you have done for me, and I will cherish you always." He wrapped his arms around her waist bringing her up against him, his fingers wove throughout her long, glorious hair as he spoke.

His words, his gestures and the emotion that emanated from him, only reaffirmed her love for him.

"Marek will always hold a place in my heart. But I know now that this was the path I was always meant to take. Marek gave me immortality, and his memory spurred me on through times when I had lost all hope. Now he has delivered me to you... my destiny." She traced the planes of his face with her fingertips, lost in his radiant emerald eyes.

After centuries of solitude, bitterness, and fear, to finally feel that she belonged, that she was loved and cared for, was overwhelming. She wanted to cry from the intensity of it. Instead, she leaned into his embrace.

"You've given me love, hope and a future I never thought I could have. With you I am finally home." Evan

343

cradled her head in his hands, clutching her hair in his fists, lost in her silver gaze.

She was his. They were bound to one another, and they had forever to spend their lives together.

Juliette smiled in response to his thoughts and lifted her face up to place her lips against his. *"Forever,"* her mind said to his as she gave herself to him… body, mind, and soul.